Advance Praise for *The Soprano Wore Falsettos*

"Thank you for your submission. Unfortunately, here at St. Martin's Press, we've recently done away with our *Really, Really Bad Book* department. I suggest you contact Bantam Books at your earliest convenience."
Walter Jacobs, editor, St. Martin's Press

"This is a book to kill time, for those who like it better dead."
Dr. Karen Dougherty, physician

"Thank you for sending me your latest book. I shall waste no time in reading it."
John Rutter, orthodontist, Great Falls, Montana

"...the funniest book since Leviticus..."
Adam Denison, Music Student

"As is the case with many burgeoning novelists, the most important thing for Schweizer to do is to write as little as possible."
Dr. Richard Shephard, Chamberlain, Yorkminster

"As a work of literature, I would recommend this book slightly ahead of the 1992 Physician's Desk Reference, but just behind the Middle Wallop telephone directory."
His Grace, Lord Horatio "Wiggles" Biggerstaff, retired bishop

"I'll have to read it tomorrow. My stigmata's acting up."
Nancy Whitmer, organist

"Laughable...and that's just his punctuation..."
Sandy Cavanah, English Professor

"This book is terrible! Who told you that you could write? There's no reason... hey...wait a minute! Don't push me into that trunk! Ack! Umphhhh!"
Beverly Easterling, soprano

"I have instructed my attorney to file a restraining order against you at his earliest convenience."
John Rutter, orthodontist, Great Falls, Montana

"If I were a tree and I knew there was a chance I could be chopped down and made into this book, I'd go ahead and throw myself on the chain-saw. Yes, it's that good!"
Gerry Senechal, Organist

"For those who enjoy this sort of book, this is the sort of book they will enjoy."
Taffi, St. James Music Press unpaid summer intern

"Pearl, get the shotgun!"
John Rutter, orthodontist, Great Falls, Montana

The Soprano Wore Falsettos
A Liturgical Mystery
Copyright ©2006 by Mark Schweizer

Illustrations by Jim Hunt
www.jimhuntillustration.com

Published by
St. James Music Press
www.sjmpbooks.com
P.O. Box 1009
Hopkinsville, KY 42241-1009

ISBN 0-9721211-6-1

Printed in the United States of America

2nd Printing May, 2007

Acknowledgements

Allison Brannon, Cathie and Ron Buck, Sandy Cavanah, Nancy Cooper, Karen and Ken Dougherty, Marty and Randy Hatteberg, Kristen Linduff, Mary Ann Martino, Rebecca Watts, Jane and Mark Wells
and
Donis Schweizer

cover photo by Tony Kirves

L

The Soprano
Wore Falsettos

a Liturgical Mystery

by Mark Schweizer
Illustrations by Jim Hunt

Dedication

For each soprano, great and small,
The Lord has loved them, one and all.

Each little flower that opens
Their echoed beauty brings,
He made them sing like angels,
(Then plucked their tiny wings.)

For each soprano, great and small,
The Lord has loved them, one and all.

Prelude

The wind slapped minte mug like a petulant

"Dadgummit," I yelled, smacking the return carriage bar on my typewriter in frustration. Baxter, sleeping on his rug in front of the fireplace, opened one canine eye and gave me a pitying look, but was otherwise uninterested. This typewriter was an antique, and I really shouldn't have been smacking it around, but this was the third time in as many days that it had locked up on me. Sure, I could have used my iBook or any one of the three other computers in the house. I could have even probably found an antique typewriter on eBay or another on-line site, one that was in better shape. But there was another reason why I put up with this temperamental piece of archaic machinery.

This particular typewriter was Raymond Chandler's 1939 Underwood No. 5 — the very one on which he wrote *Farewell My Lovely, The High Window* and *The Lady in the Lake*. When I bought the typewriter, it came with excellent documentation, complete with an actual page of the second draft of *The High Window* — a perfect match to the characteristics of this particular page mill. I had the page framed and hung it on the wall in my den.

"Problem, Hayden?" said Meg, obviously hearing my outburst. She came into the room, carrying a couple of bottles of Pete's Wicked Ale. She plopped down on the overstuffed leather sofa — if one could use the word "plop" for the way a beautiful, fortyish woman, with black hair and gray eyes, who moved with the grace of a dancer ended up reclining in front of the fireplace. I suppose it would be more accurate to say she "settled" on the sofa or perhaps she "lit" or even "ensconced herself the davenport thereupon." However she did it, when I looked up from the infuriating apparatus that was thwarting my efforts at the next great detective story, there she was, sitting comfortably and offering me a beer.

"Come sit over here," she said with a smile, patting the worn leather beside her. "Take a break. You've been working too hard lately."

"I agree," I said, messing with the hammers that had become wedged together. "But, I always think I work too hard."

7

"Typewriter jammed again?"

"Yep. I'm going to send it back to Philadelphia and get Max to have a look at it. He worked his magic on the old girl when I bought her, but that was a couple of years ago."

"A couple of years and three stories ago," Meg said. "I'm not one to quash anyone's dreams, especially yours, but your writing is not getting any better."

"Well," I said, "at least it's not getting any worse."

My '40s-style detective stories were not without their critics, but writing them was the reason I'd bought the typewriter in the first place. Raymond Chandler was the best, in my opinion. There were those that favored Dashiell Hammett or Ross Macdonald, but for my money, Chandler was the master. Hard-boiled mysteries were the favorites of millions, and they just weren't being cranked out anymore. That's where I came in. My name is Hayden Konig. I'm a writer.

"You're not a writer," said Meg.

Okay. I'm not a writer. I'm a police chief in the Appalachian mountain town of St. Germaine, North Carolina. I could be a writer. That is, if I were any good, which I'm not. I'm pretty good at a couple of things though. I'm good at being a police chief, and I used to be good at being the organist and choirmaster at St. Barnabas Episcopal Church. That church job was part-time, and I'm currently taking a "leave of absence." Police chief is full-time. Writing is on my own time. I fed a new piece of paper behind the roller and gave it one more try.

The wind slapped me in the mug

"Nuts!" I said, yanking the paper out of the carriage.

"Maybe this is a sign from God," said Meg, hopefully.

"I'm sending the typewriter off tomorrow. Federal Express. I'll bet I can have it back by the weekend."

"Isn't that a bit expensive?" asked Meg, always concerned about cost, although expenditures didn't really bother me any more. I had made a boatload of money about five years ago selling an invention to the phone company. Meg, my investment counselor, as well as my significant other, had parlayed that windfall into such a tidy sum that I really didn't even have to work, much less worry about

8

how much FedEx was going to charge me to send my typewriter to Philadelphia.

"Price is no object!" I crowed. "I'm rich as a televangelist with my own 900 number."

"Oh, stop it," said Meg, getting up with a laugh, "and try this beer. It's really good. By the way, I'm fixing sandwiches for supper. Brie and bacon." She got to her feet.

"An excellent choice."

Baxter, our Burmese Mountain dog, suspected that Meg might offer him a treat, so he bounded to his feet and followed her back into the kitchen.

I tried the beer. Meg was right. It *was* good. I settled onto the comfortable, down-filled cushions, lit up a highly illegal Cuban cigar — a *Romeo Y Julieta,* smuggled into the country by an unnamed youth on a Guatemalan Mission trip — and clicked the remote control that brought the music of Bela Fleck and the Flecktones into the room. I had built this house soon after I'd struck it rich. The den, where I was sitting, was constructed of an 1842 log cabin, twenty by twenty, with a loft. The rest of the rather large house was built to complement the cabin, but it was this room that gave me the most pleasure. There was an elk head above the fireplace. In the corner stood a full-sized stuffed buffalo that Meg had given me for Christmas a couple of years ago. There were a few thousand books and CDs, my writing desk, a WAVE sound system, the typewriter, the couch and an old leather armchair. Just right for a bachelor, I thought, even though being single was a situation that I had recently tried to remedy.

I had asked Meg to marry me last spring, and we'd tabled the proposal. She still hadn't given me a definite answer though, preferring, I had to infer, to live in town with her mother. After her divorce, she'd moved to St. Germaine to take care of Ruby in her declining years — years which, by all accounts, weren't declining very rapidly at all. Ruby was in great health and spirits and glad for Meg's company. I didn't live in town, but about twenty miles out on a couple hundred acres up in the mountains. It was a lovely drive, but I had to admit that it was rather remote.

I took another sip of the cold brew and had almost decided to try to write my story on the iBook until my typewriter was back. Nah, I thought. It wouldn't work. There was something special about

putting my fingers on the same keys that Raymond Chandler had used to write those immortal words:

"Alcohol is like love. The first kiss is magic, the second is intimate, the third is routine. After that you take the girl's clothes off."

But it would have to wait.

Chapter 1

"Have you decided yet?" I asked, taking a bite of the Brie and bacon sandwich. "It's been quite a while since I asked, you know."

Meg nodded and swallowed. "Four months, seventeen days."

"Ah, you noticed."

"I wanted to remember what day you asked me, just in case I decided to say yes. It would be like a mini-anniversary."

"Just another date for me to remember?"

"Yes. And to get me a present."

"Well?" I asked.

"Well what?"

"What might your answer be?" I asked sweetly and acting as unconcerned as I possibly could.

"Nope," said Meg, sounding as indifferent as I.

"Nope?"

"No, thank you, Detective Hayden Konig. I don't wish to marry you."

"I'm sorry," I said. "I don't understand."

I had met Meg Farthing five years ago when she had first moved to St. Germaine. I'd always accused her of setting up our first date by driving through town at sixty-five miles per hour, an allegation she strenuously denied. I pulled her over, made her get out of the car, and, after looking at her legs (and in the finest tradition of policemen everywhere) gave her a stern warning — a warning which she remembers as mainly consisting of smiling and mumbling incoherently like a thirteen-year-old adolescent. Shortly after our first meeting, she joined me for an evening of knockwurst and Bach, and the rest is history. Meg was the town beauty, as far as I was concerned — black, shoulder-length hair, blue-gray eyes and a figure that would make the Pope consider Lutheranism. Smart and beautiful — just my type — which is why I was sure she was going to jump at my marriage proposal.

"Nope. I like things the way they are," said Meg. "And so do you. Marriage might just get in the way. If we leave things the way they are, you could leave the toilet seat up if you wanted. You wouldn't have to make the bed. You could sit around in your underwear all day."

"But, I don't leave the toilet seat up," I said, a bit defensively. "Or the other stuff."

"But, you could," said Meg.

"But, I don't."

"And you'd better not, if you ever want me to come over," Meg said. "Also, let's say you wanted to go out with some floozy. If we were married, you couldn't."

"I don't want to."

"But, you still could."

"But, I wouldn't," I said halfheartedly.

"I know, but you still could."

"Okay," I said, with a sigh. "I could."

"But you'd better not," said Meg.

"So, we're not going to get married?" I said.

"No. But you can still get me a present if you want."

I walked into The Slab Café early on Friday morning. The Slab was on Main Street, just on the corner of the city square. It was an old fashioned café, complete with big black and white tiles on the floor, red tablecloths, four red-vinyl upholstered stools at the counter, and two waitresses that kept things running.

Nancy Parsky and Dave Vance were sitting at our regular table. Nancy is the other full-time officer at the St. Germaine PD. Dave works for us part-time. He answers phones, fills out reports and used to have a thing for Nancy. I say "used to" because lately, much to Nancy's consternation, he's been seen on the arm of Collette, one of the waitresses at The Slab. Nancy was peeved to say the least, but to my mind, she didn't have much of a beef. She'd never given Dave the time of day before Collette showed interest, and she still didn't. However, whenever I pointed this out to Nancy, she'd get miffed, and I didn't want her miffed. Nancy miffed was not good. So, being the chief and always trying to keep the peace, when she snarled, I'd taken to nodding understandingly and clicking my tongue in mock sympathy.

"What can I get you, Hon?" said Noylene, the other waitress, as she walked up to the table and poured me a cup of coffee as soon as I was seated.

"Just coffee this morning," I said.

"You on a diet, boss?" asked Nancy. She had ordered a short stack of pancakes with a side order of bacon.

"As a matter of fact, yes," I said. "I have three pairs of work pants, and they're still good. I don't want to have to buy new ones just because I got too fat."

"You don't mind if we eat though, right?" said Dave, talking around the half a biscuit in his mouth.

"No, you guys go ahead. I'll just sit here and watch."

"Hey," said Nancy. "Did you hear about the winning Powerball ticket? It was sold over in Elk Mills."

"Really?" said Dave. "That's only about twenty miles from here."

"Right across the Tennessee border," added Nancy. "How come North Carolina doesn't have a lottery?"

"We do. The governor just signed it into law," I said. "We should have it up and running by next summer."

Pete came up to the table, carrying a platter of waffles.

"Did you hear about the Powerball ticket?" We all nodded. "Anyway," he said, "I got a new Belgian Waffle machine and some special batter from a new supplier in Maine. Try some of these oat-maple waffles with black walnut syrup. You won't believe how good they are."

Pete Moss was the owner of The Slab, the mayor of St. Germaine and my old college roommate. In fact, he was the one who landed me this "cushy job," as he called it. It wasn't that cushy, but it wasn't bad. Pete had been my roommate in college when we were both undergraduate music majors. We'd lost touch for a while when I'd gone on and gotten a masters degree in composition. Then, after consulting the job market for composers, I went back and got another degree in criminology.

"Sorry, Pete," said Nancy. "Hayden's on a diet. We'll eat them though. They look absolutely dee-licious."

"Yeah," chimed in Dave, "it's a shame to let these go to waste." Dave turned to me with a grin. "Get it, boss? Go to waste? Go to *waist?*"

"Yes, very clever, Dave," I said. "You're a regular Henny Youngman."

"Who?" asked Nancy.

"Take my wife...please. Oh, never mind. Give me some of those waffles. I'll start this diet tomorrow."

"Hey," said Noylene, wandering up to the table looking for unfilled coffee cups and, spotting a couple of them, remedying their half-empty status. "Did Dave just tell a joke?"

"Not much of one," muttered Nancy.

"I'll bet Collette would have liked it," I said, unable to keep myself from throwing a little kerosene on Nancy's smoldering irritation. She answered me with a low growl that I wasn't even sure I had heard until I felt the kick under the table.

"Collette's off today," said Pete in all innocence. "In fact, I think she went down to Hickory for a couple of days. She's not on the schedule again until Monday."

"She's visiting her mother," said Dave.

"Glad to hear it," muttered Nancy. "Maybe we can get some work done."

The waffles disappeared quickly, and, since I was officially off my diet for the day, I ordered some grits, bacon and a couple of eggs as well.

"I thought about going on a diet myself," said Pete, "but then I made a brilliant discovery. Have you tried expando-pants? They're great!"

"What are expando-pants?" asked Nancy.

"They've got these gussets or something on the side," said Pete. He got up and unbuckled his belt. "Look here." He pulled the waistband of his seemingly normal khakis out far enough to drop a dictionary down his shorts. "They expand up to three inches."

"Wow," said Nancy, "just what the world needs. Maternity pants for men."

"I'm never going back," said Pete. "I've seen the future, and it's wearing expando-pants."

"I can't do it, Pete," I said, finishing up my coffee. "I may actually have to take up exercise."

"Don't do anything drastic. Exercise can kill you. I heard about this one guy..."

"Hey," interjected Nancy, always happy to interrupt a conversation that she wasn't interested in. "Did I hear that your typewriter was broken?"

"It was, but I sent it off to Philadelphia. It'll be back this

14

afternoon," I answered. "Have no fear. I'll be writing again very soon."

"Who's Henny Youngman?" asked Dave.

"Try to keep up, Dave," said Nancy.

The FedEx delivery guy had walked into the police station at 2:10 p.m. I know because Dave had dutifully logged him in and accepted the package. I opened the box in my office, lifted out the twenty pound typewriter, put a piece of copier paper behind the roller and clicked it into position. I didn't generally use copier paper because I didn't want to cheapen the experience. This was, after all, Raymond Chandler's typewriter. I had started using a 42 lb. bond that I ordered from California — a specialty paper that had been carried by the same stationery company since 1928. But that paper was at home, and I was itching to give the typewriter a try. I typed:

The Soprano Wore Falsettos
Chapter 1

It worked just like new.

The wind slapped me in the mug like a petulant chippy; then it threw its drink in my face, kissed me hard on the mouth, slapped me again, kissed me once more, showed me a good time, stole my wallet and banged open the door of the Possum 'n Peasel just as I walked up--it was one heck of a wind, and I oughta know.

I was meeting someone. Someone who didn't want to be seen going to the office of a gumshoe. It was all the same to me. I wasn't picking up the tab. I'm an L.D.--Liturgical Detective duly licensed by the Episcopal diocese of North Carolina and answerable directly to the bishop. At least that's what it said on my card. But, I thought as I lit a stogy and dropped into my booth, a little moonlighting on the side never hurt. The Possum 'n Peasel was still my favorite dive on the West Side even though the new

management was now offering an embarrassment of drinks
with names like "Fuzzy Smurf" and "Butterfly Kisses." The
late owner, a crusty old coot named Stumpy, wouldn't have
put up with it, and I had to admit that the only
"butterfly kiss" I wanted to see was a butterfly kissing
the windshield of my flivver on my way home from
Francine's.

I had taken up with Francine after my last case. She
was a nurse. I met her while I was visiting Marilyn in
the hospital after the last bust-up. Who could tell? I
might even be in love. All I knew for sure was that whenever she spoke, I could swear that I heard bells—like she
was a cement truck backing up.

"What'll it be, Shamus?" asked the waitress. I couldn't
remember her name, but then, I didn't know many of them
any more. Waitresses came and went at the P 'n P quicker
than Methodists in a liquor store.

"Give me a beer and a belt, Doll."

"Huh?"

"Beer," I sighed. "With a whiskey chaser." It wasn't
even any fun ordering anymore.

She snapped her gum like it was punctuation—a
misplaced period at the beginning of a sentence or
perhaps a colon, although a colon is generally used after
a complete statement in order to introduce one or more
directly related ideas, such as a series of directions, a
list, or a quotation or other comment illustrating or
explaining the statement, so it was more like a period.

"We have Bud, Bud Light, Michelob, Coors, Coors Light,
Killian's, Schlitz, Lowenbrau and Miller Light. We have
Dewar's, Jim Beam, Maker's, Dickel's, and umm…" She paused
in her litany. "I can't remember," she shrugged with a
smile cute enough to shoot, stuff and hang over the
fireplace. "I'll have to go check."

"Never mind," I growled under my breath. "Just bring
me a Fuzzy Smurf. And one of those glow-in-the-dark
swizzle-sticks."

"I'll have one of those, too," said a voice from over my
shoulder.

16

"I see that you have your toy back," said Meg.

"I do," I said. "It works great!"

"I was afraid of that. How's the new story coming?"

"It's so good, it's almost writing itself."

"That'd be a nice change."

"Look," I said, "for someone who doesn't want to marry me, you sure are critical. You haven't even read it yet."

"I'm just looking out for the literary community at large. But you make a good point. I shall refrain from criticizing until I've heard it."

"Shall I read it to you then?"

"Yes. Yes, you shall." She sat down on the sofa, placed her hands in her lap and looked at me expectantly. I raised my eyebrows and accepted the unspoken challenge. I read my opening paragraphs in my best dramatic voice, paying extra attention to some particularly well-written prose that I thought showed off my best work — my opening sentence, the part about the gum-snapping and the cute smile. This was good stuff. I could tell.

"Is that it?" Meg asked.

"So far. What do you think?"

"It's growing on me."

"It is?"

"Actually, yes. I hate to say it, but it is. I do not detest it."

"You don't?" I was amazed.

"Nope. I can definitely say that it doesn't disgust me."

High praise.

She walked past the table, her dress clinging to her torso like paint on the nose cone of a B-17 Flying Fortress, a blond bombshell with more curves than an 48/M reverse-panel throttle bracket assembly.

"Hi there," she purred, her engines dropping to idle as she lowered her flaps and glided into the booth. "My name is Memphis. Memphis Belle."

"Of course it is, Kitten," I said, taking a puff on my cheroot and tipping my hat back to enjoy the view. "Now, how can I help you?"

Chapter 2

Worship committee meetings at the church happened on Tuesday mornings and, when I was employed there, I tried to miss as many as I could. But, when feeling guilty, or when things were so slow down at the station that I couldn't find any other work to do, I would dutifully make my way to the downtown square and into the offices of St. Barnabas, where I would present myself as a ritual sacrifice at the altar of the committee meeting. Although I hadn't been the organist at St. Barnabas since November, Father George had asked me to come in on this particular Tuesday in late March. It was one of those mornings that could take your breath away, as crisp and snappish as a librarian, with the sun filtering through the budding leaves of the hardwoods. The ever-present scent of the pine and fir trees that were prevalent along Main Street was carried across the town on a light breeze. I hadn't worn a coat this morning, but was beginning to rethink that decision. I hadn't asked Father George exactly why he wanted me to come to the worship meeting, but it was a slow morning, and I was, after all, still a member of the church. Besides that, Meg had asked me to go.

Father George Eastman was the rector of St. Barnabas, beginning his ministry in St. Germaine almost a year ago. He'd come just after Easter last year, and now it was the middle of the next Lenten season with Easter looming large again. The church had muddled through the holiday seasons without me, and Epiphany had come and gone. Foremost on everyone's minds and tongues was the little matter of the St. Barnabas financial windfall. It was the five-hundred pound gorilla in the room.

St. Barnabas Church in St. Germaine, North Carolina, had been the unexpected recipient of an unusually large sum of money. It seems that, due to a bank error and some underhanded financial finagling of funds back in the 1930's by the bank's president, Northwestern Bank owed the church over thirty million dollars. St. Barnabas, not wanting to seem too greedy, had agreed to settle the matter to the tune of sixteen million, paid over four years. There was plenty of discussion about how that money could best be used, and everyone had his own ideas.

It was during the church-wide dustup in late October that I had

resigned as church organist and choir director. There were hard feelings all around, and although I was asked back repeatedly, I thought it best to take some time off. Meg, in a sympathetic gesture, had stopped singing in the choir, as did a number of others — or so I had heard through the St. B. grapevine. Meg still attended services, was on the vestry and involved in all manner of activities. I hadn't been back. The church held a meeting in November and determined that they would give me six months to decide if I wanted to remain in the position. "Take your time," they said. "And if you need a couple more months to make up your mind, just let us know." Father George found an organist to take over while I considered my options — a Mrs. Agnes Day. She was from St. Germaine and had been the keyboard player at one of the Catholic churches in Banner Elk before she retired about five years earlier. She was a nurse by trade, having worked for a plastic surgeon in Boone for a number of years, and then at the Watauga Medical Center. I think she'd been fired from the hospital, but that might have just been a rumor. I had heard she was now working in town. Home health care.

"Her name is Agnes Day?" I asked with a laugh when I found out who was replacing me. "Really?" Marilyn just smirked.

For the first time since I could remember, I hadn't had the pressure of Christmas hanging over my head like the Sword of Damocles. Meg and I took her mother, Ruby, down to Asheville and spent Christmas Eve through New Year's at the Grove Park Inn. We went to Christmas Eve services at the Cathedral and had an all-around great time.

"Good morning, Hayden," said Marilyn, the long-suffering church secretary, as I walked into the meeting room. "Want some gossip?"

"Absolutely," I said, handing Marilyn a cup of coffee and taking a sip of my own.

I picked up my own coffee at The Ginger Cat on my way to the church and one for Marilyn as well. She'd given me a heads-up. Father George had taken to making the coffee for the morning meetings at the church. We'd been used to getting Community Coffee, shipped to us from Louisiana, but the good reverend had decided that it was too expensive. Now he personally went to the Food Mart and bought the cheapest generic brand he could find. He definitely didn't have the taste buds the rest of us did. It was weak

as a baby squirrel and about the same color. He'd drink his two cups and the rest would be thrown away at about noon. The real coffee drinkers now had to walk across the square and pay for their cup of cheer.

"Squeal," I said.

"You know Benny Dawkins?"

"Sure," I said. Benny was the thurifer at St. Barnabas. The best incense-swinger around. "What about him?"

"He's suing the organist. Umm...substitute organist," she corrected. "Agnes Day."

I'm sure I looked surprised. Marilyn continued.

"It seems he brought his great-grandfather's old violin for her to look at and give him some advice on selling it."

"Did she?"

"Did she *ever*. She bought it from him for eight hundred dollars."

"That sounds like a good deal," I said. "Most old violins aren't even worth that."

"This one was," said Marilyn, "and more. A whole lot more. I don't know how much, but Benny was very upset. Anyway, she sold it in New York and he's suing her."

"I don't think he'll win," I said.

"That's what Logan told him, too, but he doesn't care."

"So, Logan wouldn't take the case?"

"Nope. Benny found a lawyer in Asheville, though. Some guy that advertises on TV."

"Hi there," said Beverly Greene, walking in to the room and cutting our conversation short. "I'm *so* glad you're back. Did you get me one of those, too?" She pointed to my coffee.

"I'm *not* back," I said. "I just came for the meeting. And sorry about the coffee. I only had two hands."

"I have some coffee here," said Father George, the next into the room. He was juggling a carafe and his stack of meeting papers.

"Umm...no thanks," said Bev. "I forgot that I already had two cups this morning."

The rest of the folks made their way into the room in the next few minutes. Bev was the new Parish Administrator. It was a part-time position that she'd taken over at the beginning of January. Even after Rob Brannon, Father George's first choice for P.A.,

had been arrested for murder and fraud, Father George was still convinced he needed an administrator. He didn't like conflict and like most folks who don't like conflict, he couldn't bring himself to be put in that position. He could make the call; he just didn't want to be the hatchet man. He'd sooner go in for a root canal than have to fire someone. He also didn't want to be responsible for making any financial decisions. The rector had a discretionary fund, but he didn't have to answer to anyone for that. Everything else he wanted out of his purview. When he interviewed Bev for the job, after she mentioned that she wouldn't mind giving it a try, he asked her if she would have a problem disciplining a member of the staff or telling a volunteer that his or her talents might be better used elsewhere.

"Hell, no," she said.

"Let's say that the sexton steals something from my desk when he's cleaning up."

"I'd fire his sorry butt," she said, then added demurely, "with your permission, of course."

So now, as Parish Administrator, Bev was in charge of writing the checks (although she didn't keep the books), scheduling the building, and all other various and sundry chores that fell under her "job description." One of them was to come to the worship committee meetings. The books had been kept, since the dark ages, by Randall Stamps, an ancient bean counter who had come to a grisly end last fall. Now they were sent to an accounting agency. Beverly was still in charge of collecting pledges, however, and making sure they were kept current by gentle reminders.

Also present at the meeting were Brenda Marshall and Joyce Cooper. Brenda was the St. Barnabas Christian Education director. She hadn't been a popular appointment with many of the old guard Episcopalians, being, as far as anyone could tell by her freely-spouted, touchy-feely theology, a Uni-luther-presby-metho-lopian. She had never even attended an Anglican church before being hired by the previous priest, something she alluded to frequently with a certain amount of pride. Bev was just itching to fire her, and she'd actually thought that Brenda was the reason that Father George had hired her — to bring down the ax. Privately, Bev had confided to me that it was going to be tough to get rid of Brenda. She'd been there over a year, she hadn't actually done anything wrong and there would have to be a very good reason for her dismissal. Brenda

had seen the writing on the wall and was already hinting at lawsuits having to do with the previous priest. Bev didn't know if she was bluffing or not.

Georgia Wester, one of my good friends, had been on the worship committee when I left last October, but she had rotated off in January and had been replaced by Joyce Cooper, a member of the Altar Guild.

"Good morning, everyone," said Father George, bringing the meeting to order. "And I'm sure we'd all like to say 'thanks' to Hayden for coming." He addressed me. "I'd really like your input on our services even though you're technically on leave."

The rest of the group nodded in agreement.

"I brought some coffee, if anyone would like any," said Father George, pushing the carafe into the center of the table.

"No thanks," said Bev.

"I'm trying to cut down," said Brenda.

"I already have some," I said.

"Me too," added Marilyn.

"I think I'm allergic," said Joyce. I snorted, but managed to turn it into a cough. Joyce, sitting next to me, whispered out of the side of her mouth, "It's all I could think of."

Father George, shuffling through his papers, didn't seem to notice.

"As you are all aware," he continued, "Easter is three weeks away." He turned to me. "We've already made plans for Holy Week."

"Of course," I said, with a genuine smile.

"But, feel free to make whatever suggestions you'd like. We'll try to incorporate them if we can."

"I probably won't," I said. "I'm sure that whatever you've decided to do during worship services will be meaningful and appropriate." I meant it. Really. In the days before my sabbatical, I had been very involved in planning the services, but now that I wasn't actually attending St. Barnabas, I was having a hard time generating any concern. If I was going to be asked for my opinion, I probably couldn't keep quiet, but I was sure going to try. Less stress, I told myself.

"How're we doing on the Maundy Thursday service?" Father George asked.

"I think I have it about finished," said Brenda.

I froze, the coffee cup just touching my lips, as an icy feeling crept up my spine; in spite of myself, I looked over at Marilyn. She was avoiding my gaze, fighting to keep a smile off her lips.

"I went over all the material Father George gave me," Brenda said to me, in that wonderful tone of voice with which she used to terrify children, "and so, when designing the service, I used the traditions of the Episcopal Church as well as incorporating some other denominational material and several ideas of my own."

The worship committee looked over at me.

"I'm sure it will be wonderful," I said, sweetly. "Sometimes it's a *really* good idea to design your own services. People will find it very meaningful." It was a sarcastic comment, but I did my best to kept all the disparagement out of my voice. If the words hadn't come out of my very own mouth, I might have thought I actually meant them. Marilyn, across the table, was not fooled. She was losing her battle and had started to chew on her tongue.

"George," I said. "Seriously. You know, you don't really have to 'design' services. It's been done. They're right there in the prayer book."

"Oh, I know, Hayden, but I thought that Brenda needed the experience of planning the Maundy Thursday service. I gave her all the literature as well as the prayer book. It'll be fine."

"That's great," I said, with a big smile.

Chapter 3

"You married?" she asked, sipping her drink with the slurping sound of a dentist's vacuum, the one that hangs on your lip like a giant fishhook and hoovers up your spit before it overruns and dribbles onto your bib.

"Nope."

"Seeing anyone?" I liked a woman that got right to the point.

"Now and then," I said. I tried to think of Francine, but my mind kept leapfrogging like a Greek sailor back to the vision in front of me. I knew I was staring, but I couldn't help myself.

She shrugged. "Well, maybe we can get together some-time. You know, off the books."

I nodded, trying to maintain eye contact.

"Anyway," she said with a smile, "I'm from the bishop."

"The bishop?" I frowned. I knew all of the bishop's gals, and Memphis Belle wasn't one of them.

"Not your bishop. The Presiding Bishop."

"Ah," I said with a nod. "The Presiding Bishop." The fog was clearing. My bishop had quite a stable, but this filly was something special. The Presiding Bishop was the bishop's bishop. The king bishop, if you will. And, as the saying goes, it is good to be the king.

Memphis Belle and I spent the rest of the afternoon up at my place, engaged in a steamy theological discourse about the American view of eschatology and dispensational pre-millennialism.

Nah. Not really.

"This is just awful," said Meg, joining me at my table at The Ginger Cat.

"I thought you said you didn't hate it."

"I wasn't talking about your writing, which is not especially awful. Just moderately awful."

"What then?" I asked.

"I just got appointed to a church committee."

"It's a bad one?"

"It's the worst one. I was put on because I'm on the vestry and someone thinks that I'd be a good chairman."

"Chairwoman," I corrected. "It's because you're so irresistible. What's the committee?"

"Chairperson. It's the committee to decide how to spend sixteen million dollars."

"Yikes," I said, "but don't you mean four million? Four million a year for four years. That's what the settlement was."

"Yes, that's exactly right," said Meg. "But the bank's accountants have now decided that it would be in their best interest to pay the entire amount this fiscal year rather than to stretch it out. They've got their reasons I suppose, and whatever their rationale, we're going to have sixteen million dollars by the end of April."

"That's good," I said. "Put it in a money market account and forget about it for a long time."

"I wish," Meg grumbled. "The congregation found out about it, and they all have great ideas on how to spend it. See what you miss when you stay at home? Speaking of money, has anyone cashed that Powerball ticket yet? It jackpot was up to a hundred and twenty million."

"I haven't heard."

Cynthia Johnsson came over to take our order. She'd been working at The Ginger Cat off and on, since it opened a few years ago. She was also a certified belly dancer, giving lessons and doing quite a number of parties around the area. I asked her once how one became "certified." She just winked, and I didn't inquire further. I'd once gotten Meg some lessons for her birthday, but had been informed, rather brusquely, that my generosity was hardly a present for *her* and *my* birthday was quite a way off. Luckily, I'd had a back-up present in hand.

"What'll it be?" Cynthia asked.

"Turkey and sprouts on whole wheat," answered Meg. "And some raspberry tea."

Cynthia wrote it down and turned to me.

"Got anything bloody? Something out of a cow?"

Cynthia shook her head. "No beef. Annie's on a health kick. Chicken salad or turkey. Hey! How about a bean curd and chive sandwich on toasted sourdough? Or maybe a portabella mushroom wrap with avocado paste?"

25

I shuddered. "Turkey," I said. "On rye. No sprouts."

"It *comes* with sprouts," Cynthia said. "And a side of baby carrots in an almond glaze."

"Give 'em to a rabbit," I griped. "Put some cheese on that sandwich and an extra slice of turkey. And make it rare."

"Our turkey's already cooked," teased Cynthia, "but I could put some strawberry jam on it. You can pretend that it's blood."

"No thanks," I said. "And get me a cup of coffee, will you?"

"I will. Anything in particular?"

"Whatever you've got made as long as the name contains four words or less."

"How about Colombia Nariño Supremo?"

"Sure. Only three words. Sounds great."

As Cynthia walked off, I turned my attention back to Meg. She'd been looking at me with that kind of expression that meant I was going to be asked to do something that I didn't want to do, something I probably shouldn't do, and something I knew I'd regret once I got into it.

"Okay," I said. "What is it?"

"Well," she started, "since I'm the chair of this committee, I get to choose the other members."

"Nope," I said. "No way. I hate committees."

"Now listen here, Hayden," she said, with more than a touch of schoolmarm in her voice. "You are a member of St. Barnabas whether or not you choose to work there. This is very important, and it can't be left to a bunch of nitwits."

"Who else do you have?" I asked, resignation already apparent in my voice and confirmed by Meg's immediate change of tone.

"Malcolm's agreed to be on it. Billy Hixon is on since he's the Senior Warden. Also Gwen Jackson and Lee Dalbey. If you agree, then that'll be six. That's what the vestry wants. Three vestry members and three lay people."

"You know, of course, that it will make some folks pretty angry. It smacks of nepotism, even though we aren't married."

"Sure, but you're still a member of St. Barnabas and everyone agrees that you're the one who got the money for the church in the first place. If you hadn't solved the crime, we wouldn't have even known the money was out there."

"All right," I conceded. "How's it going to work?"

"We're going to have a church-wide meeting for anyone who wants to come and voice an opinion. Then the committee will make recommendations, and the vestry has the final vote on the committee's proposals. If they don't take them, it goes back to the committee and we start again. The vestry can vote on the committee's recommendations, but they can't make their own."

"Pretty clever," I said, as our sandwiches arrived.

"It was George's idea. Six people are going to have a hard enough time trying to decide. The vestry's twice as big and half as smart."

"And the vestry agreed to this?" I asked, lifting up the top piece of rye and peering suspiciously into my sandwich. It looked fine, but I was always leery of some kind of tofu-esque surprise snuck into the turkey by the Health Nazis.

"Yes," said Meg. "They did. Malcolm gave them a form to sign. I don't think all of them actually read it."

Malcolm was a retired banker and had handled my investment accounts before I met Meg. Still in his early sixties, he wasn't old enough to retire — just rich enough. His second wife, Rhiza, had been a friend of mine in college. She was a few years younger than I was, and Malcolm had a decade and a half on both of us. Malcolm Walker was a savvy broker and understood money and how it worked in a way that few St. Germainians did, save Meg Farthing.

"When's the first meeting?" I asked, removing a piece of stray pine nut from my mouth and dropping it onto my plate.

"Next week. I'll let you know for sure. You know," she said, "you really should come back to church, even if you don't want the job. I'm going to start singing with the choir again." She looked at me for a reaction.

"I think you should." I lowered my voice. "You can be my spy. I want to know how they're sounding. Call it professional curiosity."

"No way. You'll have to come back if you want to stay in the loop. And anyway, you know how they sound. Everyone and his brother has been reporting to you weekly."

"Well," I said, "I can't come back just yet. It seems that I may be doing some subbing for the next few Sundays. My name got out as an available organist, and I'm getting a couple of calls a week."

"So, are you going to do it?"

"I think so. No rehearsals — just a Sunday morning service. Plus, as you know, if I'm the organist of St. Barnabas, I can't be on your committee."

27

"What about Holy Week?" Meg asked, sadness evident in her question. "And Easter? It's almost here. Don't make the church suffer through Agnes Day's rendition of *Rise Again*. They already went through *The Silent Night Calypso* on the fourth Sunday of Advent. You can't do it."

"Yep. I can and I will."

Chapter 4

I sat at my desk and went over my notes. Memphis Belle was a pro. She'd come to me because I was a pro. Marilyn was a pro. Francine was a pro. Everyone I knew was a pro. So why was I feeling like it was amateur night at the Feed and Seed Opera?

Memphis didn't have much and I didn't have to pump her like an old squeezebox for what I got. More importantly, she didn't blink at my two hundred-a-day plus expenses. I guess the big bishop could afford it.

General Convention was coming up, and there were always problems. As usual, someone was noodling with the prescribed readings for the church year. The Reformed Common Lectionary was up for the final vote, and someone had stuck John 3:16 in twelve times. I wasn't worried and neither was Memphis. They'd work it out. They always did. But there was another game afoot. The Presiding Bishop had been tricked into approving a "color" committee. He'd assumed it had something to do with racial equality. It didn't, and now he had to explain the "Presiding Bishop's Committee on New Liturgical Colors" which, not surprisingly, was a hundred and sixty-five large over budget.

The church had prescribed seasonal colors for eons. Sure, a few odd colors had weaseled their way into the yearly cycle over the years--blue during Advent, gold for special feast days, black for Good Friday--but, by and large, most churches were still working with four colors--green for ordinary time, red for Pentecost, purple for the penitential seasons, and white for Easter and Christmas. What would be the effect if the church voted to change to chartreuse for Advent? Or burnt umber for Epiphany? I shuddered to think.

The Color Committee was looking for an up or down vote at convention and, if they played their cards right, the vote could be scheduled right after the Senior Liturgical Limbo finals. It would be easy to pack the house, swing the vote and set new colors for the next millennium.

"Marilyn," I called. "How about some java?"

"I think she's dead," said Nancy. "And it wasn't an accident. She was killed."

"Not again," said Dave with a shake of his head. "For a populace this small, there certainly have been a lot of murders lately."

"I don't know if I'd call it murder," I said. "It may just be an accidental death or even a plain old homicide."

"You mean an ichthyocide," said Nancy, scooping poor Gertrude out of the tank. "I think it was one of the other fish. She was just fine yesterday."

"I don't trust those two angel fish," Dave said, tapping on the glass. "Look how they're huddling together. It's like they're planning something."

"You know things are slow when you're trying to figure out which fish is the murderer," I said as I went into my office. I sat down behind my desk, put a CD into the player and the sounds of Mozart's *The Abduction from the Seraglio* filled the room. It was an old favorite that I revisited every few years and the first opera recording I ever bought. I had purchased the three-record set with the first money I had ever made at a church job. Last year, I finally found the same recording reissued on CD.

"Who's your favorite composer, boss?" asked Nancy, leaning against the doorjamb.

"Why?"

"I just wondered. Plus your birthday's coming up. A CD is a pretty cheap present."

"It's hard to say," I said. "Depends on my mood. I always like Mozart, though."

Nancy pulled her notepad and pen out of her breast pocket and jotted something down, presumably my taste in birthday music.

"Hey, guess what?" said Nancy, putting her pad back and buttoning the flap over her pocket. "You remember the Passaglio wedding back in February?"

"Sure," I said. "I didn't play for it, though. I was taking a break, as I recall. Wasn't it in Boone? Something about our church being too small?"

"I only know one thing about it," said Nancy. "I heard this

morning on the radio that it was going to be featured on *America's Funniest Videos.*"

"Is that show still on?"

"Syndication," answered Nancy. "Anyway, check it out. Sunday night, seven o'clock."

Meg was right. I did have several people filling me in on the services at the church. Bev came by at regular intervals to complain bitterly. Georgia would see me in the street and tell me about the latest anthem disaster. Elaine had taken to going to early mass at eight o'clock and skipping the musical service altogether. JJ would come by the police station on occasion and laugh. Where Bev was appalled by the Christmas Eve communion performance of *O Holy Night* with Agnes Day on accordion and Shea Maxwell squeaking away on the clarinet, JJ found it hilarious and couldn't wait to tell me about it.

According to the information that had come my way, the choir had dropped from around twenty members to about eight, with two of them being new. One of the new ones I knew. He was a church member who had come a couple of times when I first started with the choir, but he informed me that he didn't like to come to rehearsal. The latest choir member had joined a couple of weeks ago. She was a retired junior high school music teacher, going by the name of Renee Tatton, who had recently moved to town. Bev was informed that Renee Tatton was her "professional" name. Renee didn't share her real one. She had given Bev her life story over lunch one afternoon. When she was younger, she had sung opera in Austria and Germany. After returning to the United States, she'd gotten her teaching certificate and taught school in Maryland until she decided to retire in January. She had vacationed in Boone many times through the years and had fostered the notion that this area would be a lovely place to live. So, upon her retirement, she moved to our beautiful city and set about making friends and finding a niche for her musical talents. That niche included the St. Barnabas choir. It also included hanging out a shingle for voice lessons.

Bev was not impressed, but I thought it was a soprano thing. I had met the lovely Ms. Tatton, and although I hadn't actually heard

her sing, I did know one thing about her. Renee was quite a devotee of the cosmetic surgeon's art. As Bev so delicately put it, she'd had more tucks than a hospital bed sheet.

I was listening to the end of the first act duet when Nancy came in and interrupted.

"We gotta go, boss. It's Ruthie Haggarty. She finally killed him."

"Little Bubba?"

"Yep. She called it in herself. I sent the ambulance over, but she said he wasn't breathing."

"Okay, you go ahead," I said. "Let me call down to Boone and tell them we're coming. I'll be right behind you."

Ruthie Haggarty was married to the meanest man in three states. His given name was Bob Wayne, but everyone called him "Little Bubba." This was to distinguish him from his father "Big Bubba," who was older but not larger than his son. Little Bubba was about six foot six and weighed close to three hundred pounds with two hundred eighty of it being muscle. I had seen him lift the front end of a tractor and hold it in the air while Ruthie changed the tire.

Ruthie, a good church-going gal, was the only one who wasn't intimidated by him. She'd dress him up and make him go to church with her twice a year, once at Easter and once on her birthday. Ruthie, with or without Little Bubba, was in her pew at St. Joseph's Catholic Church every time the doors opened.

Ardine McCollough had made friends with Ruthie some years back. Ardine had been in a bad marriage that involved quite a bit of abuse, and I suspected that she had solved the problem in the traditional mountain way — a nice cup of oleander tea. Her husband, PeeDee, disappeared one night and hadn't been heard from since. I had asked Ardine about Ruthie and Little Bubba.

"She told me," said Ardine, "that he never hit her. Not once."

"Hard to believe," I said. "He's got a volatile temper. I've had to lock him up more than a few times."

"I know it. That's just what Ruthie told me."

"Did you...give her a few tips?" I asked with a hard smile.

"I don't know what you're talking about," sniffed Ardine.

That had been several years ago. All I knew for sure was that for the past several months Ruthie and Little Bubba had been going at it hammer and tongs. I had been called out on three separate occasions by neighbors who had heard gunshots coming from the trailer. The first time I knocked on the door, Ruthie apologized to me and said that the rifle had gone off by mistake. The second time, I arrived to find Ruthie standing on the stoop with her arms crossed and Little Bubba sitting down, digging a slug out of his bicep with a hunting knife. When I walked up, Ruthie spun on her heel, went into the trailer and slammed the screen door after her.

"She just nicked me," he muttered as the bullet popped free.

"Yeah, I can see that," I said. "You want any help?"

"Nah. I don't know what she's always on about. I married her, didn't I?"

"Yes, Little Bubba, you did."

"I ain't hit her much."

"That's good."

"She's always on me about my girlfriend. Walleena don't even live in this town."

"It's good to keep your wife and your girlfriend separated if you can," I agreed.

"There just ain't no pleasing that woman."

"Well, if you're okay and she's okay, I'll be on my way," I said. "Just let me say hello." I knocked on the door. Ruthie came up to the screen, but didn't invite me in.

"You all right?" I asked. She nodded.

"Do me a favor, will you? Stop trying to shoot him." She nodded.

The third time I had been called out, Ruthie was washing her face and hair in the kitchen sink. There was a lot of blood. Little Bubba was nowhere to be seen, and his truck was gone as well.

"Can you tell me what happened?" I asked.

"He cut me," she said, still washing up. "Not bad, I don't think. Look at it and tell me, will you?"

I looked. "It's not bad, but you're going to need some stitches. You want me to take you to the hospital?"

"Nah. I can do it myself."

"What about Little Bubba? Did you shoot him?" I asked.

"Missed him. I hit the truck, though."

33

"You know, I can arrest him if you'll press charges."

"How long will you keep him locked up?" she asked.

I had to answer honestly. "Probably a couple of weeks if we're lucky. Then I can get a judge's order to keep him away from you."

"You think that'll work out here?"

"No, not really."

"Don't do it then. It'd just make him madder," she said.

That was a couple of weeks ago. I had heard from Ardine that he'd come back and that they were getting along. But now, apparently, she'd killed him. I hoped it was justifiable. I liked Ruthie.

Chapter 5

I was about three minutes behind Nancy when I left the station, but her lead had increased to about ten minutes by the time I drove up to the Haggarty trailer. I would have beaten her in the winter; my '62 Chevy pickup truck making pretty good time on these mountain roads. In the winter, Nancy drove a little Nissan whose four-cylinder engine could barely make it up her driveway. When the snow was off the roads, though, Nancy took to her motorcycle, a Harley-Davidson Dyna Super Glide. She was the fastest thing in Watauga County on these mountain roads.

Nancy was already inside. I could see her through the screen door with her pad out, taking notes. I walked up to the door and pulled it open, surveying the inside of the small living room. There was an old couch, a lamp, and a big-screen TV that served as a display for all kinds of religious *objets d'art* — everything from a Virgin Mary TV antenna to a prayer cloth blessed by Reverend Ike himself. But it was Little Bubba, as the designers say, that was the focal point of the décor. He was sitting in a blue recliner, the footstool flipped out, the chair pushed slightly back. He had half a cookie in one hand and a remote control in the other. There were scraps of paper scattered around the chair. His eyes were open and so was his mouth. I had seen dead folks before, and this was one of them.

"He's dead, ain't he?" said Ruthie, asking for confirmation. "Nancy said he was."

"I believe so," I said. "Did you tell Nancy what happened?"

"Sort of," Ruthie answered.

"Well, if you don't mind, could you tell it again so I can hear it?" Ruthie nodded and took a long breath.

"Little Bubba hadn't been back here for a few days. I guess he was staying with his girlfriend up in Sugar Grove. So anyway, he comes back, and I'm in the kitchen making Easter cookies for church."

"Easter cookies?" Nancy asked.

"You know. Shaped like bunnies and eggs and such. So anyway, I had this idea to make one shaped like Jesus on the cross. It turned out pretty well, so I made enough for the whole Sunday School class. I thought we'd decorate them at our party this Sunday. Look here. I've got red-hots for the blood and all colors of sparkles."

"Hmm," I said.

"Then I wrote up all these devotions to wrap around the cookies. I thought we could keep these by our beds and read the devotions while we nibbled on the cookies. I get very hungry while I'm talking to Jesus."

"So, what happened?" Nancy asked.

"Little Bubba came in and took the whole platter while I was in the bathroom. He plopped down in his chair and started eating. He just threw the devotions on the floor. Look there," she said, pointing at the half-eaten cookie in his hand. "That's the last one left."

"So what did you do?" I asked.

"I yelled at him and told him to get out. He said he wasn't going anywhere and to shut up before he shut me up for good. So I hit him."

"You hit him?"

"Yep. I hit him with the skillet. Two hands."

I walked over behind the chair and looked at the back of Little Bubba's head. I heard the ambulance drive up outside.

"You certainly did hit him," I agreed. "And maybe more than once."

"Maybe," said Ruthie. "Do I have to go with you?"

"I'm afraid so," I said.

"He shouldn't have eaten those cookies. I get very hungry while I'm talking to Jesus."

"Well, that's as much excitement as we've had for a few months," said Pete.

"And thanks to brilliant police work, the culprit has been apprehended and is safely in the Watauga County penal system," I added.

"Yes. Brilliant indeed. It's a shame that all the criminals in our fair city don't call the police department to report their crime and wait in their homes to be arrested."

I chose to ignore him. "Where's Noylene? I need to get something to eat."

"Over at her shop. She's opening up in about a month. I think she's going to call it *Noylene's,* even though I tried to talk her out of it."

Noylene Fabergé was Pete's head waitress, albeit "head waitress" was strictly an honorary post. He had given her the title so he wouldn't have to give her a raise, but Noylene had finally graduated from Beauty Correspondence School and was ready to open her own shop. She was now a licensed beautician.

"Anyway," said Pete, "Collette's in the kitchen. She'll be out shortly. I thought you'd taken to eating lunch over at The Ginger Cat."

"I can't do it anymore. The soup is good on Thursdays, but there are only so many watercress and blueberry duck finger sandwiches you can eat."

Collette came strolling up. "What'll it be, Chief?"

"Reuben sandwich," I said, my mouth beginning to water. "Fries and coleslaw. And don't skimp on the corned beef."

"You'll find the fixings in the walk-in," said Pete. "The recipe's hanging on the salad fridge."

"I've made them before," said Collette. "I remember."

A Reuben sandwich wasn't on the menu, but Pete kept the corned beef, sauerkraut, Swiss cheese and Russian dressing on hand for special orders.

"There should be a couple of beers in the walk-in as well," Pete called after her. "Bring those out, too, will you?"

"Are you allowed to serve beer?" I asked.

"If the cops don't catch me."

"You should be okay. I'm pretty busy today," I said. "Hey, did you hear about Kenny Frasier?"

"Nope," said Pete.

"He'd been given a prescription for medical marijuana by some quack doctor back in 1985. So last month, he calls the FBI and asks them if he can get another one. He tells them that his prescription expires in a few months, and he'd like to keep growing his crop. He says that the doctor told him that the prescription was good for twenty years."

"I always wondered how Kenny could afford a new truck every November. I figured he was stealing tobacco out of the barns," said Pete, as our beers arrived. "What did the feds do?"

"Well, they got his phone number and his address, and they told him that they'd bring his prescription right over."

"I'll bet they did. Was medical marijuana *ever* legal in North Carolina?"

"From '79 to '87," I said. "I had to look it up. Anyway, the feds showed up at Kenny's farm, and guess what? He had a whole field of the stuff growing behind his barn. You believe that?" I laughed. "He'd been raising and selling about a thousand pounds a year for the past twenty years. He told the feds that he only used what he needed and sold the rest to other medicinal users."

"How did he distribute it?"

"He used to sell it mail order through some group of medical users in California. Now he sells it over the Internet. He's got a guy on the west coast that packages it up for him and ships it from out there."

"Amazing," said Pete. "A real entrepreneur."

"Well, not any more," I said. "Ah, here comes lunch." I picked up the corner of the rye bread to peer inside. The ingredients were all there and looked to be in correct proportion. All was right with the world.

"Hey," said Pete, "what kind of pants are those?"

"Regular pants," I said. "Nonexpanding."

"You'll come around. It's only a matter of time."

"Is Bud working today?" I asked, through a mouthful of fries. "I need a recommendation for a nice, reasonably-priced Chablis."

"Yeah," said Pete, getting up. "I'll get him. This soldier's dead anyway." He picked up his empty beer bottle and headed back to the kitchen.

I was two bites into the sandwich when Bud came out. Bud McCollough was Ardine's oldest son. He was fifteen years old and had gotten a job at The Slab washing dishes and doing odd jobs, but his passion was wine. He'd been studying it for years. Ardine had two other kids as well as Bud. Her husband, PeeDee, in his paternal wisdom, had named them all after beers. In addition to Bud, there was his thirteen-year-old sister, Pauli Girl, and the youngest boy, Moose-Head, who was seven. We all did him a favor and called him "Moosey."

"Hi, Bud," I said, when he walked up to the table. "Listen, I need something good for Saturday night. I was thinking of a Chablis."

"What's on the menu?" asked Bud.

"Grilled salmon with capers, couscous, spinach salad, maybe cheesecake for dessert."

"Appetizers?" asked Bud.

"I think so, but I don't know what. Meg is bringing them, and I think I heard talk of mushrooms."

"Okay," said Bud. "Here's what you need to do. Got a pencil?" He waited while I dug one out of my pocket and grabbed a napkin to write on.

"For the main course, I think you'll want a Las Brisas Rueda. It's a Spanish white from the central region of Spain. Las Brisas has a wide-open array of flowery and grassy aromas that almost attack the nose at first sniff. The taste is bright, fruity and filled with white peach, apricot, Granny Smith apples, grapefruit and just a hint of lime, but it's got a touch of acidity that lets it really complement the salmon, especially if it's grilled. I'd also recommend that you grill some yellow bell peppers, by the way. They'd set the Las Brisas off nicely. Got that?"

"Yeah," I said. "How do you spell 'Brisas'?"

He ignored me. "For dessert, you'll want a tawny port. Graham's 20 Year Old is a good choice with cheesecake. But just a small glass — don't overdo it — and serve it with coffee. It's a true port; you know, from Portugal." Bud got a faraway look in his eyes. "It's wonderful: mixed aromas of cola, pecans, brown sugar, citrus peel and crème brûlée. It's a bit shy at first, but then quite daring: spirited and charming, with an elegant nose."

"Got it."

Collette had wandered over to the table and was looking at Bud as though there were lobsters crawling out of his ears.

"The appetizers are tricky, since we don't know exactly what Miss Farthing is planning, but I'm going to go out on a limb and steer you toward a Luis Felipe Edwards Carmenere. Very earthy. We're talking wet leaves, dirt, and maybe just a hint of tobacco."

"Sounds...lovely," I said, probably sounding a little leery.

"No, really," Bud replied, full of sincerity. "It's one of the new Chileans. Old wood and earth, blackberries, pepper. It reminds me of a dirty Merlot. A bit scouring on the back end, but with enough fruit and balance to pull it off. It's great with mushrooms. I think you'll like it a lot. Plus, it's pretty cheap."

Got it," I said again, finishing my notes. "Speaking of cheap, how much is this going to cost me?"

"The port is the most expensive at eighteen bucks a bottle, but you'll only need one. The other two are under ten, but depending on

39

how many people you have, you may have to get several bottles."

"Great!" I said. "Now, where do I get it?"

"You can call the Wine Market in Asheville. I think they'll ship it up. You can have it tomorrow."

"Thanks, Bud," I said, handing him a ten dollar bill. "You know, if you ever want to go into business, I'll be happy to set you up."

"I can't until I'm twenty-one," said Bud.

"You can't sell wine until you're twenty-one. But you can certainly sell advice."

"Maybe. Let me think about it."

Collette watched Bud walk back to the kitchen, wiping his hands on his apron.

"Well, paint me pink and call me Porkchop," exclaimed Collette. "I never saw such a thing in all my life."

Chapter 6

I was still thinking, something I do slowly and carefully, so I won't have to do it twice, when the door to my
office banged open and in swished three men wearing neck
scarves. They struck the traditional pose--elbows in,
wrists out. I recognized decorators when I saw them.

"Mornin', boys," I grunted. "What brings you to this
side of town?"

They were a stereotype waitin' for a bus. The blonde
California-boy was wearing a pink button-down tied up
around his midriff. The Latin egg was draped in red
leather, and the muscle was a huge black man with a
shaved head and I didn't want to know what else.

"Do not toy wis us," said the egg, in broken English
with just a hint of a lisp. "It is WE who are in charge
of the coloration project."

"Settle down boys," I said. "Have a squirt of eel juice."
I pulled four glasses out of my top drawer, spit in them
and wiped 'em out with my used handkerchief. I watched
the boys shudder as I poured myself a shot.

"No sank you," snarled the egg. "My name is Raoul."

"And who are your friends?"

"Zese are my associates, Biff and D'Roger."

"D'Roger?"

"DO NOT TOY WIS US!" screamed the egg, snapping open a
six-inch blade.

"Now don't start anything, boys," I said, reaching into
the other drawer for my heater. "You're just here to talk,
right?"

"Remember when I said that I didn't hate it?" asked Meg.

"Yes," I said. "That one comment has been my inspiration to
continue."

"I changed my mind. You now have a character named D'Roger,
and you're writing with a lisp. All bets are off. And let me ask you
this," she continued.

"Okay, ask."

"You don't have the choir any more, so you can't be writing this

41

story for them. Just who are you writing it for?"

"I think you mean 'to *whom* for am I writing it?' But that's okay. Don't feel bad. I *am*, after all, a writer. Many people mix up who and whom."

"Answer the question," she growled. It was a sexy growl. "*Whom* are you writing it for?"

"Well, I may have a choir again someday," I said. "But, to tell the truth, I just like to type on this old typewriter."

Meg relaxed. "Okay then. If that's the reason, you go on ahead. I suppose it can't hurt."

"Plus," (and I was saving this news for last), "there's a murder mystery blog that's going to publish my collected works," I said, "called *The Usual Suspects*. I already sent them the first three novelettes."

"Oh, no."

"Oh, yes! The first one is coming out next month."

"Let's call this meeting to order, please," hollered Billy Hixon, simultaneously banging the silent microphone on the podium. "Is this stupid thing working?"

For a church that averaged about eighty in worship, there was quite a turnout. Everyone who called himself or herself a member of St. Barnabas had showed up for this parish meeting. There were about eighty chairs set out. The other two hundred people were standing around the periphery of the room.

"Please, people," said Billy, after someone walked to the front and showed him how to turn the mic on. "Let's get started."

The crowd settled down, and Billy called on Father George to open the meeting with a prayer.

"Is there a prayer for spending sixteen million dollars?" I asked Meg under my breath.

"I think so. There'd better be."

It was a quick prayer that began by beseeching God, in His infinite wisdom, to leave us open to His will in all things and ended with an impatient muttering of amens sprinkled throughout the room.

"It is the vestry's decision," said Father George, "and let me just

say that I agree with it, that the disbursement of the funds recently acquired by St. Barnabas will be decided by a committee of six knowledgeable people. It is not a job for the vestry, and it certainly is not a job for the priest."

"Why not just invest the money, and we can use the interest to pay all of our bills?" asked Bear Niederman.

"That's a good question, Bear," Father George said. "And we certainly may do that with some of the money. But it is my feeling and the vestry concurs that making St. Barnabas a self-sustaining corporation would be a mistake in the life of the church. It is important for the people that are St. Barnabas to know that they are needed, that their gifts and their tithes are what sustain the church and that their talents are appreciated and invaluable. What would become of us if we decided that we were so rich that we didn't need an Altar Guild? Why not hire someone to come in and fix the flowers every week? Or what if we decided that we were all too busy to bother to fix church suppers? It certainly would be easier to have every meal catered by the Hunter's Club. Or why not have the choir replaced by a professional choral group?"

"Hey...what a good idea," I whispered, just prior to an elbow hitting my ribs.

"The reason that we don't do this is because St. Barnabas is its people," he continued. "We are all connected and involved. It's what makes this a wonderful place to be and to worship. We don't want to change that."

"But shouldn't we put a couple million away in case the furnace breaks again?" asked Rebecca Watts, to laughter from the crowd.

"Well," said Father George, as the laughter subsided, "the furnace has been replaced, and the physical plant is in good repair. I want you all to understand this. It is as important to the giver to be allowed to give, as it is to the church to be able to use the gift. We, as a congregation, need to give, and we are blessed in the giving."

He looked around the room. "How many of you would continue to tithe and give to St. Barnabas if you knew that there was sixteen million dollars in the bank and all of the bills were paid?"

About half of the folks in the room put their hands up.

"Now, remembering that I am, in fact, a priest and that you are in church," he continued with a smile, "I ask you the same question again."

More laughter. Then, around the room, hands began to drop as people began to seriously consider the question.

"What are we going to do then?" asked a woman, whom I had never seen in church before. "Just give it away?"

"Some of it, certainly," said Father George. "There is a lot of good we can do in the area. The Appalachian region is one of the poorest areas in the country, and we can certainly make a difference. And we certainly can plan for the future of the building itself and put away enough for any major repairs or work that needs to be done. But I think we can go much further."

He looked around the room, his eyes bright. "I see this as a great opportunity. It might be a good idea, for instance, to create a scholarship fund. Not the entire amount needed to perpetuate it, but a beginning; something in which we can all have a part. Or perhaps we might launch a concert series or start a food kitchen for the needy in our community. But that's what our committee will decide."

"Very eloquent," I said to Meg, under my breath. She nodded.

"There is nothing about this process that will be done secretly," said Father George. "It will be as transparent as possible. The members of the committee are Meg Farthing, Malcolm Walker, Lee Dalbey, Hayden Konig, Billy Hixon, and Gwen Jackson. Once the committee has made its recommendation, the vestry will vote on it. Yes or no. If the vote is no, it goes back to the committee. Now, if any of you have any ideas or comments, and I'm sure a few of you do, I'll open the floor to suggestions."

The first one to come to the front was Russ Stafford. Russ was on the vestry and was a real estate agent and developer. He lumbered to the front, carrying an easel, several poster-sized drawings and a folder. He took a minute to set up his props, put his folder on the lectern and begin his presentation. Most people in the meeting weren't prepared for such an elaborate presentation, assuming that this was going to be more of a brainstorming session. But Russ, ever the salesman, wasn't going to be caught flatfooted.

"I have a proposal," he began, "that, I think we will all agree, would be one of the most advantageous uses of this money. I

recommend that we take some of this money and invest in building a new rectory for the church."

I looked around the room. Everyone was listening politely, which was a change for St. Barnabas. Russ took this as a good sign.

"As you know," he continued, "the current rectory is over seventy-five years old."

This was true. Our rectory, the house provided to St. Barnabas' priest, was built in 1927, but it was a beautiful old house constructed mostly of stone. I had never heard a priest complain about his or her living arrangements. There was one priest who chose to buy his own house rather than live in the rectory, and that was fine with everyone. In those years, we simply rented it out to another family. The house had ten-foot ceilings, hardwood floors, a newly designed and remodeled kitchen, fireplaces in the bedrooms, and was situated one block off Main Street — just a five-minute walk from the church. I thought it was a wonderful house.

"I propose that we begin construction on a house in The Clifftops. There are many advantages to this as I think you will see..." Russ flipped the first board over. It was an artist's rendition of what I presumed was the clubhouse at The Clifftops, nicely drawn and professionally colored. "The Clifftops," Russ explained, "is a gated community with two professionally designed eighteen-hole golf courses. It's located eighteen miles from St. Germaine on two thousand acres. It's going to have six hundred home sites, two clubhouses, tennis courts...the works. Very upscale. All the homes will be in the one to six million dollar range." He grinned a toothy, real-estate grin and flipped to the next board. It was a picture of a grand house overlooking a stunning gorge view. At the bottom were the words "St. Barnabas Rectory." A murmur went through the crowd.

"If we get in now, on the ground-floor, the price of the house we build will double in the next three years. And I'm here to tell you, people, that's a darn good investment!"

I looked around the room again. People were nodding their heads just a little — not committing themselves, but acknowledging the unabashed and obvious genius of Russ' plan.

Russ smiled a big smile now, the smile of the closer. "What do y'all think?" He directed the question to Meg, Malcolm and me, who were all sitting together. The other three members of the committee were behind us somewhere.

"We can certainly take your idea under advisement," said Meg, diplomatically. "I'm sure there will be a lot of ideas coming forth over the next month or so."

"No, I mean it," said Russ. "This is a great idea, isn't it? Look around. Everyone thinks so. So, tell us. What do y'all think?" The room was very still.

"It's a bad idea," I said, finally.

"It's a really bad idea," said Meg.

"It's a terrible idea," agreed Malcolm. The other three committee members kept quiet.

Russ was startled, and his smile faded. He was getting angry now. "Why is this a bad idea? This is guaranteed! Everyone knows that the price of real estate in this part of the country is going up and up! If we had a rectory out at the Clifftops, the value would double, even triple in just a few years. Not only that, but if we could offer a priest a chance to live out there in a three or four million dollar home, we could attract a really good one." He'd said it before he realized it, but there it was. "Hmm...sorry, Father," he said. "But you all know what I mean. It's all fine and good to give all our money away. But just tell us: why isn't this a good idea?" He stood with his arms crossed in front of him in defiance.

Meg, Malcolm and I looked at one another like three contestants on "What's My Line," deciding who was going to be the one to stand up. Finally Malcolm said, "I'll do it," stood and walked to the front.

"First of all," said Malcolm, "let me say a few things. Father George is right in many of his views about the money, but I don't agree with him wholeheartedly. It seems to me to be financially prudent to take a significant portion, if not all of that money, and invest it wisely so that St. Barnabas no longer has to worry about any financial problems either now or in the future. But I am just a sixth of this committee. I'll be happy to state my views, but I'm only one person.

"As far as investing in real estate, and especially in a new multimillion dollar rectory, is concerned, here are the reasons that it's a bad idea. Number one. We already have a beautiful rectory. It's a short walk from the church and, more importantly, it's in the historic district. As most of you know, homes in the historic district have been grandfathered in as far as taxes are concerned. As long as we own this property, we will never pay more than fifteen dollars a

46

year in city taxes. To give up this house that we own free and clear would be the height of foolishness, but to keep it as a rental house is not a good option either. We are not in the landlord business, nor do I think we want to be.

"Number two. A house, as an investment, is only a good idea if you plan to sell it. A two million dollar house that appreciates into a four million dollar house is a bad deal if you're planning on keeping the property, and I don't think we want to be building a new rectory every five years. At the current tax rate, the annual real estate tax on a four million dollar home would be $21,200."

There were audible gasps throughout the room. It always amazed me how fast Malcolm could do the math. I had figured it at twenty plus, but I always used big, round numbers.

"Number three. The Clifftops are simply too far out for our rector to be effective. Eighteen miles on those roads is about a fifty-minute drive. That's a long way. Maybe not in a big city, but up here it sure is. Not only that, but remember that this is an investment in a gated community that may or may not make it as a viable association. I've been out to the Clifftops. Right now, it's little more than some dirt roads pushed in with a bulldozer. There's no infrastructure, and no electricity; there are no clubhouses, no tennis courts, and no golf courses. At this point, it's all real estate speculation, and although it might be a good investment, and one that I might make as an individual, to have the church build a rectory at the Clifftops wouldn't make much sense."

"But that's what makes this a great deal," said Russ, desperate now. "We can get in on the ground floor! You just said it would be a good investment."

"Yes, it might well be a good investment, but only if the church is intent on investing the money. I'm not sure it is. Of course, that's just my opinion," said Malcolm, gently. "The rest of the committee might feel differently. By the way, Russ," he said, taking his chair, "aren't you one of the developers involved in the Clifftops?"

"Yes, I am!" steamed Russ, grabbing his boards and his easel. "That's how come I know a sweet deal when I see one!"

"That went well," I whispered to Meg.

"Hush."

47

"It seems to me," said Jed Pierce, coming forward and speaking in a slow drawl, "that the members of this committee are all already of one mind."

Jed Pierce was a pharmacist in Boone, although he lived in St. Germaine, and had been elected Senior Warden in the fall. He had resigned when a certain traffic accident, in which he was involved, was made public, and Billy had taken over his position. I think he still felt that I had something to do with disclosing it, even though I assured him that I did not.

"It also seems to me," he continued, "that the people on this so-called committee are the *richest* members in the church. I'd like to know who formed this committee and who decided who was going to be on it."

"I ain't rich," said Billy, but there were more than a few heads nodding in agreement.

Father George got up and addressed the crowd. "I chose Meg Farthing to head up the committee. She chose the other members, and the vestry approved them. I told Meg to choose people she knew would consider their task prayerfully and use their expertise to guide us in these decisions."

"So she chose her rich friends," Jed said. "That figures."

"I said, I ain't rich," said Billy, a little louder, and this time to more than a few chuckles from the crowd.

"Well," said Father George, "it is probably true that most of the committee members are well-off, financially speaking, but they have experience with these kind of funds that most of us do not." I admired Father George for not making Meg defend herself.

"It's obvious that Malcolm's got the best idea," said Jed. "Put the money in the bank, and we don't have to ever worry again."

"That's not exactly what I said," explained Malcolm, getting to his feet.

"Why do we need a committee anyway?" asked Bear Niederman. "All this talk about spending all this money is going to split us right down the middle. Nobody's ever going to be happy. If we just put it in the bank like Malcolm said, we could pay our bills, buy what we needed and never have to worry about it again. Goodbye pledge drives!"

There was laughter and applause to that suggestion.

"But, that's the worst thing that could happen!" said Father George. "We need to be able to give to the church."

"We can give to other stuff," said Jed. "We could give to the Red Cross. Or Habitat for Humanity. We'd actually have *more* money to give."

"But you wouldn't," pleaded Father George. "You just wouldn't give it."

"Here's what I propose," said Jed. "I think that we should put one person in charge of this; somebody who knows what he's doing. And I think we all know who that is."

Father George was desperate. "We've got to have a committee. One person only has one viewpoint. We need more than that!"

"Tell you what," said Jed, ignoring the priest. "Why don't we do it this way? Whoever's given the most money to St. Barnabas over the years should be in charge of deciding what to do with the sixteen million dollars. That seems fair. Whoever that may be has been a good and faithful steward. It's only right that he should decide what's to be done."

"Sounds like a good idea to me," said Bear.

"Me, too," said Steve DeMoss.

"I think it's a good idea as well," said Phil Camp.

"I second the motion," said Russ Stafford, seeing a ray of hope return. He sure wouldn't talk the committee into a new rectory, but he might be able to talk Malcolm into an investment opportunity.

"There is no motion on the floor," said Billy, standing up.

"This is a parish meeting, ain't it?" asked Bear. "And we can take a vote of all the members, can't we?"

"Yes, we can," said Billy. "But there's still been no motion."

"I move we let the person who's given the most money to St. Barnabas be in charge of deciding what to do with the sixteen million dollars," said Jed in a loud voice.

"I second it," said Russ quickly. "And we mean real money, too. Not that 'in kind' stuff that Hayden does where he gives his check back to the music fund."

"Yeah," came the reply from the crowd. "None of that stuff." I raised my hands in a gesture of innocence. It wouldn't make any difference to me, one way or the other. I was staying out of this one, but the crowd wasn't. They were well involved now, and the noise in

the room was intensifying moment by moment.

"All in favor," shouted Jed.

"Just one dang minute," yelled Billy. "Y'all just hang on for a second."

"I call the vote," shouted Bear.

"I second that," hollered Jed. "Call the vote, call the vote..."

"Call the vote, call the vote," echoed the chant from the room, the congregation falling easily into the cadence as the rabble became roused. I looked at Father George. He was sitting, despondent, his head in his hands.

"Fine," yelled Billy, now flustered by the increasing cacophony. "All in favor signify by saying...?"

"AYE!" came the enthusiastic reply.

"All opposed?"

There were a few "nays" scattered around the hall including Meg's and my own, but it was evident who had carried the day. Malcolm stood up and walked to the front. The crowd quieted.

"You all know it doesn't work that way," said Malcolm. "This is a vestry decision. That's how we do things."

"Then let's have a vestry vote," called Russ. "We're all here."

Malcolm shrugged and gestured toward Billy. Billy cleared his throat.

"Mark Wells isn't here," he said, "and Logan's on vacation."

"It's still a quorum," said Malcolm. "We can vote."

Billy nodded. "All vestry members in favor of the motion, raise your hand." I (and everyone else in the room) counted seven hands.

"That's a majority," said Malcolm with finality. "I'd like to say that I'll do my best to prayerfully consider what is right and prudent for St. Barnabas..."

"Hang on a second," said a voice from the back of the room. It was Beverly Greene. "Hang on, Malcolm." She made her way to the front.

"We already voted," said Jed, loudly. "It's a done deal."

"Oh, I realize that," said Beverly, facing the crowd. "There's just one thing. As you all know, I've been doing the pledge cards for a couple months now, and since I started in this job in January, I've been astonished by people's giving. I must confess that when I

began this job I was curious as to what some people had given over the years, so I added some figures up."

She looked pointedly around the room and people started staring at their shoes.

"Malcolm gives a lot of money," Bev said. "In fact, he gives more money every year than anyone else. I didn't want to tell you how much because it's no one's business but his, but he's been a very generous member here for eighteen years."

There were murmurs of approval across the room.

"But he hasn't given the *most* money. Since this has to be out in the open, I'll tell you that Malcolm's given a little over $800,000 in his time here. That's a lot, but there's someone here who gives St. Barnabas $1259 every month and has been doing it for sixty-seven years. I added it up the other day because I was just amazed."

I watched Malcolm as he did the math in his head. He did it quickly, and, although his expression changed ever so slightly, to most observers, he seemed as interested as the rest of the congregation.

"When I asked her about it," Bev continued, "she told me that her tithe is one half of the settlement pension she receives from the Georgia Pacific Lumber Company. It comes to her every month since her husband was killed in a mill accident in 1938, and she'll continue to receive it until her death. Every month she receives $2518, and she gives half of it to the church. She told me that she just didn't need that much money to live on. Anyway, when you add it up, it comes to a little over $1,012,000."

I looked over at Malcolm. He smiled and answered with a slight inclination of his head. No one said a word.

"The person who has given the most money," Bev said, in her sweetest voice, "is Lucille Murdock."

Two hundred heads turned toward the back of the room. There, sitting in her usual place in the corner, was a tiny, eighty-seven year old woman, both her hands tightly clutching a black purse in her lap. Her snow-white hair was tied back in a bun, and she peered cautiously across the room through two gigantic, coke-bottle lenses that magnified each of her frequent blinks, making her look like a frog in a fishbowl.

"Thank you," she said in a shaking voice as she rose slowly to

her feet. "I will certainly pray about it." Lucille Murdock walked out of the parish hall to complete silence.

"Could this be the hand of God?" I muttered with a smile.

"I hope so," said Meg.

Chapter 7

"Tell me boys," I said, my roscoe dancing back and forth between them like a nervous ballerina on opening night. "Just how do you go 165,000 clams over budget?"

"Fabric samples," said Biff. "They aren't cheap, you know."

"Don't give me that malarkey!" I barked. I had 'em scared now--scared as a bad writer in a roomful of English majors--so scared that I thought Biff was going to jump right into D'Roger's arms. The egg started to cry.

I needed answers and I needed them pronto. A little bird told me I smelled a rat, and when I smell a rat, there's usually a red herring around. Also rats.

"Something's fishy," I said with a sniff. "You're not pros. You boys smell like last week's perch pie."

"What?" said Biff, obviously hard of herring.

"Don't shoot, mister," the egg blubbered. "She paid us to come up here. She said you were a pushover."

"Guess what?" I said.

"What?" said D'Roger and Biff in unison.

"I ain't."

"Did you happen to take any of those wandering musician church jobs, yet?" asked Meg. We were working in the kitchen of her house, whipping up some lunch. Actually, Meg and Ruby were working. I was sipping a Long Island Ice Tea and contemplating the two women with my number six ogle — the one that got me banned from Myrtle Beach. Meg looked a lot like Ruby, whose hair was still mostly black, although now, as she neared seventy, it was becoming streaked with silver. She was still a striking woman, tall and statuesque.

"Quit looking at me like that," said Ruby. "You should be ashamed. I'm old enough to be your slightly older, very good-looking second cousin."

"Which is legal in North Carolina," I added, ducking a piece of celery aimed at my head by Meg. "And, to answer your question, my dear, yes, I did take one of my many offers, but only for the Sunday after Easter. The job was too good to turn down. The chance-of-a-lifetime, if you will."

"Really. What, pray tell, is it?"

"You'll laugh," I said, taking another sip of my very refreshing drink.

"I promise I won't laugh."

"Okay then," I said. "Remember when we did that Clown Eucharist last year?"

"How could I forget? *Crown Him You Many Clowns...The Clown Imperial March*...it was awful."

"Yes, well...I got a call from Holy Comforter in Morganton. They heard about our Clown Eucharist."

"You're not doing another one?"

"Of course not. I told them a Clown Eucharist was a bad idea, and it didn't work that well."

"That's a relief."

"Then I might have mentioned another option for them to try," I said, sheepishly.

Meg's head dropped. "What did you suggest?" she asked in a quiet voice.

"A Pirate Eucharist."

"WHAT?!"

"Really, Meg," Ruby said. "You shouldn't scream. Use your 'indoor voice.' What will the neighbors think?"

"They're not going to do it, are they?" asked Meg. Then she comprehended the meaning of my maniacal grin. "You may *not* play for a Pirate Eucharist."

"I'm sorry," I said. "You misunderstood. I'm not only playing for it; I'm *writing* the Pirate Eucharist."

"It sounds like fun," said Ruby. "Can we come?"

"Arrrgh-solutely," I said, dropping into me best piratese. "Yar, me proud beauty, I be honored to take ye wi' me!"

"But you can't!" said Meg.

"Listen," I said. "Clowns scare little kids to death. Pirates are much more fun. If you can have a Clown Eucharist, why can't you have a Pirate Eucharist?"

"No reason I can see," said Ruby.

"Lots of reasons," said Meg. "Lots."

"The priest thought it was a great idea. They're advertising it."

"Oh, no..."

"Oh, *yes!*" I said.

Ruby and Meg finished up the sandwiches in short order.

"Well, if I'm going to a Pirate Eucharist," said Meg, "then you may go with me to church on Palm Sunday. We're singing *The Palms* by Fauré."

I snorted. "You realize that this particular Fauré is not Gabriel Fauré," I said. "It's by his musically challenged half-nephew Jim-Bob Fauré. It's an awful piece."

"Well, I haven't heard it yet since I skipped rehearsal last week, but I'm sure you're exaggerating because you, as we all know, are a musical snob. It's probably lovely."

"Oh, yes, I'm sure you're right," I agreed, eyeing my lunch.

"And speaking of awful writing," Meg said in her most pitying voice as she handed me a roast beef sandwich, "your story is not going well, is it? The plot seems to be a little off course."

"Not a bit of it. I'm right on target. Every word a gem. Every nuance a nugget of pure gold."

"I'd like to read it," said Ruby, sitting down next to me. "Do you have a copy?"

"Not with me, but I'll make sure you get one as soon as I finish," I promised.

I got the skinny from the boys and set out just after the sun went down. It was a dark night, as nights here in the city usually are, and, in fact, I couldn't remember a sunny night since my twelve-hour layover at Juneau International in the middle of August. It was also stormy, but that was a given. I pulled the lapels of my trench up over my ears, tucked my head down and turtled down the street at a leisurely pace.

The decorators were a front for a scam--that much was clear. One hundred sixty-five large for fabric swatches? Who did they think they were dealing with--Martha Stewart's prison consultant? After a little friendly persuasion, they'd given me a name. I didn't hurt them. I just pinched them a little.

I walked into The Slab on Thursday morning, bright and early, early for me being eight-thirty. I had taken my time driving in, enjoying the scenery and listening to the *Ninth Symphony* of Vaughan Williams. It was the symphony about which Aaron Copland quipped, "It's like watching a cow for forty minutes." Aaron Copland was right, but it was beautiful music for driving through the mountains on a crisp morning in March.

"I thought you said we were meeting at eight sharp," said Nancy as I walked in.

"It *is* eight," I said, sitting down. "Isn't it?"

"Close enough," said Dave.

"You got here three minutes ago, Dave," said Nancy.

"Well, I knew that the chief wasn't going to be on time. He's always here at eight-thirty. And I was right, wasn't I?"

Collette filled his coffee cup and looked at him adoringly. "You're really smart, Dave," she said.

"Oh, puh-lease!" said Nancy to no one in particular. "I think I'm gonna..."

"Coffee for me, Collette," I said, hastily interrupting Nancy's outburst. "And some of those Belgian waffles."

"Has anyone heard from Lucille Murdock since the meeting on Tuesday night?" asked Pete, pulling up a chair. Pete was always a de facto member of our staff meetings whenever we met at The Slab Café. He was, after all, the mayor, and since he was the owner, he also comped our breakfasts. It was a good deal all around.

"How did you hear about Mrs. Murdock?" I asked.

"Everyone's heard about it. Are you kidding?" said Dave. "It's big news. How do you think she's going to spend the money?"

"I'm sure I don't know, Dave, but she's certain to have a lot of help deciding."

"I'm sure Agnes Day will have a few suggestions," said Nancy.

"Why do you think that?" I asked. "Why would a substitute organist even care?"

"I heard that she was bucking for your old job, boss. If you didn't decide to go back, that is."

"Yeah, I heard that, too. So?"

"Well, if she's the regular organist, she might want to finagle some of that cash into the music fund."

"She might," I agreed. "But what does that have to do with Mrs. Murdock?"

"Don't you know?" asked Nancy. "Agnes Day is Mrs. Murdock's home health care nurse."

Meg and I entered the front doors of St. Barnabas on Palm Sunday at precisely 10:32. The service started at 10:30 or was supposed to. As usual, things were slightly behind schedule. Meg had decided to forego singing in the choir after the rehearsal on Wednesday night. I accused her of being a "fair-weather" singer and threw in a few "I told you sos" for good measure. I didn't get to use them very often, so when I had the opportunity, I jumped on it like a Schnauzer on a schnitzel.

"Hush up," Meg said, putting one lovely finger to my lips, "and I'll make it worth your while."

I hushed up.

I hadn't been back to St. B.'s for almost five months, and I had mixed feelings as I walked into the nave. I missed playing the organ in church. I missed playing, period. Then I heard Agnes Day's prelude. This was Meg's plan, of course, and a ruse that I saw through immediately.

"It won't work," I said. "I'm not coming back."

"I'm sure I don't know what you mean," Meg said. The sounds of what I thought might be *All Glory Laud and Honor*, the Palm Sunday processional, came crashing down from the organ loft.

"What on earth is that?" I whispered.

"Agnes Day is improvising," said Meg. "It's her musical gift to the congregation. Each Sunday in Lent, she's been improvising on hymn tunes for that particular day."

"My God! I've never heard anything like it."

"It's not over yet. Here," she said, handing me a hymnal. "Bite down on this."

We sang the Palm Sunday processional and watched as Benny Dawkins, the world-class thurifer, worked his magic with the incense pot. He really *was* world-class, having finished in the top five for three years running at the International Thurifer Invitational in London. Benny had told me that he had perfected a couple of new moves that he picked up at the competition — the *Three-Leaf Clover* and the *Double Gerbil.* He executed them flawlessly.

We joined in on the *Kyrie* and the Psalm and listened to the sermon. At the offertory, we were treated to a heartfelt, if not completely accurate, choral rendition of *The Palms* by Jean-Baptiste Fauré.

"I thought you said his name was 'Jim Bob' Fauré," said Meg, as the offering plate went by.

"Jean-Baptiste translates to Jim Bob."

"No it doesn't."

"It should."

During communion, the musical offering was *The Holy City,* sung by Renee Tatton. I hazarded a glance back up to the choir loft. Ms. Tatton wasn't wearing a robe, but instead had chosen a lavender, diaphanous gown covered in sequins. I thought that her arm waving was rather extreme for that particular piece, but Meg said that those bird watchers returning from communion would certainly appreciate it. Other than that, it was a pretty good performance.

"At least she chose to wear something purple," I commented. "It is a penitential season, after all."

The service concluded, and the congregation made their way out of the sanctuary and headed to the parish hall for coffee, cookies and the latest gossip — gossip which chiefly concerned one Lucille Murdock. Meg and I were almost the last to leave, hanging back to listen to Agnes Day's postlude. Finally, we had to admit that enough was enough, and we followed the lemmings to the coffee pot. We had just finished our second cup — real Sunday morning coffee, not Father George's anemic brew — and were getting ready to leave when Georgia pulled on my arm.

"You'd better come," she said. "Something's wrong."

Meg and I followed her through the kitchen, out the door into the alley and back into the sacristy. Elaine was waiting. She and Georgia were helping prepare the homebound communion.

"Come here," said Elaine, grabbing my arm and pulling me into the nave. Meg and Georgia followed.

The organ was still playing. Agnes Day had been improvising on *What A Friend We Have In Jesus* as the postlude. I'd heard enough of it, before we left the first time, to know that it wasn't going to be a virtuoso performance. Now, amid the din of the organ, I noticed the zimbelstern, a set of seven bells played by a rotating hammer and activated by a toe stud on the pedal board. The zimbelstern was great for effects — very pretty — and I used it liberally on Christmas Eve, but I hadn't ever heard it used in *What A Friend We Have In Jesus*. Then again, I'd never heard an improvisation on that particular hymn tune.

"Listen to her," said Georgia. "That's just awful, even for her. She's been playing the same thing for ten minutes."

"Maybe she's still improvising," Meg said.

I shook my head. "I don't think so. C'mon."

I was down the aisle and up the stairs to the choir loft in short order with the three women following me. I stopped in front of the big stained-glass window that framed the loft and looked at the organ. There, draped across the console, was Agnes Day. I took out my cell phone and called for an ambulance as Meg, Elaine and Georgia joined me in front of the window.

"Is she dead?" asked Meg. "She's not moving."

"I don't know." I stepped down to the console, followed closely by Meg. I pulled Agnes Day back from the console and looked at her face. Her eyes were open and unseeing. I let her slump back gently where I found her, then reached around and turned the organ off.

"She's not breathing," said Meg, "Shouldn't we do CPR or something?"

I shook my head. "Look here," I said, pointing to the right side of her head. "If we'd gotten here ten minutes earlier, maybe. Even then..." I left the sentence unfinished.

"Then who was playing the organ?" asked Georgia. "A ghost?"

I pointed to the MIDI recorder. "She was recording her improvisation. I suppose to play it back at some point — maybe listen to it."

"What's that thing?" asked Elaine.

"MIDI is short for Musical Instrument Digital Interface. Basically, in this application, it records all of the aspects of a pipe organ's performance."

"So it will play it back exactly as it was recorded? All the stops and wrong notes and everything?" asked Georgia.

"Everything."

"When did *that* get installed?"

"A couple of years ago," I said. "I bought it and had it put in so I could hear how the organ sounded out in the church. Just to check myself. A practice tool, mostly."

"But you could record a postlude or something, and we could play it back later?"

"Sure. I did it a couple of times." I turned to Meg. "Remember when I got that call half-way through communion? You just put the disk in for the hymn and the postlude, punched the 'play' button and the service never missed a beat."

"You recorded the music for every service in advance?" Elaine asked.

"No," I said. "Just an emergency hymn and an emergency postlude. Father George and I had a signal worked out. If I had to leave before the end of the service, we'd skip the middle hymn if we hadn't already sung it, announce the last hymn as *Be Thou My Vision* and finish up. Communion would be silent, but that didn't really bother anyone."

"Hey, can we go downstairs?" said Georgia. "This is creeping me out. I mean, just look at her. Aren't we being disrespectful?"

"Sorry," I said. "I guess I'm used to it. You can go on down if you want." Georgia just shrugged.

"I still don't get it," said Elaine. "So what happened?"

"Agnes Day was recording her improvisation. When she got hit, her foot kicked the zimbelstern on and her hand fell on the playback button. Look here. The MIDI played back everything she'd recorded along with the notes that her body and left arm were playing as they rested on the keys."

"So when it finished..." Elaine nodded, finally understanding.

"The recorder simply played it back over and over. Until we came up and turned it off."

"How long do you think it took before she died?" asked Georgia,

edging slowly toward the stairs.

"I can't tell for sure. Like I said before, it could have been ten minutes, maybe more. Meg and I were in the parish hall for almost twenty."

We were all quiet for a moment.

"If only she hadn't been such a bad organist," said Elaine, sadly. "We might have saved her."

Nancy arrived at the church a matter of minutes after I had called her. Dave was right behind her. The ambulance was on the way.

"You ladies stay up here for a little while," I said. "Dave, you go wait for the ambulance and send them up here with a gurney. Hopefully, most of the congregation has gone home, and we won't have to explain any of this until tomorrow. Is Father George still here?"

"He didn't even stay for coffee," Georgia said. "He had a couple of hospital visits to make, and he wanted to see the ball game this afternoon."

"Fine. We'll tell him later. Nancy? Let's you and I have a look around before the EMTs get here."

I explained the series of events to Nancy as we quickly searched the choir loft. It didn't take long to find the murder weapon — a G3 handbell that I remembered being used to give a pitch for the Psalm. It was heavy — about four pounds — and had noticeable blood on the finish. The killer hadn't even tried to clean it off, just set it back on the shelf by the organ.

The organ console was clean, nothing out of the ordinary at all. I took off the pedal board, and we looked under the organ. It was clean as well.

I called Elaine and Georgia over. "Did either of you hear a handbell clang during Agnes Day's recessional? Maybe a dull thud, following by a ringing sound?"

"Who could tell?" said Georgia. "All I heard was just a bunch of wrong notes."

"I might have heard it," said Elaine. "No," she decided. "I guess not. Not that I remember anyway."

"Any idea who might have wanted to kill her?" asked Nancy.

"Anyone who heard her play," answered Georgia.

Chapter 8

"Did you talk to Father George?" Meg asked me on Sunday evening.

"Yep. I called and told him this afternoon. He actually answered his cell phone. I must say, he was quite upset."

"Rightfully so." Meg was sitting at my kitchen table watching Archimedes eat his supper and contemplating recent events. "Don't you find it odd and a bit unnerving that St. Barnabas has had such a crime wave in recent years?"

"Not really," I said. "You forget. I heard her play." I held up another mouse, and Archimedes took it gently from my hand with his beak.

"Your bad joke aside, isn't it weird? And this is the second person to be murdered in the choir loft."

"That's why I used to keep my 9mm Glock under the organ bench. You never know who's going to take offense at a Hammerschmidt passacaglia. I wanted to be prepared."

"Well, *I* think it's weird," said Meg.

"It's coincidence," I said. "It's not really a crime wave. There have been a couple of murders, sure, but not anything outside the realm of statistical probability for a town this size. And accidents happen all the time."

I gave Archimedes the last of the three mice I had taken out of the freezer to thaw. Archimedes was a barn owl that had shown up at the cabin a couple of autumns earlier. I fed him regularly and, over the years, he had become quite used to us. So much, in fact, that I had installed an automatic window in the kitchen so he could enter or leave as he pleased. In the freezer, I kept a supply of mice and a few baby squirrels that I got from Kent Murphee, the coroner in Boone. Where he got them, I never asked. I opened the fridge door and got out the last of Pete's Wicked Ales, turning back around just in time to see the owl hop up into his windowsill and disappear silently into the dusk.

"He's amazing, isn't he?" said Meg. "I never get tired of watching him. I'm glad he's stayed around, but I guess he'll vanish one of these days, and we'll never know what happened to him."

"I guess," I agreed. "But he's not that old yet. He may be around

for a while. Lord knows, he doesn't have to scavenge much for food. And he does look pretty well fed."

"Speaking of 'well fed,' did Father George talk to you about playing this week?"

"Yes. And what has 'well fed' got to do with anything?"

"Nothing. I just thought it was a nice transition," said Meg. "That, plus you need to go on a diet."

"What?"

Meg giggled. "It's called 'stream of consciousness.' It's a book I'm reading. You're supposed to say whatever you're thinking."

"Well, stop it," I said.

"Speaking of diets," Meg continued, "do you think you might consider playing this week? Just through Easter?"

"Only if you stop," I said.

"Done and done," said Meg, holding out her hand for me to kiss. I missed her hand entirely.

I walked down to the corner and turned right, then right again, left, then right, right, straight, right, straight and a quick left. I popped a mallard into a hotel lobby and looked around for the lounge. It wasn't hard to find. I'd been here before. I strolled up to the bartender.

"What'll it be, Mac?" he snarled in a low grunt, casually wiping down a glass.

"A shot of Four Roses and an answer," I said, laying a sawbuck on the bar. "I'm looking for a palooka that goes by Pedro LaFleur. Big guy, about two eighty. Cauliflower ear. Flat nose. Three-inch scar under his eye. Sings counter-tenor for the Presbyterians. Hard guy to miss."

"Sorry Mac, I ain't heard or seen nobody like that." He reached for the sawbuck, but I covered it with my badge-- the one I'd swiped from Detective Krupke. He gave a nod toward the back of the bar and slid the bill out from under the badge. I smiled and took my drink for a little walk.

Pedro LaFleur and I had been partners in a past life. We had been closer than two cousins in a Kentucky hayloft, but went our separate ways about ten years ago.

There were ideological differences. He couldn't get past my understanding of the doctrine of Divine Simplicity as applied by St. Thomas Aquinas, and I didn't see his need for wrestling with the hermeneutic problems of tri-theism in reformed theology. Now I needed his help.

"Hello, Pedro," I said, sitting down across from him.

He smiled at me—a smile that would make my blood run colder than a penguin's pizzle if I wasn't on the same side of the draw.

I filled him in on what I knew. He didn't say much, but then, he never had to. He just sipped his drink.

"Sounds interesting," he finally said. "I'm in. But let's get something to eat. I'm hungry as Kate Moss' tapeworm."

Monday morning was rainy, cold, windy, and, by and large, one of the nastiest days we had seen for quite some time. When you get used to a couple of weeks of beautiful spring weather, it's always a shock to be shoved back into winter by a nasty Mother Nature who doesn't want to be taken for granted. And, to top it all off, we were in for two inches of snow, if you could believe the weatherman on Channel Four, which no one did. If he predicted two inches of snow, it was a cinch that we'd either get ten or a heat wave. The odds were about even. I pulled up in front of the police station just in time to see Nancy get out of her Nissan and slam the door angrily.

"I just got my bike out, and now this," she growled. "I hate Channel Four."

"Me, too," I agreed. "Let's go see if we have anything from Kent."

I doubted that Kent would even be in his office this early, much less have a coroner's report ready on Agnes Day. I was right. Nancy and I headed over to The Slab after leaving a note for Dave. We always left a note, even though he knew where to find us, especially on a miserable Monday morning with murder lurking in the air.

"Do you feel it?" I said to Nancy, sniffing the air like a bloodhound as we walked the two blocks to the café.

"Feel what?" asked Nancy. "All I feel is cold and wet."

"It's murder in the air," I said. "Lurking."

"Yeah, yeah," Nancy grumbled. "Lurking. It's definitely lurking. You love this stuff, don't you?"

"The weather?" I asked. "I don't mind it so much."

"No, not the weather. The crime, the chase, figuring it out."

"Well, I must admit, it does put a spring in the old detective's step."

"Mine, too," Nancy said, with a wicked grin.

We sat down at our table in The Slab, although, on this particular Monday, we could have had our choice of any of the tables. The weather was keeping all of Pete's usual patrons inside. Noylene Fabergé was sitting at the counter having a cup of coffee. Pete was in the kitchen, I supposed, just waiting for our order.

"Hi, Noylene," said Nancy, as she took her seat. "Is your beauty shop open yet?"

"Not yet. If it was, I wouldn't be working here anymore." Noylene stood up and came over to the table with her coffee pot.

"I thought you liked it here," I said, holding out a cup.

"I like it fine. I just wouldn't have time to do both. What can I get you?"

"Whatever's easy," I said. "Dave's coming, too. He'll be here in a bit."

"I'll tell Pete you're here and that you're hungry."

"As Kate Moss' tapeworm," I added.

"Huh?"

"Never mind," I said, as Noylene headed for the kitchen. I turned my attention to Nancy. "Did you hear anything from the lab?"

Nancy had taken all of our crime scene evidence to the state police lab in Boone last night. It wasn't CSI Miami, but it was certainly better facilities than we had in St. Germaine. Unfortunately, we didn't have much evidence. We found the murder weapon, of course — the handbell, but our subsequent search of the choir loft turned up nothing except quite a few sequins scattered on the floor in front of the organ. I suspected they came from the soloist's gown, given the way she was flapping about. I picked one up and turned it over. It hadn't been sewn onto her dress, but rather, applied with hot glue. There were probably so many of them on there that twenty or so wouldn't be missed. Nancy had diligently collected them and sent them to the lab with the other evidence.

I doubted that the handbell had anything to tell us except that it was, in fact, the murder weapon. Kent Murphee could match the indentation to the bell and there was probably enough blood on it to make an irrefutable match. I didn't think that there would be any fingerprints. That would be just too easy.

Dave walked into The Slab. The door caught the wind, yanked it out of his hand, and banged it against the jamb with a force I thought might break the glass, but didn't.

"Lovely weather, isn't it?" said Pete, bringing some country ham biscuits to the table.

"I like it," said Dave, taking off his coat and dropping it over a neighboring chair.

"To the case at hand," I said. "Nancy, what do we know?"

Nancy pulled out her pad, flipped a couple of pages and checked her notes.

"Agnes Day was killed yesterday sometime between noon and 12:20. The choir came down from the loft after the service was over. She was still alive at that point."

"I listened to the MIDI recording," I said. "It was just about six minutes long before it was cut off. So, if she started at noon, or close to it, she was killed six minutes later. We didn't find her until 12:20."

"Right," said Nancy. "I haven't heard from Kent, but we're presuming that she was killed by blunt force trauma — a handbell to the head. I interviewed most of the choir last night. Plus a couple of members of the vestry, Beverly Greene, and Father George. No one saw anything unusual. Everyone says they left the choir loft after the benediction, put their robes up, and went straight to the parish hall. All eight of them. I haven't gotten to talk with the soloist. She wasn't available, but I'll catch up with her this morning."

"Renee Tatton," I said.

"Yep."

"How about motive?" I asked Nancy. "Did you come up with anything?"

"She wasn't well liked. No one I talked to had anything good to say."

"No one?"

"Nope. Mighty peculiar. She was, by all accounts, singularly unpopular."

"We need to talk to Benny Dawkins," I said. "He had a disagreement with her. I heard something about a lawsuit."

"I'll check it out," said Nancy.

"There's something else. Lucille Murdock, the lady who is making the decision about how St. Barnabas will spend the sixteen million dollars, was Agnes Day's home health care patient."

"That's quite a coincidence," said Dave.

"Yes, quite," I said.

"Another thing," said Nancy. "Did you happen to watch *America's Funniest Videos* last night?"

"Is that show still on?" asked Pete.

"Syndication," I said. "I didn't watch it."

"Me neither," said Dave. Pete shook his head.

"Last night they played a video of the Passaglio wedding."

"Really? Was it funny?" asked Pete.

"It was freakin' HILARIOUS!" said Nancy, laughing at the thought of it.

"What's it got to do with the murder?" I asked.

"You've got to see it," Nancy said. "I'll see if I can get a copy of the tape. It was sent in by a videographer in Boone. I got his name."

"Yeah," I said, impatience creeping into my voice. "But what does it have to do with..."

"Agnes Day," interrupted Nancy, "was the organist."

Chapter 9

Pedro and I made our way to Ramelle's, an all-you-can-eat buffet on the next block. We were greeted by the Maitre d'Porcelet and shown to our table.

"So, who's the brains?" Pedro asked, looking at me over a huge platter of fried squab and probable equine parts. Ramelle's was known for their vast quantities of food, most of it unidentifiable once it hit the grease.

"The boys gave me a name. Miss Bulimia Forsythe. Know her?"

"I've heard of her," said Pedro, slurping down what might be a lung, or perhaps a forelock. "Soprano, right?"

"Yeah."

"Skinny? Red hair?"

"Really skinny," I said.

"I don't know how she does it. I've seen her in here putting down enough to choke a Sumo wrestler on Fat Tuesday."

"It's a puzzler, all right," I said.

I met Annette for lunch at The Ginger Cat. She was waiting for me at a table in the back and waved at me as I came in. Annette Passaglio was a long-time member of St. Barnabas and had been on the vestry a couple of times since I had been organist. She was the closest thing St. Germaine had to a socialite, if our town could claim to even have such a class of folks. Her husband, Francis, was an orthodontist, but Annette was from old money, and I always had the feeling that she merely tolerated his profession, believing that it was beneath the societal position to which she aspired. She'd rather that he had been a surgeon or an investment banker or, better yet, a congressman, and she wouldn't have minded funding any one of those dreams, had Francis shown even the smallest amount of ambition.

I made my way past the other diners and sat down across from Annette.

"It's nice to see you, Hayden," said Annette, holding out her hand palm down, as if to be kissed. It was the second hand that

I'd had offered to me in the last two days, but this time, I reached across the table and shook it, hoping I'd made the correct decision.

"It's nice to see you, too." I said. "Have you ordered yet?"

"No," she said, with a pitying look. "I thought I'd wait for my dining partner." It took me two beats to comprehend the unspoken rebuke at my faux pas. I smiled in self-defense. Oops.

"Ah, well...ahem," I stammered, clearing my throat and noticing that she'd already placed her menu down on the table. "What would you like?"

"I'll have the duckling and wild rice," she said, ordering the only entrée on the menu with a price tag of twenty bucks. "And raspberry tea. Iced."

Meg had given me some etiquette tips for my lunch meeting with Annette, and one of the things she prepped me on was ordering. It was my job and mine alone. Cynthia walked over to our table with two glasses of ice water and set them down warily. Then she stood back and looked at them for a moment before reaching across the table and moving my glass a quarter inch to the right. She'd obviously encountered Annette as a customer before.

"Are you ready to order?" she asked. "Or would you like more time?"

I think we're ready," I said. Annette just smiled.

"Mrs. Passaglio will have the duckling and wild rice. And raspberry tea. Iced."

"And for the gentleman?" said Cynthia.

"I'd like the wild rice as well. But I don't care for baby ducks. May I have piglet with mine?"

Cynthia made a snorting sound as she tried to stifle her laugh. It was not a lady-like snort. "I'm sorry, sir. We're out of piglet."

"Then I shall have a sandwich. Sprouts and mushrooms, I guess. Maybe some other fungi, if there's some lying around the kitchen. You choose. Hey! What about the feet from the duckling? Can you put those on there, too? Maybe a little Grey Poupon?"

"No feet," said Cynthia. "We put those in the soup, but I'll check on the availability of fungi. They may be out of season."

"They're never out of season in my shower."

"That's more information than I need," laughed Cynthia, heading toward the kitchen.

The cold smile never left Annette's face.

I had seen the wedding video an hour earlier at the station. Nancy had gone down to Boone and gotten a copy from Todd Whitlock, Watauga County's foremost wedding videographer. The whole thing had been very entertaining, and I smiled in spite of myself as I remembered it.

As wedding videos went, the beginning was pretty typical. Nancy fast-forwarded to the homily and handed me the program that went with the video. Father George was one of the two ministers involved in the service, the other being someone I didn't recognize and who the program identified as Rev. Caleb Latimer, minister of St. Matthew's United Methodist Church in Greenville. I assumed that this was the groom's minister.

Misty Passaglio's wedding was the social event of last winter. Even though a February wedding in St. Germaine was rare, Misty's fiancée, Jerry, who worked for the State Department, had been assigned to the American Embassy in Italy beginning in April. It was a job of which Annette approved, and although it would have been preferable for Misty to have her wedding in June, or even late May, Annette thought that a winter wedding might be distinctive enough to offset the seasonal awkwardness. I had been invited, of course, but in reality, only as "the help." Once Annette found out I wouldn't play for the wedding, both Meg and I were quickly relegated to inconsequential status, and since I make it a policy not to be present at any weddings that I am not paid to attend, we both skipped it entirely.

I had heard that, although Misty wanted to be married in St. Barnabas, Annette had decided that the church was just too small for the number of guests that would be attending. There were any number of churches available, but Annette had chosen Covenant United Methodist Church in Boone. The sanctuary was white and crisp, they had a piano as well as a pipe organ, and, most importantly, it could seat about twice the number of people as could attend if the wedding were held in St. Barnabas.

I turned my attention back to the tape. Rev. Latimer had just finished his homily as Nancy and I watched intently.

"Here it comes," she said. "This is just great!" Nancy hated Annette.

71

According to the program, it was time for the vows and, after they had been recited, the soloist would sing *O Promise Me,* not my favorite, but then, it wasn't my wedding. The videographer was in the back balcony with a good telephoto lens. He panned back for a wider shot. The soloist, who was sitting in the first pew, walked up to the piano and stood in the crook, waiting for his cue. The piano wasn't on the dais, but placed on the floor of the sanctuary, nestled into a niche constructed for just that purpose. The organ console, on the other hand, was up on the platform, the entrance on the same level as the minister's overstuffed furniture, and separated from the congregation by a raised panel that mimicked the choir railing stretching across the front of the church.

It might have all gone smoothly if the organist, who was also the pianist, had left the music for the soloist on the piano when they rehearsed. She did not. Although the camera had zoomed in on the wedding couple — they were now facing each other — to their left, clearly visible in the shot, the organist was frantically sorting through sheets of music. The soloist waited patiently, knowing that they still had time, but noticing that his accompanist was not yet seated at the piano. He finally glanced over his shoulder and saw what the rest of us were privy to: Agnes Day rooting through a pile of music sitting on the console of the organ. Finally, she apparently found what she was looking for, disappeared out a door into the sacristy and appeared a minute later through a side door that put her at the piano. The videographer, meanwhile, had widened his shot again, his microphone up at the front, picking up the vows of the betrothed.

"Will you, Jerry, have Misty to be your wedded wife? To have and to hold..."

The congregation, as is always the case in a religious service when something out of the ordinary happens, had turned its attention to Agnes Day. She had turned out to be much more entertaining than the wedding. The videographer, for whatever reason, kept his shot wide enough to include her unintentional antics.

Agnes Day sat down at the piano, as the minister, having gotten the correct answers from Jerry, now switched his traditional interrogation to the bride.

"Misty, will you have Jerry to be your wedded husband, to live together in the holy estate of matrimony? Will you love him, comfort

him, honor him and keep him..."

Agnes Day sat down at the piano, opened her music, looked at it blankly for a moment and then closed it again to a few titters. It was obvious to everyone that she had brought down the wrong song. The crowd wasn't paying the least bit of attention to the bride and groom, entranced, rather, by the drama that was taking place at the piano. The soloist smiled politely, rolled his eyes slightly and took a deep breath as Agnes Day got up from the piano bench to fetch the correct music. He looked nervous. Time was running out. He would have to sing as soon as they finished their vows.

"Jerry," Father George said, "repeat after me. In the presence of God and before these witnesses..."

Jerry started repeating at the same time Mrs. Agnes Day did something extraordinary. Instead of going back out the door and around to the back entrance to the choir loft, she walked up the steps and leaned over the railing to pick up her whole stack of music. Perhaps she was thinking that it would be quicker to get all the music down to the piano and sort through it there. Perhaps she was thinking that it was almost time to play, an extra minute or two, an absolute *eternity* in wedding time, would be intolerable and this course of action would be quicker. Whatever she was thinking, I'm pretty sure she changed her mind when she over-balanced and tumbled head first into the organ pit.

"...as long as we both shall live," finished Jerry.

Nancy laughed. "No, no. Wait...just wait..." she said. "It gets better."

Anyone who has ever fallen in public knows, in that awful moment, that there are two things you can do. You can either fall, make a fool of yourself, and get it over with, or you can somehow catch yourself, try to save your self-respect, and maybe maintain a shred of dignity. At least that's what goes through our brain in that split second of terror we experience as we begin to topple. In reality, the second option almost never exists. And it didn't for Agnes Day.

"In the presence of God and before these witnesses," said Misty. "I, Misty, take you Jerry, to be my husband..."

Although we couldn't see it, I was pretty sure that Agnes Day held onto her music, at least part of the way down. It's what an organist would do, I thought, although she probably dropped it before her hands hit the pedal board. I don't know why the pedal stops were

on, but they were, and they made quite a racket.

"Watch this," said Nancy. The entire wedding party turned to face the organ and see what was going on, but there was no help for Agnes Day. The soloist was frozen in place, and no one in the party seemed to know what to do, this event not having been planned for in the two-hour wedding rehearsal. Father George, his view being blocked by eight bridesmaids and enough flowers to bury a crown prince, did the only thing he could. He continued.

"For better, for worse."

"For better, for worse," Misty growled, not having a clear view either, but knowing that on her "special day," she was no longer the center of attention.

Agnes Day wasn't a particularly sturdy woman, and she was so far over that her arms were simply not strong enough to push the top of her body back over the rail. One option, and one she might have made had she been practicing by herself, was to slither ignominiously over the rail and onto the pedals. Even then, it was quite a drop into the pit, especially head first with not much arm strength to break the fall. This was not an option she was willing to take, so Agnes Day did the only thing she could. She started kicking her legs and bouncing her hands on the pedals hoping to move herself back far enough to allow her center of gravity to tip her out of the pit. It was a slim chance, made slimmer when her dress flopped up around her waist. The videographer made no more pretense of trying to photograph the wedding and had zoomed in on Agnes Day's assets, modest though they were.

"Holy cow," I said, looking closely. "What is that thing?"

"That's what we call a 'foundation garment.'"

"Why is she still kicking?" I asked.

"She doesn't know that her dress is up around her waist."

"How can she not?" I asked.

"Look," said Nancy, pointing. "She's wearing support hose, and that long-line girdle thingy. She can't feel anything below her waist anyway."

The congregation, that had been chuckling politely at the beginning of the episode, was now laughing like it was the audience at a stand-up comedy act. A good one, not one of those HBO specials. Above the laughter, due to the judicial placement of the microphones, we heard Misty finish up.

"...to love and to cherish, as long as we both shall live."

Finally, after the vows, one of the groomsmen mercifully crossed the platform, reached over the railing and helped Agnes Day out of the pit. Her hair was disheveled, but she held onto a piece of music — the solo. She walked back to the piano to another round of laughter mixed with growing applause.

"That's it," said Nancy, clicking off the tape. "Of course, it was even more hilarious with the network narration dubbed onto the tape. That, and they announced the wedding couple's names and the city. I swear, I haven't laughed so hard in a long while."

Annette and I sat across the table, eyeing one another. Finally, she spoke.

"Well, what did you want to see me about?"

"I think you know, Annette."

"No, I really don't."

"It's about Agnes Day."

Annette was silent, but her icy smile faded.

"You know she was killed yesterday."

"I know she's dead. I didn't know she was killed."

"Killed," I reiterated, "in the choir loft. You didn't have a whole lot of good feelings toward Agnes Day, did you? By the way, before you answer, I saw the tape of last night's show."

Annette reddened. "I don't have a whole lot of good feelings toward *you*, either," she said. "You were the one who refused to play for my...for Misty's wedding. If Agnes Day was killed, that old cow got what was coming to her."

I looked at Annette and waited without saying anything. It was an old detective's trick. Sooner or later the "interviewee" becomes uneasy with the silence and volunteers information you wouldn't normally get. It worked like a charm.

"That wedding and the reception cost over $65,000, and she ruined the whole thing. It's all anyone could talk about. Then that idiot Todd Whitlock..." She spit out his name, venom dripping from her lips. "...didn't bother to tape any of the vows, preferring instead to zoom in on Agnes Day's underwear! And to top it off, he wouldn't even give me the tape — a tape *I* had paid for. He said it would be

worth more to him to send it in to the producers of the TV show." Her eyes narrowed. "That was *my* tape."

"It sounds as though you might have more of a beef with Todd than with Agnes Day."

"Oh, I do, and you can bet that he's being sued for a whole lot more money than he'll ever see from that television show."

"Why didn't you sue Agnes Day as well?"

"My lawyer said I didn't have a case, or I damn well would have. She'd be living in a refrigerator carton under the Blowing Rock overpass, if I had my way."

"Well," I said, "she won't be living anywhere now. Were you in church yesterday?"

"I was."

"Did you go up to the choir loft after the service?"

"I did not."

"Here's your duckling," said Cynthia, placing a plate down in front of Annette. "And here's your sandwich."

"Thanks, dear," said Annette, her icy smile returning. She looked back at me and concluded our conversation in her sweetest voice.

"I do so hope that she had the good grace to die horribly."

Chapter 10

"I talked to most of the old choir members. They're excited about your return," said Meg. "Even more so when I told them you had a new detective story."

"I'm not coming back. I'm just subbing until Easter. One week."

"They still want to see your story," Meg coerced, sitting down on my lap and pulling my copy of *Audiophile* magazine out of my hands. "I told them all about it."

"Hmm. I think this is a trick. I am a highly trained detective, you know, and not susceptible to flattery."

"How about bribes? You do take bribes, don't you?" Meg asked, running her hand through my hair.

"Yes, being a highly trained detective, I do take bribes."

"What'll it take?" she said softly in my ear. "For you to come back?"

"Umm." I was pretty sure that I had an answer, but all of a sudden, I couldn't remember the question.

Miss Bulimia Forsythe was a legendary ringer in choral circles, making the rounds of most of the church choirs in the city. An interior decorator by day, she spent Wednesday nights driving choir directors wild. She could read anything at sight from eight-part Gesualdo motets to the solo cantatas of Scarlatti to Messiaen's "Trois Petites Liturgies," a piece so hard that it made choir directors weep like Tammy Faye Bakker at a Merle Norman display. She had perfect pitch and a voice like a Waffle House full of angels. She could make your soprano section sound like the Holy Ghost Choir with Jesus on cymbals--IF she showed up on Sunday.

Sure I'd hired her. Who hadn't? The director that tamed her could pretty much write his own ticket. It was like having a tetchy, musical Michael Jordan on your high school choir team. If you could get her to play, you were home free. You could go 25/0 without breaking a sweat and move right to the top of the choral league. But Miss

Bulimia Forsythe was a fickle mistress. She could make you look good or, like I found out the hard way when I scheduled the world premiere of the Distler "Te Deum" for the second Sunday of Easter, she could put the last nail in your musical coffin. It wasn't her fault, she said later as I was cleaning out my desk. She'd gotten a run in her stocking.

Still, one question nagged at me like Mr. Ed's wife. Why was Bulimia involved in the Presiding Bishop's Committee on New Liturgical Colors? I knew she was a decorator, but what was in it for her?

Pedro had heard of her, all right. They had been an item over at First Prez for about six months--the happiest six months of that director's life. Their interpretation of the Purcell duets for soprano and counter-tenor had become renowned over the years. Six months of musical bliss--then it was over. But I don't think Pedro had seen her for a while. No one had.

Nancy came into my office bright and early on Tuesday morning. "I talked to Benny Dawkins," she said.

"Yeah?"

"Agnes Day screwed him over big time."

"How so?" I stopped penning my monthly report to the city council and sat back in my chair.

"Benny had an old violin that his great-grandfather had left him. He wanted to sell it, so he took it up to the church about a month ago and let Agnes look at it."

"Did he say why he did that?"

"Well, he said that you weren't around anymore, and he wanted a musician to give him an opinion. Anyway, she offered him eight hundred bucks for it, and he took it."

"That's what Marilyn told me," I said. "Eight hundred bucks. I assume it was worth a lot more than that."

"She sold it last week at an auction in New York. Guess how much."

I shrugged.

"Two hundred fifty-five *thousand* dollars!" said Nancy, as she

pulled out her pad and flipped a couple of pages. "The tag inside the violin said Guadagnini. It seems that Agnes Day didn't mind telling folks about her acquisition. One of the choir members told Benny. He called the auction house once he found out and got the auction information. Here's the auction flyer that he got off of the Internet." Nancy handed me a printed sheet and continued talking, as I looked it over.

"It was an original G.B. Guadagnini made in Piacenza, Italy, in 1745. Benny said that his great-grandfather brought it over in 1925, and it had been sitting on the mantle ever since. He only considered selling it because he's three months behind on his farm loan. He's pretty desperate."

"What did he do when he found out?"

"He said that he went over to Agnes Day's and told her she owed him that money. He even said he'd pay her a finder's fee. Agnes Day laughed at him and showed him the bill of sale she'd made him give her. Benny says he didn't threaten her, but I don't know if I believe him."

"It doesn't pay to make Benny mad," I said. "You remember a couple of years ago when Greg Hardesty ended up taking Benny to court over that three acres of land that Benny said were his."

"I don't remember," said Nancy. "What happened?"

"Greg's barn mysteriously burned down the night after the verdict."

"Did you arrest Benny?"

"No proof. And Benny had an alibi. He was at church."

"That's a good alibi. Who was the witness?"

"Me, of course."

"You think he'd kill Agnes Day just to get even?"

"Well, he can't get the money back," I said. "And it sure sounds like motive to me."

"So," I said, "Agnes Day, who we assumed was one of the working middle-class, all of a sudden, seems to be quite well-heeled. Do we know who are the beneficiaries of her estate?"

"No, we don't. Net yet."

"Let's find out, shall we?" I said, using the imperial "we" that

Nancy knew meant that she'd be doing all the work.

"I'll check," said Nancy. "How about Annette Passaglio?"

"Oh, there's no doubt that she hated Agnes Day."

"Enough to kill her?"

"Never underestimate the fury of a status-seeking Monster-of-the-Bride, who wants her husband to run for Congress and has been publicly ridiculed in front of the entire county on national television."

"I see your point."

"I think that *if* Annette had been in the choir loft, and *if* she had tried to get an apology out of Agnes Day, and *if* Agnes Day snubbed her because she was playing her postlude, and *if* Annette saw the handbell sitting on the shelf...she might well have clunked her with it."

"I know I would have," said Nancy.

"There you go," I said, holding up my hands in a there-you-have-it gesture. "But that's a lot of *ifs*."

"On the other hand," said Nancy, "*if* I was Benny Dawkins, and *if* I went up to the choir loft to beg Agnes Day to reconsider, and *if* I was going to lose my farm, and *if* she blew me off because she was playing her postlude and *if* I saw the handbell and *if* I was really at the end of my rope...I might have been so pissed off that I might have clunked her with it."

"Quod erat demonstratum," I said, holding my hands up again. "Still a lot of *ifs*."

"I went through her house yesterday, but I'll check with the county attorney on her estate," said Nancy. "Maybe that will turn up something."

"Hi, Kent," I said, when the coroner finally picked up his phone. "Hayden Konig, here. Did you find anything interesting?"

"Just finished," said Kent. "Hang on a second." I heard the rustling of papers. "Here we go. Caucasian female, sixty-three years old with a touch of emphysema. Her heart was in good shape, though."

"What about the ding in her head?" I asked.

"Good choice of words. That bell you brought in? That was the

murder weapon. A clear match to the imprint, and there was blood on the bell as well."

"How about the sequins?" I asked.

"Just sequins. They had remnants of hot glue on the back."

"Did you send the bell to the lab?"

"Yes. No prints at all. The lab sent it over to Durham to get it checked for DNA. Just in case. My guy says that the bell was probably wiped down."

"Probably, but maybe not. Those handbell players are fanatics about fingerprints on their bells. They wear gloves anytime they touch them."

"Really? I had no idea," said Kent.

"I doubt if you'll find a fingerprint on any handbell in the church," I said. "Thanks, Kent."

"Anytime. You guys at St. Barnabas are keeping me in business."

Chapter 11

Francine was in my office the next morning, as bright and early as the bird after that worm, or maybe even ants, the occasional spider or even a wasp, if you happened to be a grackle and up as early as Francine.

"I hear that you're looking for Miss Bulimia Forsythe," she said sweetly--a sweetness I recognized instantly as the candy coating on a cake listed in the Relationship Cookbook as "Strychnine Surprise."

"Well...yes, I was," I answered, as innocently as I dared.

"Listen, Bub," she said in a low growl. "You'd better not have anything to do with that floozy, or I'll turn you inside out quicker than the sock matron at Wanda's Wash 'n Wear."

"Take it easy, doll," I said. "She's a suspect. I think she's involved in the coloration scam."

"If I find out you're lying..."

"Francine," I said with an unabashed ogle. "How could I ever step out on you?" I almost think I meant it. There she was, standing in front of me in her hospital whites, that little hat perched on top of her no-nonsense, short blonde hair, a thermometer tucked neatly behind one ear, a blood pressure cuff dangling tantalizingly from her waistband, the seams of her white support hose running in precise vertical symmetry from the perfect hem of her starched dress straight down into her sensible shoes. It was a sight that would make any red-blooded man with a nursing fetish slap his mother.

"I was just checking," said Francine, smiling coyly at my leer before sitting down on the couch, crossing her nylon-covered, alabaster legs and giving me a glimpse of one white garter belt. "I saw her yesterday. She was at the hospital getting a post-op check."

"Post-op?" I asked. "Post-op for what?"

"Miss Bulimia Forsythe just had another...procedure. It's the third one in a couple years. Apparently she thinks that a bigger chest will give her more breath support."

"So," I said, "she's packing a couple of falsettos."

"Yep."

"Hey, guess what?" Pete said, banging open the door to the station. "I have a clue!"

"A clue for what?" said Dave, who was working the desk. "Hey, is Collette back from Hickory yet?"

"Yeah, she's back. A clue to the murder, that's what!"

"Well, come on in," I said. "And tell us of this wondrous clue."

Since Nancy was in the official "visitor's chair," Pete flopped down in my old, blue leather wingback. "You see," he began, "I was talking with a guy who knows a guy..."

"Names, Pete. We need names."

"Okay. I was talking with Molly Frazier."

"That's not a guy," said Dave from the doorway.

"I was changing the names to protect the innocent," said Pete. "They do it all the time. I have to protect my sources."

"You're not a reporter, Pete," said Nancy. "You don't have sources."

"Anyway..." I urged.

"Anyway," continued Pete, "Molly comes into The Slab, and I happened, in the course of our conversation, to ask about her brother, Kenny."

I nodded. "The feds got him for growing pot," I explained, for Nancy and Dave's benefit. "Medicinal."

"Yeah," continued Pete. "Medicinal."

"Did you ask her out?" asked Nancy. "She's pretty cute."

"Maybe," said Pete, hesitantly. "Okay, sure, I asked her out," he acknowledged with a smile. "She's *very* cute."

"Back to the clue," I said.

"Right. So I ask her about Kenny, and she says that Kenny's out on bail. She said that Kenny told her that something bad was going to happen to Agnes Day. He said that bad karma will get you every time."

"So?" said Nancy.

"Kenny's aunt is Lucille Murdock. Agnes Day, the organist, was Mrs. Murdock's home health care nurse. So, this is what Molly tells me. Kenny, when he's trying to get his prescription for medical marijuana refilled, visits his aunt, sees Nurse Day in her dress whites, and asks if she can get him the prescription. She says she

can't, but she suggests that he contact the Feds and maybe they can do it for him."

"Holy smokes," Dave said. "She set him up."

"I don't imagine she thought that he'd actually do it," I said, "but you can never underestimate the sheer perspicacity of someone that's been taking medical marijuana for twenty years."

"Perspicacity?" said Dave.

"Ingenuity," I said. "Perspicuity, intellect, cleverness, astuteness." I pulled the top page off my "Increase Your Vocabulary Desk Calendar," a Christmas present from one of the choir members, and handed it to Dave.

"How often does *that* work?" Dave asked.

"Almost never," I admitted.

It was late in the afternoon on Tuesday when Nancy came back into the office. I was still filling out forms, my once-a-month penance for taking the city's paycheck.

"You almost finished, chief?" she asked.

"A couple more," I replied. "Did you find out anything?"

"I did. It's Tuesday, two days after Agnes Day was killed and, so far, there's only one claimant for her estate. There wasn't any will that I could find, and I doubt she had one. She had a quarter million in a savings account, but that was deposited a couple of weeks ago. She probably hadn't even thought about a will. Anyway," said Nancy with a sigh, "I turned everything over to the county attorney. He says it'll all go to probate."

"Who's the claimant?"

"That's the interesting part. Her only living relative, that we can find, is a niece."

"Does she live in town?" I asked.

"Well, just outside. It's Ruthie Haggarty, Little Bubba's distraught widow."

"Ruthie? She's in the lock-up, right?"

"Nope. She made bail Sunday morning."

"What time?"

"About eight," said Nancy. "Her attorney got to a judge on Saturday. He pled spousal abuse. You have to admit, it's a pretty

compelling argument. Anyway, the judge let her put her trailer and the three acres up as bond."

"So now she's in line for a cool quarter million."

"Is that motive?"

"Did she know about the money?" I wondered.

"If she didn't, she wouldn't have put in a claim with the county attorney, now would she?" said Nancy.

"That's motive."

"Do you think that's everyone?" I asked Meg, after I had filled her and Ruby in on the day's revelations. We were relaxing on Meg's porch, listening to the *Sanctus* from Bach's *B-Minor Mass* and enjoying the remainder of the port that Bud had recommended for my dinner party last Saturday. The guest list had included Malcolm and Rhiza Walker, the Sterlings, Meg and myself.

Malcolm had been very impressed by the wine selection. He was used to drinking spirits that sold upwards of five hundred dollars per bottle. I didn't tell him how much these bottles cost or that my sommelier was a fifteen-year-old wine snob who was washing dishes at The Slab Café. It made the wine taste all the sweeter, especially when he asked for the label information.

"I'll just write these down," he said, pulling a six hundred dollar pen out of his two thousand-dollar cashmere blazer.

"Nice coat," I said. "Nice pen, too, but you're going to be surprised by the price of the wine."

"Thanks," said Malcolm, clicking his pen open and pulling a business card out of a solid gold clip. "Rhiza got them for me for Christmas. The card clip, too. Nice, eh? It matches the pen. And I don't mind spending a little more for a good vintage."

"You're such a show-off, Malcolm," laughed Rhiza. "I don't think that's what Hayden meant."

The more I thought about it, the more I figured Malcolm was chapped at the prospect of having Lucille Murdock decide what should be done with the church money. From what I knew of Malcolm, this would have irked him to no end.

"Is that all?" I repeated to Meg. "I've got four people with motive and opportunity. Most of the time, I can't even find one suspect. Now I have four."

85

"Five," said Meg.

"Five?"

"Yep," she said. "Russ Stafford."

I'm sure I looked confused. "Why Russ?"

"I asked Malcolm about The Clifftops this afternoon. I thought it might be a good opportunity for a couple of my more risk-taking clients. Malcolm told me that he went over Russ' numbers, and there's no way he'd invest any money out there. Russ hasn't sold even one lot. He's over-extended, and unless he sells something fast, he's going to be in bad shape."

"How bad?" I asked.

"Bankrupt."

"That's bad," I agreed. "So what does this have to do with Agnes Day?"

"I'm so happy you asked. Since Lucille Murdock is in charge of making the decision about the new rectory, Russ has to convince her that investing in The Clifftops is a good idea. Unfortunately for Mr. Stafford, Agnes Day was Lucille's nurse."

"So?"

Meg looked over to her mother.

"Agnes Day hated Russ Stafford," said Ruby. "She thought he was a crook and hated him with a passion."

"Why?" I asked.

"Russ sold her a house about ten years ago, but he was acting as both buying and listing agent and didn't tell her. Agnes Day found out he was working both sides of the deal after the contracts were signed and it was too late, but she could carry a grudge like nobody's business. She had *nothing* good to say about Russ Stafford. And she told him on Saturday, over at The Ginger Cat, that if she had anything to say about it, he could choke on his Clifftops Properties. I know this," Ruby said, "because I happened to be there having lunch one table over. Not that I was listening in," she added.

"It's good you weren't," I said. "Did you not happen to hear anything else?"

"Well, Russ bent down and said something to Agnes. I couldn't hear what it was, but she went white as a ghost."

"Very interesting. So, if Russ was hoping to get Lucille's okay on the real estate deal, he had to get her away from Nurse Day."

"That's about right," said Ruby. "By the way, your cell phone's ringing."

"Man," I said, fumbling through my pockets. "Is there anyone in this town who didn't want to see her dead?" I found my phone on the fourth ring.

"Hi Nancy," I said, flipping the cover up. There were two people who had my cell phone number, and I was sitting with one of them. "What's up?"

"Go turn on Channel Four. Right now. Hurry up!"

"Turn on Channel Four," I called to Meg. She walked into the living room and clicked on the television. Ruby and I followed her in and stared. There, on Channel Four Eyewitness News, was footage of the one hundred-twenty million dollar Powerball winner accepting her check in Nashville.

It was Malcolm Walker's wife, Rhiza.

Chapter 12

"Marilyn," I called out. "Bring in the liturgical color chart, will you?"

She slithered with a lurching movement, sort of like a snake with one bad leg.

"What's with the slithering?" I asked. Marilyn was a good secretary, but changed her stripes quicker than a tiger didn't.

"I'm trying a new look," she said, dragging one shapely gam behind her like a Quasimodo Junior-Miss. I read in 'Hymns and Hers' that church musicians find this alluring."

"Not so much," I muttered, taking the chart from her outstretched hand.

This was the latest chart--approved just three years ago. I didn't even remember it coming up for a vote. It was as cut and dried as a rogation salami and sailed through all the committees without a second look. It was the same old thing, but with just a couple changes. There were a few more choices than in the "good old days." Gold, several shades of green, dark blue, light blue...these were all options.

"Do we have a chart of the proposed colors?" I yelled after Marilyn as she lurched back to her desk.

"Not yet," she hollered back. "It should be here this afternoon."

"When's the vote scheduled?"

"How should I know?" she yelped. "You're the detective."

I hadn't been to a staff meeting because I wasn't on the staff, and I hadn't been to a worship meeting because I didn't want to go. I explained all this to Marilyn on Wednesday of Holy Week.

"You see, Marilyn," I explained, patiently, "I'm not on the staff, so I don't have to go to the meeting."

"That's fine," she said. "I just think you might want to know what's going on."

"I actually don't even *care* what's going on. It has nothing to do with me. I'm just coming tomorrow night for the Maundy Thursday

service and Sunday morning for Easter. That's it. Then, for the next two weeks, I'm playing at two other churches."

"Okay," said Marilyn. "I guess you'll just have to be surprised."

"Nothing surprises me anymore. Just tell me what the hymns are and I'll ask the choir what they've been working on. I presume that they're still having rehearsal tonight?"

"As far as I know. Have you heard from Rhiza yet?"

"Nope. No one has. I think she's in hiding."

"You know that Agnes Day's visitation is tonight as well. Over at Swallow's Mortuary."

"I'd heard that. I think I can get over there before choir rehearsal."

"I think everyone that was in her choir is going. I guess I'll head over there, too. It's sad, really. She has no family at all, and Mr. Swallow said there were no inquiries from friends. I hope I don't end up like that."

"No chance of that," I said, with a smile. "I'll make sure there's standing room only at your funeral, even if I have to pay people to come."

"You're sweet. Thanks."

"By the way, is there any word from Lucille Murdock? How is she going to spend the sixteen million?"

"No one knows," replied Marilyn, "because nobody's heard from her. When Agnes Day was killed, Lucille went down to visit some family members in Hickory. There's been a lot of talk, but we haven't heard anything." She paused for a moment before continuing. "Umm...Hayden?"

"What's up?"

"You know I wouldn't normally repeat anything that I heard in the church, right?"

"You are the soul of discretion. Now, spit it out."

"I was in the sanctuary, taking the Palm Sunday bulletins up to the choir loft. The soloist and Agnes Day were rehearsing, and I didn't want to interrupt them, so I stood on the stairs, up at the top, waiting for them to finish before I went into the loft."

"Okay," I said. "Then what happened?"

"Well, I dropped some of the bulletins. So I was picking them up off the stairs and Agnes Day said to the soloist..."

"Renee Tatton," I interrupted.

"Right. Renee Tatton. She said that she recognized her from when she was the office nurse for Dr. Camelback in Boone."

"The plastic surgeon? That Dr. Camelback?"

"I guess so. It's the only one I know. He's got that infomercial on TV running every hour on the hour."

"Makes sense. I understand that Ms. Tatton is quite an ardent enthusiast."

"So I've heard. Anyway, Renee sort of hems and haws and says 'Oh yes, how are you?' and Agnes Day says 'Do you still have your special friend? I sure wish I had somebody to take care of my doctor bills. I'd be in there every month. He's a great doctor. An artist.'"

"She called Dr. Camelback an artist?"

"That's what she said. Then she asked — and I swear this is what I heard — how her voice-lift was working out."

"Her what?"

"Her voice-lift. That's what she said. Do you know what a voice-lift is?"

"I have absolutely no idea," I admitted. "But I'll find out."

I was walking back to the police station when it started snowing. A spring snowfall wasn't an uncommon event in St. Germaine, but it certainly was an unwelcome one. Most of the flowers that had peeked their faces out a week ago in anticipation of an early spring and some easy cross-pollination were now doomed. I'd put on my jacket when I left the office for the church. Now I zipped it and turned up the collar as I headed back.

Skeeter Donalson met me just as I turned the corner. He was wearing a sweatshirt that proclaimed "I saw 'The Immaculate Confection' at The Slab Café," (one of Pete's marketing ploys), and he had a handful of flyers that he was giving to anyone who went by.

"What's this, Skeeter?" I asked as he thrust one of the lime-green handbills toward me.

"Noylene's Beautifery," Skeeter said. "She's opening up on Friday. A 'grand opening,' she says. There's gonna be balloons and pie."

"An excellent combination," I agreed. "I wouldn't miss it."

"There's a coupon there, too. It's good for three dollars off your first stylin'."

"A first-rate opportunity," I said. "I could use a haircut. Thank you, Skeeter."

Since The Slab was on my way back, I was happy to drop in for a cup of coffee. Now that I had the monthly reports out of the way, the world was my oyster. I went in the door, brushed the snow from my hair, shook my coat from my shoulders and tossed it over an empty chair. It wasn't hard to find one. They were all empty.

I went behind the counter, took the coffee pot off its warmer and poured myself a cup. Pete must have heard me come in because he came out of the kitchen a half-beat later.

"Did you see this?" I handed him the flyer.

"Noylene's Beautifery?"

"I'm hoping she's ordered a neon sign," I said. "Something in reds and yellows."

"Noylene's Beautifery?"

"Look, Pete. It's her shop. She can call it what she wants."

"I'm the mayor. We have tourists. She cannot call it Noylene's Beautifery!"

"I believe that she's already incorporated and has her business license with the state."

"Arrrgh!" said Pete.

"Look on the bright side," I said. "With a name like Noylene's Beautifery, she'll either go out of business in two months, or it'll become a bizarro, cutting-edge, cult-like, styling salon that people will flock to. Noylene will be charging four hundred dollars a haircut. Either way, it's win-win."

Pete nodded. "Yeah. It might just work. That's really, really clever. Hey, wait a minute. Do you think she's that smart?"

"Could be," I said, sipping my coffee.

"Have you heard from Rhiza? Who'd have thought one of us would win something like that?" Pete was referring to the three of us, he and I and Rhiza Walker née Golden, who were in the music department together at Chapel Hill. "The rich get richer, I suppose."

"I suppose," I said. "Now, let's see." I held up three fingers. "I'm rich, Rhiza's richer, and you're..."

"Hush your mouth and stand up for a second," said Pete.

"What for?" I asked.

"Just stand up."

I stood up, an impish grin spreading across my face.

"Are those?" Pete grabbed hold of my waistband. "Yep...I knew it!" he laughed. "Expando-pants! You got yourself a pair!"

"Let's just keep this between us," I said, feeling like the kid caught with his hand in the cookie jar. "No need to spread this around."

He lowered his voice conspiratorially. "It's just between us. But how do you like them?"

"You were right," I said. "I'm never going back."

Nancy was brushing the snow off the windshield of her car as I walked up to the station. It was still coming down and the temperature was dropping.

"Did you get a chance to talk to the soloist?" I asked. "Renee Tatton?"

"Nope. She didn't answer the phone, and I can't find her. I talked to Meg, though. She said that she thought that Ms. Tatton would be at choir practice tonight. Maybe you can ask her a few questions after practice. Or send her down here tomorrow."

"I'll do one or the other," I said.

"That's something about Russ Stafford, isn't it," said Nancy, as she got into the Nissan. I had filled her in on Meg and Ruby's exposé this morning. "By the way, I also got a call from the state police. They want to know if we need any help. Do you think we poor mountain folk can figure this one out?"

"Yassum," I said, in my best hillbilly-ese. "But, what we sorely needs, Mizz Parsky, is some clues."

Chapter 13

I was on my way to see Memphis. I didn't tell Francine. Not that she would have minded. No, I was sure she wouldn't, I told myself. But I was lying like a Welsh shepherd at an ASPCA inquiry.

Memphis lived in midtown. A penthouse suite. Apparently the Presiding Bishop had extended his influence into the real estate market. The name on the building was Bishop Towers. A nice address. An address you could hang a shingle on and say you made it or a couple of million of them if they were a buck apiece.

The doorman was only a Right Reverend. I had expected a Very Reverend at the least--maybe an Extremely Reverend. Still, once the epaulets had been sown on the cassock, you had to kiss the ring.

"I'm the Right Reverend Sherman," he said with Anglican snoot dripping from every pore. "Do you have an appointment?"

"You bet I do, bub," I said. "Tell Memphis I'm here, will ya?" I lit a stogy.

"I'll call Miss Belle, and there's no smoking," he said, flipping his purple cassock as he executed a perfect ecclesiastical pirouette and headed toward the concierge desk.

I lit two more cigars just for spite and looked around. The lobby was as opulent and obvious as a Southern Baptist's gold eyetooth. There were fountains, jabats, torchieres, pedestals, swags, cornices, sconces, tassels, finials and a whole bunch of other decorations that I could only guess at. It was worth a fortune, or I wasn't smoking out of all three sides of my mouth. In a moment, the Right Reverend called me over and pointed to the elevator.

"Top floor," he said with obvious disdain. "See if you can manage to find it." I could feel my ire starting to swell like week-old roadkill on hot asphalt in the Texas sun, but then I remembered that Dr. Phil said that it wasn't good to keep anger bottled up, so I walked over and slapped the priest in the head with a fermenting mackerel I kept in my coat for just such an occasion.

"Pay attention, Padre," I said, slipping the fish back

into my trench. "I ain't sayin' this twice. Next time I see you, you'd better have read The Confession of St. Ambrose. Especially the part about humility. Capice?"

He nodded and wiped a loose fin from his hair.

"Now beat it," I said, punching the button for the penthouse.

Meg and I walked up to the choir loft together. We turned the corner at the top of the stairs and entered the loft to see a person in every chair and three basses sitting on the steps. Twenty-three people, several of them actual singers.

"Welcome back," they called, as I walked down to the organ. I felt guilty, but not *that* guilty.

"I'm not back," I groused in my best curmudgeonly intonation. "I'm just subbing for myself until Easter."

"Huh?" said Rebecca. "How can you sub for yourself?"

"Never mind," I said. "Now tell me what you guys are working on."

"Didn't you pick something out for us?" asked Georgia.

"No. I'm just subbing. I'm playing tomorrow night for the Maundy Thursday service and Sunday Morning for Easter. Then I'm off to Morganton the next Sunday and maybe Hickory the week after that."

"I heard you were playing for a Pirate Eucharist," said Randy. "I think we all might take a road trip. It's Low Sunday anyway."

"What's a Pirate Eucharist?" asked Marjorie.

"It's like a Clown Eucharist, except with pirates," said Michelle.

"That sounds great," said Rebecca. "Arrrgh. Let's plan on it."

"Arrrgh," said the rest of the choir in unison. All except Meg, who closed her eyes in silent prayer.

I struggled to regain control. Control that I'd never had, as I recalled — not in all the years I had been choir director.

"I don't know what you're singing tomorrow night and Sunday," I said, "but you must have been rehearsing something."

"Here's our folder," said Fred. "This is what we were practicing. By the way, did you bring your latest detective story? I'm really looking forward to it." Fred was one of the four choir members who

94

stuck it out when Agnes took over. I opened the folder and flipped through the music. There was a piece entitled *Love Grew Where The Blood Fell*, a two-part arrangement of Beethoven's *Hallelujah* from *Christ on the Mount of Olives,* and something called *Feel The Nails.*

"I'm sorry. I didn't bring it," I said, flipping through the three pieces. "But I'll have some copies tomorrow night."

"He's not getting any better," Meg whispered to Fred, just loud enough for me to hear.

"Can't we just sing what we sang last year?" Michelle said. "No one's going to remember what we did. We still know it, and most of us have never rehearsed this other stuff."

"Good point," I said. "What did we sing? Anyone remember?"

"We did the Shephard *Tenebrae* service on Thursday," said Mark Wells, "but we had a couple of pieces for Palm Sunday we didn't do last year."

"I remember," I said. "The Shephard piece is too long for the service this year. We could do Casals' *O Vos Omnes* tomorrow night if a couple of the sopranos can still sing the high notes, and some *Messiah* choruses on Easter. Would that be okay with everyone?"

No one was used to me asking their opinion about the choir's repertoire, and they were too surprised to do anything but nod.

Elaine, Rebecca and Fred went down to the choir room to get the *Messiah* scores and *O Vos Omnes* while the rest of the choir chatted. The console had been cleaned, and I took the time to change most of the presets on the organ. We had managed to make it through most of the anthem when Renee Tatton made her entrance in a whirl of angora, capri pants, and high heels, carrying a snifter of white wine.

"Sorry. Sorry I'm late," she announced loudly as she came into the loft, drowning out the choir's attempts at pronouncing "attendite et videte." The rehearsal ground to a halt as most of the choir encountered Ms. Tatton, up close and personal, for the first time. She swooped down to the front row, her arms arched in semi-graceful dance movements, her snifter pointing her way.

"Lovely to see you, dear," she said to Rebecca and the other altos by default, as she floated by the section. "So good of you to join the choir." I could actually feel Rebecca bristle from three chairs and an organ bench away.

It was Raymond Chandler who wrote, "From thirty feet away, she looked like a lot of class. From ten feet away, she looked like something made up to be seen from thirty feet away." He might well have been talking about Renee Tatton. I would have guessed that she was in her early fifties, but looked, from a distance, to be about thirty — the key words being "from a distance." From closer, however, her liberally applied makeup couldn't hide the tightness around her eyes, the face that might be riding a very fast motorcycle or the plumped lips that could have once belonged to a duck. But her most astounding attribute was her chest, hoisted proudly aloft like a photo finish in a dirigible race.

"Holy cow," whispered Steve from the bass section. "How does she stand up?"

"And why would she want to?" muttered Mark, with a leer. I could tell that the bass section was on a roll. "Hey," he said, "did you guys hear about Rhiza?" Everyone grunted in the affirmative.

"What are we singing?" Renee asked, taking a sip of her wine and picking up the Casals anthem. "Oooo, I love this one."

"Great," I said. "Then let's get back to it, shall we? Measure sixteen, please."

Renee Tatton was on the front row, and, since she'd already made enemies of the entire soprano and alto sections, I was ready to make myself a hero and call her down for an overactive warble that I suspected was skulking behind the facade of youth. But alas, it was not to be. Renee, it turned out, had quite a lovely choral singing voice. There was a bit of age to be sure, but nothing like I had expected from a woman in her sixth decade, especially an opera diva. When we switched to the Handel choruses, she managed the moving lines with ease and flexibility. I'd never heard anything like it — certainly not from a woman pushing sixty. I was shocked. The sopranos actually sounded pretty good. I looked over at Meg. She was glowering. I made a few pointless suggestions to flex my choir director muscles and decided to call it a night.

"Do you know what's going on tomorrow night?" asked Elaine. "During the service, I mean."

"No, I don't," I said, suddenly remembering Marilyn's warning.

"Regular service music, I guess, and the anthem. We'll figure it out when I see the bulletin tomorrow."

"There's a foot-washing," said Elaine. "Are we singing any foot-washing anthems?"

"Nope. I'll just play something."

"Then we'll be going down to the front and nailing our sins to the cross," Elaine continued.

"Excuse me?" I growled, amid laughter from the choir. Then I regained my composure and said calmly, "I shall have to play some 'nailing' music for that as well. I'm just the substitute. By the way," I added, "is there anything...umm...out of the ordinary for Easter?"

"I don't think so," said Elaine. "But you never know."

Chapter 14

The door to Memphis Belle's penthouse suite was ajar which struck me as odd because the rest of the penthouse, from what I could see through the glass, reminded me more of a carafe or perhaps a decanter. The door was definitely ajar—a big No. 25 pickle jar or one of those Mason jars, the kind with the wide mouths like that joke about the wide-mouth frog everyone keeps telling even though it isn't funny. I screwed off the lid and went in.

It didn't take long to locate Memphis. I had suspected that she was a swinger, and now she was proving me right, hanging from the balcony of the second story landing, swaying back and forth like a metronome set on andante or maybe molto allargando or even piu lento if the killer happened to be Mozart which I was pretty sure it wasn't because Mozart had already been dead for over two-hundred years, murdered himself by someone as nasty as the person who killed Memphis Belle. I was convinced it was a homicide because no woman I knew would be caught dead in a lime green pants-suit ensemble after Labor Day. It was one of those things called a clue, and I was, after all, a trained detective. I shook my head in time with the beat. This was going to be a long weekend.

I answered the phone on the second ring on what turned out to be a snowy Maundy Thursday morning. I'd already been up for a couple of hours and had done some good work on my detective story.

"Hayden," said a familiar voice on the other end of the line. "It's Rhiza. Mind if I stop by?"

"Not at all. I was hoping you'd call."

"I'll be there in twenty minutes."

"I'll start breakfast."

I had a couple of omelets almost ready when Rhiza came in the front door. She didn't knock, but then, she never did.

I had known Rhiza for over twenty years. We'd met at UNC Chapel Hill. She was a good pianist, but not a great pianist, and she knew her academic and professional path lay in history and research rather than performance. Our romance lasted a couple of years,

until I graduated and moved on to my next career in criminology. She and Pete were the reason I came to St. Germaine in the first place. They teamed up and talked me into taking the job as Chief of Police.

Rhiza and I kept our sometime romance going, strictly off the books, until she'd decided to marry Malcolm Walker. She was his trophy bride, his arm candy, and she played the part well, even dyeing her hair blond and raising her voice a diminished fourth to a decidedly Betty Boopish pitch. She was a gal who knew what she wanted, and Malcolm was it.

"Hi, Babe" she said, her voice back down to her normal contralto. "Man, what a week!" She flopped down into a chair at the kitchen table.

"Yes, I heard. It's all everyone in town is talking about. Well, that and Agnes Day's recent demise."

"I couldn't believe it," said Rhiza, ignoring my mention of the murder. "It was absolutely amazing. I stopped to get gas on my way home from Kingsport, bought a five-dollar ticket and forgot about it. Then when I heard that the winner bought their ticket in Elk Mills, I checked my ticket on the Internet. It was the winning ticket. I couldn't believe it."

"So, where have you been?"

"Well, I told Malcolm, of course. He set up a corporation and did a bunch of legal stuff before he'd even let me go claim the ticket. Then we called the Lottery headquarters, took a limo down to Nashville, and got the check."

"The check?"

"It wasn't a real check. Just one of those giant checks you see on TV. They deposited the money straight into the corporation checking account."

"How much was it? A hundred and twenty million?"

"Nothing like that," Rhiza said. "I took the cash option. With that and federal taxes, it came out to a little over thirty-four million."

"You still have to pay North Carolina taxes as well."

"They already got it. You think the state government's going to miss a chance like that?"

"Still, that's a pretty nice payday."

"Yep," she said. "Now hand over that omelet and get me some coffee, will you?"

"Coming up."

"Did you ever tell Meg about us?" Rhiza asked, finishing up the last piece of toast.

"No, I did not," I said. "She never asked about any past girlfriends, and I never offered any information."

"Did you ever ask her about her pre-Konig flings?"

"Nope."

"You just..." She paused before she continued. "Trust each other?"

"Yep."

"That'd be something," she said, wistfully. "Trusting each other."

"Trouble in paradise?" I asked.

"He's having another affair." Rhiza shrugged and took a sip of her coffee. I looked at her. She was, for lack of a better word, stunning: ash blonde hair, with the face of an angel and a body to match. If there was anyone as pretty as Meg in St. Germaine, it was Rhiza.

"How do you know?"

"A girl knows. First of all, he's after me to have some plastic surgery done."

"You're kidding!"

"Nope. Breasts, chin, tummy tuck...the works."

"Is he crazy? You're absolutely..." I hesitated, suddenly aware that I sounded like a kid with a schoolboy crush.

"Go ahead and say it," Rhiza laughed. "I'm beautiful. I admit it."

"Well, I mean *really*."

"But I'm not as young as I used to be. Forty-seven next month. I guess I'm due for some nipping and tucking."

"Rhiza, I ask you this as your friend and as someone who looks at you, albeit from a distance, with lust in his heart. Please, do *not* do it."

"Well, not yet anyway," she said, with a smile.

"Is that all?" I asked. "That hardly seems like enough evidence."

"No. There's also the usual stuff. Lying about his whereabouts, money missing out of the accounts. He thinks I don't know, but I

found the password to his accounts years ago. I used to check them every couple weeks or so."

"Have you checked them lately?"

"Not for about a month, but over the past couple of years, there's been about a hundred thousand or so taken out."

"Wow," I said. "That's a lot."

"It's not that I mind so much. I know why he married me. Don't forget. I *was* the other woman. But, you know, I've been with him for ten years now. I love him I guess, but I think it's about over. You remember his fling with Loraine Ryan?"

"Yeah," I answered. "The Reverend Mother Ryan. That was a mess."

"Well, he still sees her, I think. She's up near Greensboro somewhere."

"She was defrocked, as I recall."

"Yes, she was," Rhiza said. "But she opened a counseling office. Last year, he decided he didn't trust me to be faithful to him, so we decided to arrange a post-nuptial agreement."

"You agreed to that?" I asked.

"Sure," said Rhiza, holding out her coffee cup for a refill. "I'm sure it was Loraine's idea, and I have no intention of being unfaithful to Malcolm. Sex is just sex. I can take it or leave it, and if it's going to cost me a few million dollars, I'll leave it." She sighed. "It's just sad."

"It is sad," I agreed.

As I drove up to the station, the snow was still falling — big wet flakes that stuck to whatever they touched.

"Any new suspects today?" asked Nancy, as I walked in.

"I don't think so. How many do we have now? Five?"

"Five."

"Make it six," I said. "I talked to Dr. Camelback's office this morning."

"The plastic surgeon?"

"Yep. Did you know you could get a voice-lift?"

"Umm...no, I didn't," said Nancy. "What is it?"

"It's a procedure whereby the plastic surgeon tightens your vocal folds, thus making your voice sound less old than it really is."

"Okay. What has that got to do with us?"

"Marilyn heard Agnes Day ask Renee how her voice-lift was working out. Agnes Day used to be the office nurse for Dr. Camelback, and she recognized Renee from one of her visits. Now, I couldn't get any info out of Dr. Camelback's current nurse, but I'm betting that Renee had that voice lift done and doesn't especially want anyone to know about it."

"Who would care?"

"You haven't met many operatic sopranos have you?" I asked. "Having a voice-lift would be the professional death-knell if anyone found out. It would be like using steroids if you were a baseball player."

"Well, *that* never happens."

"You get the point."

"I get the point. So," Nancy said, "you'd think she'd kill to keep that secret?'

"Well, it's embarrassing, certainly. But, if it were me, I wouldn't kill anyone. Then again, I'm not a soprano."

"I'll put her on the list. That's six then."

"Can we count any of them out?" I asked. "Do any of them have alibis?"

"Let's see," said Nancy, pulling out her pad. "I don't know about Renee Tatton yet, but at the time of the murder, Annette Passaglio was in the parish hall. She had gone in for coffee."

"I didn't see her, and I was there," I said. "She might have gone in earlier than we did, but she certainly could have gone back upstairs."

"Russ Stafford says he was out at the Clifftops. No witnesses. Benny Dawkins was at the service that morning. You remember. He was swinging the incense pot. He says he put the pot back in the sacristy after the service and went home. He lives alone. No one saw him after the service, and no one saw him leave."

"Of course not."

"Ruthie Haggarty made her bail and got out of jail at about eight on Sunday morning. I talked to her neighbors. She didn't go home. She told me that she did, but changed her mind when I asked her why her neighbors never saw her car. Then she remembered that she went shopping in Boone."

"On Sunday morning?"

"That's what I thought, too. She says she spent the morning in Wal-Mart, but didn't buy anything."

"She's lying. No one goes to Wal-Mart and doesn't buy anything. Does the store have any surveillance tapes?"

"Nope. It's been too long. They record over them if they don't need them."

"Figures," I said.

"I can't find Kenny Frazier anywhere. No one's seen him since Saturday."

"How many is that? Six? And we can't rule anyone out."

"That's everyone," said Nancy. "So far."

I had sworn off staff meetings, but I made an exception on Thursday afternoon. I thought it might be advantageous to know what was going to happen during the upcoming services, and Father George had called a meeting for everyone who was involved.

"Thank you all for coming," he began. "I'm sure that your participation will help make our worship during Holy Week meaningful for everyone." We all smiled politely and nodded our heads.

"Now Brenda needs to fill us in on a few last-minute details."

Brenda was carrying quite a sheaf of papers, all stapled neatly in separate stacks, and bulletins for everyone, all which were handed out in short order. When everyone had received his or her handouts, she pulled out her clipboard and began.

"Let's begin with tonight's service," she said, flipping through her pages. "It's pretty straightforward. We're doing a dramatic reading of the Passion. All you readers make sure you read over your passages beforehand. Bob? There's been a change. You'll have to read Pilate's part as well as Peter's. Chuck can't be here." She looked over at me. "Unless Hayden wants to do it."

"No, thanks," I said, still looking over the bulletin. "I've got enough to worry about."

"Fine," said Brenda, in her huffity, put-upon voice. "Then Bob will have to do it."

"Bob's not here," said Georgia.

"I called him a month ago. He said he was coming."

"That may well be," replied Georgia, "but he's not here."

"I'll deal with it later," said Brenda. "Let's talk about the rest of the service. After the dramatic reading of the Gospel, we're going to have a foot-washing service."

"Foot-washing?" I said. "Will you actually be the one washing the feet?"

"No," said Brenda.

"Oh, Father George, then," I said.

"No," said Father George.

"We went back to the original intent of the service of foot-washing," Brenda explained. "As you know, in Biblical times, it was important for travelers to have their feet washed when entering a house. They wore sandals and the roads were very dusty, so the servants would wash the guests' feet."

"I remember," I said. "Making Jesus' act of washing his disciples' feet all the more significant. It's a very moving experience, both for the clergy, who assumes the role of the servant, and the person for whom it is done."

"Well, I'm not very comfortable with that," said Father George. "And neither is Brenda. We didn't think that many people would come up to get their feet washed and quite frankly, with that outbreak of toe-nail fungus that's been on the television every five minutes, it's probably very dangerous."

"That's a commercial for *Lamisil,* not a news report. I doubt that toe-nail fungus has reached epidemic proportions in Watauga County."

"It really doesn't matter," Brenda explained. "You see, Hayden, since we now have modern footwear, paved roads, and cars, it's no longer important for people to have their feet washed after traveling. We've decided to update the service."

"Ah," I said.

She continued. "We'll be using the traditional liturgy, but instead of washing people's feet, we're going to shine their shoes."

"Ah," I said.

Father George jumped in. "They will have, metaphorically speaking, gotten dust on their shoes on their way to the gathering of the faithful."

"So you two are going to shine all our shoes?"

"Don't be silly," he said. "We could hardly do that. There wouldn't be time. When people come up for communion, they'll

take the bread and wine, then move off to either side where we will have two stations set up."

"Stations?" I asked, still not comprehending.

"For heaven's sakes, Hayden," said Elaine, with a smirk. "Get with the program. Two stations of electric shoe polishers."

"Of course," I said. "I understand perfectly. Electric shoe polishers."

"It's much more relevant to today's society," Brenda said defensively.

"I'm sure it will be very special to many people who need their shoes shined," I said.

"No need to be so condescending," said Elaine, trying to raise my ecclesiastical ire. "We're all looking forward to the service."

Elaine could make all the snide comments she wanted. I wasn't going to rise to the bait. I turned back to Brenda. "You'll want me to play during communion, right?"

"Yes," said Brenda, "and also during the Nailing Service after the choir sings." I looked at her blankly.

"I gave Agnes Day the song I wanted the choir to sing during the nailing service," she said, her eyes narrowing. "I'm *sure* you rehearsed it last night. *Feel the Nails?*"

"Actually, we had to change that one," I said, with an apologetic shrug. "I didn't know anything about a Nailing Service."

"Look at your bulletin," she said in exasperation. "See these post-it-notes?" She pointed to a lavender note stuck inside the front page. "After the stripping of the altar, we're going to write down our sins."

"All of them?" I asked, as I peeled the two by two-inch note off the bulletin. "On this?"

She ignored me. "Then we're going to take them up to the altar and nail them to the big wooden cross."

"Nail them to the cross?"

"Everyone that wants to."

"Do we have enough nails?" I asked. Elaine stifled a giggle. "No, really," I said. "That's a lot of people. It's going to take a while."

"We thought of that," said Father George, proudly. "That's why we have a nail-gun."

Chapter 15

I called the coppers and told them what I knew. Not everything, of course, just enough to get me out of the door and back on the street. They thought it might be suicide, but then, they were being paid by the city, and it didn't do them any good to think too hard. The coroner said she'd been dead for a couple of hours.

Pedro met me at the corner. He had heard about Memphis. News traveled fast in the district.

"C'mon," he said. "I know a new place. We'll go and get a drink."

"Will you be handing out the story-so-far to the choir?" Meg asked.

"Yep. I must keep my public happy."

We were down in the workroom of St. Barnabas where the copy machine was housed. I was copying a few pages of my music to avoid page turns, and I had put my latest opus on the machine as well. The story wasn't finished yet, but it was far enough along to make for good reading. Or so I thought.

"When is this one going up on the blog?" Meg asked. "What's it called again?"

"*The Usual Suspects. The Alto Wore Tweed* should be up next week. Then I'll be famous."

"What about your other efforts?" Meg asked.

"*The Baritone Wore Chiffon* comes out the first week of May. *The Tenor Wore Tapshoes* in June. This one in August. I've already signed the contract."

"You get paid for this?"

"Actually, no. Not exactly."

"What? You get a T-shirt or a coffee mug or something?"

"Well...no."

"Wait a minute...you don't pay *them*, do you?"

"Umm..." I said. "Not much. It's more of a contribution, really."

"A lot?"

"No," I said, shaking my head. "Not a lot. Certainly not a lot. Besides, my work will be read by literally millions of people."

Meg's eyebrows went up.

"Okay, thousands. I'm sure it's thousands. Maybe even hundreds. And, as you know, I'm tuning up for the Bulwer-Lytton Competition in June. I think I have a real shot this year."

"You're *tuning up* to write the world's worst sentence?"

"We athletes need to keep up our training."

The service started at six. I played the prelude and then followed along in the bulletin. There was a hymn — *Seek Ye First The Kingdom Of God* — that I thought was an odd choice for a Holy Week service, but then, I was just the reserve backup substitute organist, and it was my job to play 'em, not comment on 'em. We sang the *Kyrie,* heard the Old Testament reading and chanted Psalm 78. Then we skipped the Epistle in favor of the dramatic Passion Gospel, which was going pretty smoothly until the Apostle Peter was due to speak. Then there was silence.

"I tell you I don't know him," said Brenda, finally breaking the lull by denying Jesus in her lowest voice. Obviously, Bob hadn't shown up. I guessed that Pilate would be a low alto as well. I wasn't disappointed.

"Are you the King of the Jews?" Brenda growled, when Pilate's line came up.

"Yes, it is as you say," replied Father George.

Brenda hadn't given herself a part in the drama, there being very few roles for women in the Passion Gospel. In fact, much to her dismay, the only woman that she was able to cast was Lynn Askew as the narrator. Now that Brenda had a part to play, however, it was apparent that she was going to make the most of it.

"What shall I do, then, with the one you call the King of the Jews?" Brenda asked the congregation, her voice rising. "WHAT SHALL I DO?"

"Crucify him?" the congregation muttered, following along in their programs, but not quite into the spirit of the narrative and apparently, not quite sure exactly *what* to do with the King of the Jews.

"Why? What crime has he committed?" Brenda called out, her voice climbing.

"But they shouted all the louder..." said Lynn, trying to match Brenda's enthusiasm, yet tempered by a genteel southerner's restraint.

"Crucify him?" mumbled the congregation, still unsure of their stature as a mob.

Lynn continued narrating. "Wanting to satisfy the crowd, Pilate released Barabbas to them."

"The rabble could have used a little rehearsal," said Meg, under her breath.

"I notice that *you* didn't yell 'Crucify him,'" whispered Georgia.

"I'm sorry. I don't yell in church," said Meg, sweetly. "You didn't yell either."

"I had a tickle in my throat," said Georgia.

"I think that Marjorie yelled," said Bev, looking over to the tenor section. "At least once."

"I think that's because she fell out of her chair and woke up," Meg said.

"Be quiet," I whispered, "and stand up for the next hymn."

"The gifts of God for the people of God," said Father George. "Take them in remembrance that Christ died for you, and feed on Him in your hearts by faith, with thanksgiving."

"This story's pretty good, and by that I mean really bad," said Rebecca as she stood up to go downstairs. "You might just win this year." I smiled and nodded. This was high praise from a librarian.

"Are you going down for communion?" whispered Meg.

"I don't think so," I said. "Tonight, I'll just play. I'll come back tomorrow when the electric shoe polishers are finished whirring."

Our anthem during the offertory had gone very well, and Brenda had given the congregation instruction and their spiritual motivation for having their shoes polished. I looked down from the balcony before I began my variations on *Herzliebster Jesu*. There were two ushers standing like soldiers behind the electric shoe polishers in case anyone needed help, but Elaine had told me that the shoe polishers were automatic. You just put your foot under the black, fuzzy roller, triggered the switch, and the apparatus went into action. I could play a couple of stanzas before I had to pay attention

to the score, so I kept shifting my gaze back and forth between the front of the church and the music that was in front of me. As was our custom, the whole choir had gone downstairs to receive communion first, before heading back to the choir loft to lead the post-communion hymn.

I immediately saw that there were a couple of major flaws in Brenda's plan. Firstly, the electric shoe polishers were not silent. They sounded like two high-powered hair dryers. It was pointless for me to play anything with all that racket going on, and by the end of stanza two, I pushed the organ up to warp five.

Secondly, there was really no option for people *not* to have their shoes shined. They received communion, stood up, and were herded automatically into the shoe-shining line.

Thirdly (and this was unfortunate), there was no way for anyone to tell when his or her shoes were finished. The polisher kept going as long as there was a shoe underneath it, so, where as communion usually takes all of thirty seconds per person, shoe shining took a minute or more. Before long, the line wound all the way around the church, and I could now hear the shoe-ushers shouting and herding the customers over the noise. But I was just the reserve backup substitute organist, and I launched into another variation with gusto.

"Look at this!" hissed Meg, thrusting a shapely leg in my direction, as the sopranos made their way back into the loft. "Just look at this!"

I looked down at what had once been a pair of red high-heels. The toes of the shoes were now black.

"They're ruined! Those idiots didn't even get new buffers! They still have black polish all over them! And it was too dark to see."

"Oh my," I said, not daring to smile. I looked at the rest of the ladies coming back into the loft. Each and every one of them had black toes except for Georgia who, thanks to a stroke of luck, had worn black shoes to the service.

"What a tragic development," I gulped, trying to keep the tears back. It was no use. I kept playing as I stuffed my handkerchief in my mouth, snorts of laughter, I'm pretty sure, coming out of my ears.

Renee Tatton glared at me with the eyes of a snake. "These shoes cost four hundred dollars," she spat. "Who's going to pay for these?'

I could only shrug my shoulders and shake with what I hoped was silent merriment.

"Okay, Hayden. This is not funny!" Bev said, holding up her pumps, one light-brown and one now two-toned. Mark cackled, and the rest of the men, who, by this time, had joined us in the loft, started laughing as well. The shoe polishers were still making enough noise to wake the real St. Barnabas, and I pulled another couple of stops on the organ and opened the swell box just to keep up.

Marjorie was the last one up. She walked up beside me and looked down at her feet. I followed her gaze and howled with laughter. Marjorie had one white sandal and one black foot. Now, even the women started to giggle, and in three beats everyone in the choir loft was snorting into their hymnals.

"I don't know what's so funny," said Marjorie. "Next time, I'm not waking up."

The shoe-polishing service had finally finished up, the altar had been stripped and we had all sung *Were You There* in semi-darkness. This was, traditionally, where the Maundy Thursday Service at St. Barnabas ended. The congregation usually left in silence to return again on Easter morning. Father George held a Good Friday service as well, but there was no organ playing involved. The organ fell silent after the second verse of *Were You There* — the third being sung unaccompanied — and wasn't heard again until Sunday.

Tonight, however, we still had the "Nailing Service" to finish. Father George got up to make the announcement.

"It will be very meaningful," he began, using a word that had become less and less "meaningful" as this service wore on, "if all of you will find the purple post-it-note in your bulletin and write down one sin that you have committed in the past week. Then we're going to take them to the altar and nail them to the cross. When we come back on Easter, our sins will be removed and replaced by flowers. What a perfect metaphor for what Jesus has done for us."

"Now, as the organ plays softly, please come forward and give your sins to Jesus Christ. After you've nailed your sin to the cross, please go in peace to love and serve the Lord."

That was my cue. I had flipped the hymnal open to the Holy Week section and began to play as the choir jotted their sins on their pieces of paper and, as they finished, made their way down the stairs.

I was halfway through the first hymn when the first sin was nailed up.

KA-THWAACK! went the nail-gun. KA-THWAACK! KA-THWAACK!

I glanced down to see the nail-gun being passed from one person to the next as they tacked their sins to the big wooden cross that St. Barnabas brought out once a year. At least, I thought, Brenda had the good sense not to use a nail-gun that needed an air compressor. This one was self-contained. I looked at the bright-orange contraption as closely as I could from up in the balcony. The Altar Guild had decorated it with some thorns interspersed with purple ribbon. There was also someone (I couldn't see who) helping folks with the nailing. A carpenter, I hoped.

KA-THWAACK! went the nail-gun again. KA-THWAACK! KA-THWAACK! KA-THWAACK!

I started into another hymn. This was going to take a while.

When I survey the wondrous cross, KA-THWAACK! *On which the prince of Glory died;* KA-THWAACK! *My richest gain* KA-THWAACK! *I count but loss,* KA-THWAACK! KA-THWAACK! *And pour contempt on* KA-THWAACK! *all my pride.*

Chapter 16

"Where are we going?" I asked Pedro, not really caring.

"A new dive just opened up across from St. Gertrude's. It sounds like our kind of place. Good looking beer-fräuleins in tight shirts, lots of German brews, and Baroque organ music from a three-manual Flentrop with a sixteen-foot heckelphone you can really hang your hat on."

"Sounds sweet," I agreed, suddenly interested. "What's this place called?"

"Buxtehooters."

"Buxtehooters! You're going to get it for that one," said Meg.

"It's brilliant," I said. "A new pinnacle in my writing career. I don't know how I do it."

"Neither do I," said Meg. "But the more important question is, *why* you do it?"

I ignored the barb. "Hey!" I said, changing the subject as neatly as a Democrat in a tax debate. "Do you want to go to the grand opening of Noylene's Beautifery?"

"Noylene's what?"

"Noylene's Beautifery. She's opening her shop tomorrow."

"I just have two questions. Do we have to get our hair styled and is 'Beautifery' actually a word?"

"The answer to both questions is 'I don't think so.' We may get some coupons for haircuts at a later date. But Skeeter says there will be balloons and pie."

"What kind of pie?" asked a suspicious Meg.

"Does it matter?"

I had decided to start exercising. My decision wasn't based on the thought of a future in expando-pants, but rather a realization that I wasn't getting any younger, and if I was going to keep some semblance of my current non-pear shape, while still eating copious amounts of pie and Belgian Waffles, I'd better do something about

it. So, after much procrastination, I'd begun jogging a couple of miles every morning. At least I told myself it was a couple of miles. It was probably closer to a mile and a half. Friday morning, I had already finished my run, taken a shower, and was having my second cup of coffee when the phone rang.

"Hayden," someone whispered. I realized it was Marilyn. "Hayden, you'd better get in here."

"What's up?" I asked.

"Just come in as quickly as you can." The click on the other end was abrupt and final.

"Well, that was cryptic," I said to Baxter, as I gave him a biscuit. He wagged his tail in appreciation and walked to the door to be let out for a full day of chasing squirrels, beavers or whatever else crossed his path.

"Didn't you think that was cryptic?" I yelled after him, as he bounded away. "Well, *I* thought so," I said to myself. I grabbed my coat, locked the door to the house and climbed into my truck. It was still cold out, but the snow had stopped, leaving a couple of inches of slush on the ground. I slipped my new recording of Monteverdi's *1610 Vespers Service* into the CD player, turned it up, dropped the truck into four-wheel drive and headed toward St. Barnabas Church.

"Thank goodness you're here," whispered Marilyn. "Let's go into the kitchen and get a cup of coffee."

"No thanks," I said. "I just..."

"Come...into...the...kitchen," she repeated, this time accompanied by "the look" and a nod toward Father George's closed office door. I'd seen "the look" enough times in my life to know when something was up.

"Right. The kitchen." I followed her down the corridor, through the parish hall and into the kitchen where we found a couple of mugs and filled them with coffee. I took a sip and poured it into the sink.

"I see Father George is still buying the cheap stuff," I said.

"You get used to it after a while," said Marilyn. "Now pay attention. I came in this morning at eight o'clock."

"Yeah?"

"And there was a manila folder sitting on my desk. I opened it up. It was full of post-it-notes."

"From the service last night?"

"That's what I thought. Extras. But they weren't. They were the ones that were nailed to the cross."

"Brenda must have taken them all off after the service," I said. "We have a Good Friday liturgy at noon. Maybe she didn't want to come in this morning and clean up, so she did it last night. It would be pretty unsightly to have all those notes nailed up for today's service."

"I thought so, too. But that's not why I called you."

"Then why?"

"I pulled the notes out of the envelope. I...umm...thought it would be good to straighten them up."

"Marilyn!" I laughed. "You just wanted to read those people's sins."

"I did not! I just thought that I'd give them to Father George and...and...oh, fine," she admitted. "Well, who wouldn't? I admit it."

"I'll bet Brenda didn't read them," I said. "She's a better person than that. More scruples."

"She probably didn't have time," sniffed Marilyn.

"That could be the another reason," I said. "Anything good in there?"

"As a matter of fact, yes. There was quite a lot of juicy stuff. All unsigned, of course."

"Of course. But you recognized some handwriting? Had some unsubstantiated rumors confirmed?"

"Of course," Marilyn said. "But that's not why I called you. One of the notes that I happened to see while I was straightening them out..."

"Straightening them out?" I interrupted.

"Yep. One of the notes said *I killed the organist. I had no choice. Please forgive me.*"

"What?!"

"It said *I killed the organist. I had no choice. Please forgive me.*"

"Where's the note?"

"Father George walked in, and I shoved it into the envelope with

the others. He took them into his office. You can't tell him, Hayden. He'll know I was going through them."

"What if I told him you saw that one by accident."

"He won't believe you. He'll fire me."

"Yeah, probably. Listen, the service is at noon. There's no organ music, so I don't have to play. You'll have to let me into his office during the service."

"I don't have a key. He changed the locks when you left. I think he thought you had a master key to the whole place."

"He was right," I said with a grin. "Let me think about it. I need that note. There may be a fingerprint, some DNA, we might get a handwriting sample — any number of things. By the way," I added, "you didn't happen to recognize the handwriting did you?"

"Nope. It was written in cursive though. And it was in black ink. Can't you just subpoena all the notes?"

"Well, if I were him and I didn't want to show them off, I'd say they were protected by priest-penitent privilege. We could get them, I think, but it'd take a while before some judge decided we were right."

I went out the back door, took the long way around the church and came back into Marilyn's office about five minutes later.

"Good morning, Marilyn. Is the good Father in?" I asked with a wink.

"Why, I believe he is," said Marilyn, then hissed under her breath, "Don't you tell him!"

"Have no fear," I said. "Would you buzz him please?"

A minute later, Father George opened his door and ushered me into his office. "Good morning, Hayden," he said, stiffly. "What can I do for you?"

"I had a thought, George. You know, we have quite a list of suspects for the murder of Agnes Day."

"I had heard that, yes. It's a terrible thing." He shook his head side to side.

"And, although I wouldn't have thought that the Nailing Service was a particularly good idea for Maundy Thursday, it occurred to me this morning that since most of our suspects are St. Barnabas

communicants, maybe one of them wrote down that particular sin and nailed it up on the cross. May I go into the church and look through them? They're unsigned, aren't they?"

Father George blanched. "I don't know if they're signed or not," he said. "We've already taken them down, but I haven't read them and I won't. Whatever is in those notes is between that person and God."

Excellent, I thought. I'd already caught him in a lie, and now he was trapped. He'd read those notes as soon as he came into the office. It was as plain as the nose on his face.

"Since you haven't read them, George, what would be the harm in me looking through them? Just to make sure."

"A confession to a priest is sacrosanct. Every court in the nation has upheld the sanctity of the confessional."

"I agree totally. But nailing a post-it-note confession onto a cross in a public building is hardly a confession made to a priest."

"I'm prepared to defend my argument. In court, if necessary."

"What's the big deal, George? Wait a minute. Did you read those notes?"

"Umm...no, of course I didn't. It's the principle of the thing."

I looked at him for a long minute. He tried to keep his eyes locked on mine, but they kept flitting around the room. Finally I spoke. "Here's what I think, George. I think you read those notes, and someone wrote something that you don't want me to read. There may be any number of notes with some illegal or embarrassing admissions. I don't care about them. There's only one note that I would be interested in, and that note has to do with the murder of Agnes Day. If you tell me now that you didn't read them, I'll believe you, and I'll go and get a subpoena for all of the notes. You know as well as I do that they're not protected by the priest and penitent privilege. Then I'll go over them all with a fine-tooth comb and, since I've told you that I'm going to do this, if you destroy the notes before the subpoena gets here, you will be committing a felony by destroying evidence. However, if you want to change your story right now, I'll understand that you were in a difficult spot and didn't know how to react."

I stood in front of his desk for thirty seconds before he opened the top left drawer and handed me a purple note, folded in half. I pulled a baggie that I'd purloined from the kitchen out of my pocket

and had him drop the note inside.

"Aren't you going to read it?" he asked.

"I don't want to touch it yet. What does it say?"

"It says *I killed the organist. I had no choice. Please forgive me.*"

"And you weren't going to give it to me?" I asked, incredulously.

"Probably. I had to think about it. I didn't know *what* to do."

I opened his office door. "I'll need to get your fingerprints and a DNA swab for exclusionary purposes." Father George looked shocked. "Since you touched the note," I explained. He relaxed and turned back into his office.

"You, too," I mouthed to Marilyn. She smiled and nodded.

I took the note down to the station after alerting Nancy to the find, then sent her down to the church with a couple of DNA swabs and a fingerprint kit. Dave greeted me as I came in.

"I hear you have a clue," he said.

"That's what we've got, sure enough," I replied, pulling the bag out of my pocket. "We need to do a couple of things. Call Gary Thorndike in Durham and see if he can get some DNA off this note — tell him I need it fast. You may have to drive it over to him. But first, we need to get a copy of it and get a handwriting analyst up here from Greensboro. Just put it on the copy machine. Got all that?"

"Got it," said Dave, opening the bag.

"And Dave," I added, with a sigh. "Don't touch the note, okay?"

"Oh...yeah. Sorry."

I was getting ready to meet Meg at Noylene's Beautifery when Nancy stuck her head into the office.

"The handwriting guy is coming down this afternoon. He'll be here at about four o'clock. You must really have some clout, boss."

"Oh, yes. Lots of clout. You going over to Noylene's? I hear there's going to be pie."

"Wouldn't miss it," Nancy answered. "I'll walk over with you."

The slush had melted in the afternoon sun, and although it was

still cold, you could sense spring trying to shove the last vestiges of winter aside and muscle its way back to the front of the line. The wind had stopped and, if you weren't standing in the shade, the weather almost seemed to have reverted to its pre-snow, vernal condition. The buds on the trees were quite visible, although the actual leaves had steadfastly refused to be fooled by what the hill folk called "blackberry winter."

It was a short walk across the park in the center of the town square. Noylene's Beautifery had its doors unlocked, its sign lit, and, true to Skeeter's promise, inside, we were treated with balloons and pie.

"Here's a coupon," said Skeeter, greeting us as we walked in. "Three dollars off."

"Three dollars off how much?" asked Nancy.

"Jes' depends," said Skeeter. "The prices are on the board over yonder."

"Thanks, Skeeter," I said. "We'll be sure to take a look. But let's get to the important matter at hand, shall we? What kind of pie do you have?"

"Pies are in the back," said Skeeter, gesturing toward the back of the shop. "I can't talk. I gotta hand out these coupons."

Meg came in and received her three-dollar coupon while we were deciding whether to wait or head for the pie table without her. Luckily, we didn't have to make that decision.

"Hi, Meg," said Nancy. "We were just going to try some pie."

"I'm sure Hayden was, anyway," said Meg. "You couldn't keep him away from a free piece of pie."

"True," I said, "but why would you want to?"

"Be polite," said Meg, under her breath. "Let's look around first."

"I knew we should have gone for the pie," I said to Nancy. "Now we're stuck."

"You mean, *you're* stuck," laughed Nancy. "I'm having pie."

Meg slipped her hand into mine and dragged me to the counter where Noylene was greeting her new prospective clientele.

"Hi, Noylene," said Meg. "Tell me about your shop."

"We do just about everything," said Noylene, pride evident in her voice. "From pedicures, to styling and coloring, to fingernails. And," she pointed to the back of the store, "we got somethin' no one

else has. We invented it. It's called the Dip 'n Tan."

"Dip 'n Tan?" said Meg. "What's that?"

"Come on with me, and I'll show you," said Noylene, leading the way.

"Gee," I said to Meg, under my breath. "I wonder what *this* could be."

"I'm afraid I know," whispered Meg. "I was being polite."

"Polite enough to give it a try?"

"Nope."

Noylene opened the door that was between the two styling bays — the door marked "Dip 'n Tan" in large white letters. We followed her into the rather small room that featured a large tank, about six feet tall and about four feet in diameter. The raised letters on the side of the tank said "564 gallons." Off to the side of the tank was a platform that someone had built, and above the tank hung a trapeze bar. Attached to the bar was a cable that ran across the ceiling, through three pulleys, down the far wall and terminated at an electric winch.

"See this?" said Noylene. "This is the Dip 'n Tan. We applied for a patent, but we haven't heard back from the government yet."

"Who's we?" I asked.

"Well, I designed it, but Skeeter and D'Artagnan did the actual building.

"What's in the tank?" asked Meg.

"Tanning fluid," said Noylene. "It ain't cheap either. I got it for fifty-five dollars a gallon. That's the bulk-rate price for us distributors. Otherwise it's about a hundred bucks. Most places spray it on, but this gives you a much better tan."

"How many gallons are in there, Noylene?" I asked, gingerly peeking into the barrel. "How could you afford it?"

"I got me a government grant for Appalachian women to start a small business. A lady over in Boone helped me fill out the papers. It paid for about two hundred and fifty gallons of tanning spray and a hundred gallons of alcohol. I asked the manufacturer, and he said we could cut it with alcohol. You just have to stay in a little longer."

"My," I said, "this is really ingenious. Let me see if I've got this right. First you take off all your clothes..."

"Well, you've got to put this hair protector on first," said Noylene, holding up a shower cap. "Either Skeeter or me will be in

here depending on if you're a bull or a heifer," said Noylene. "You won't have to worry about that."

"I wasn't worried," I said. "Okay, you put on the hair protector. Then you hang onto the trapeze and Skeeter, or you, Noylene, if I was a heifer, would switch on the winch, and I'd be lowered gently into the tanning broth."

"That's all there is to it," said Noylene, proudly.

It looks like it's only about four feet deep," I said, looking into the tank. "What about the upper parts?"

"Well," Noylene admitted, "until I get enough money to buy some more tanning spray, you'd sort of have to squat down there in the tank."

"Ewww," said Meg, quietly.

"Well that certainly would get some places tanned that God probably never intended to see the sun," I said. "I applaud your efforts, Noylene, and I wish you the best of luck. I, personally, don't see any need to be tanned artificially, but I'm sure there are many that do. Meg, here, for instance, has been known to darken in the dead of winter, much to my amazement."

"How often do you change the fluid," asked Meg.

"There's no need," said Noylene, with a big smile. "The alcohol kills all the germs. We just need to add a gallon every now and then, to keep the level up. See?"

"Yes," said Meg, with a shudder. "I see."

"This pie is good," I said. "Strawberry Rhubarb. You should try it."

"Nope. I got a piece of Pumpkin and some Blackberry Cobbler," said Nancy.

"Here's the EMT boys," said Nancy, and then whispered to Meg, "I'm dating the tall one. His name's Mike."

"'Bout time," I said, as the two ambulance drivers made their way into the shop. "He's been asking you out for two years. You invited them to the pie-fest, I presume."

Nancy ignored me, smiled and made her way up to the front to greet them.

Mike and his partner Joe got their coupons from Skeeter and fell

in line for the next Dip 'n Tan tour. I suspected that they thought it was the line for pie. The ambulance that Mike and Joe were assigned to was sent out of Boone but covered all of Watauga County. It was a lot of area.

"I'm going to try the blackberry cobbler next," I said.

"I thought you were on a diet," said Meg.

"Well...I am. But I've been saving up for this afternoon."

"What about your three pairs of pants?" asked Nancy. "They were getting too small, remember?"

"Yes, I remember."

"Wait a minute," said Nancy, looking me up and down. "Those are new pants. Hey, are those..."

I was mercifully saved an embarrassing admission by a deafening crash outside the Beautifery. An old red truck had plowed through a parking meter and hit a streetlight. We watched from Noylene's window as Kenny Frazier opened the driver's side door, got out of the truck and staggered through Noylene's front entrance. The front of his red-plaid shirt was more red than plaid. He dropped to his knees without a word and fell forward onto his face.

"Mike! Joe!" I yelled. "Get up here! Fast!"

I turned Kenny over and yanked his shirt open. He was covered in blood, and I could see buckshot holes in his chest.

"He's not breathing," said Meg as Mike and Joe came running up. Mike took one look and raced out the front door for the ambulance.

"Pick him up," said Joe to me, lifting Kenny from under his arms. "Get his legs."

"Shouldn't we..." started Nancy, remembering her emergency training.

"No time," said Joe. "He's not breathing, and we can't do CPR until we know the extent of his injuries. We can get him on the respirator, though. Get the door, will you?"

Nancy held the door as Mike came tearing up in the ambulance. Joe and I had Kenny out the door and to the back of the ambulance just as Mike lowered the gurney. Kenny Frazier was into the ambulance and off to the hospital before you could say "Welcome to Noylene's Beautifery and Dip 'n Tan." The whole episode took less than two minutes.

"Do you think he'll make it?" asked Meg, as the ambulance sped off, lights flashing and siren set on "stun."

"I have no idea. It looked pretty bad. He was shot by a scattergun."

"You'd better clean up," said Nancy. "You've got blood all over you."

"What happened?" asked Noylene, finally making her way to the front of the shop. Nancy told her.

"Oh my God," said Noylene, "They've killed Kenny."

"Those bastards," said Skeeter.

Chapter 17

We walked into Buxtehooters to the sound of Bach's little G-minor fugue. The place was packed. The music was good but that wasn't why the customers were lined up three deep at the bar gazing up at a trio of waitresses singing along with the countersubject. The waitresses, as well as the bartenders, were all young women of exceptional talents--if you consider being able to stand upright despite tremendous gravitational obstacles a talent.

Six beers later, the three waitresses singing on the bar had improved dramatically, and I was feeling much better.

"By the way," said Pedro, pulling out a sheaf of papers. "I have a copy of the pork amendments included on the Liturgical Color Bill that's coming up. There's the usual parking lot repaving for the cathedrals and a 'retreat center' for the bishop of West Virginia. There's also a couple of hundred thousand allocated for the study of the effect of incense on hair loss in priests, ages forty to fifty-five."

"That's a new one," I said with a grin.

"But, here's something interesting," Pedro continued. "The contract for all new fabrics would be awarded to 'Naves by Raoul.' I did some checking. 'Naves by Raoul' is a wholly owned subsidiary of Bulimia Forsythe Enterprises."

"And somebody's doing a brisk business in soprano development," I said as Helga, our beer-fräulein, jiggled another round of Wienerzuckers up to the table.

"Looks like it to me, too," said Pedro. "But maybe it's just a coincidence."

"Maybe. You believe in coincidence?"

"Nope."

"Me neither."

"Let's get Kenny's truck off the parking meter and haul it behind the station. We'll look at it this afternoon." I had washed up in Noylene's bathroom, but I still felt the need of a hot shower.

"Will do. I'll call the tow truck," said Nancy.

"Then you'd better get out to Kenny's farm and see if you can find anything. He might not have been shot out there. Probably not, in fact, but it's a place to start."

"I'll head out as soon as we get the truck squared away."

"I'll get back to the office and call over to the hospital." Maybe he'll be okay." I didn't sound or feel very confident about the prognosis.

"Yeah, maybe," said Nancy.

When I walked into the office, I could tell that Dave had been waiting anxiously for my return.

"I heard about Kenny on the scanner," he said. "What happened?"

"He ran over a parking meter and crashed his truck into a street light. Then he staggered into Noylene's and collapsed. He'd been shot. Luckily the EMTs were there. Nancy had invited them over for pie."

"Man, that's just awful. Did you bring me any?"

"Any what?" I asked.

"Any pie," said Dave.

"Sorry, Dave, I was preoccupied."

"Oh yeah. Anyway, there's some news. I called over to Durham and talked to your friend Gary Thorndike. He said that if I could get the note over to him today, he could do the tests and have something by Monday or Tuesday."

"You'd better get going then," I said. "It's a three hour drive."

"Yeah, I'm going. He also said that he had news on the bell."

"The bell?"

"The handbell. Dr. Murphee sent it over to check if there was any DNA on the handle."

"Oh, yeah," I said. "I didn't know it was going to Gary's lab."

"It did. Anyway, Dr. Thorndike pulled three samples off the bell." Dave picked up a piece of paper and read from his notes, making sure he got his information correct.

"One of the samples was the victim, Agnes Day."

"Of course."

"The other two samples are unknown — one female, one male. If he had a sample to compare them with, Dr. Thorndike said he could match them."

"That's great! Now all we have to do is find out who we need to get a sample from."

"Can't we just test everyone?"

"Nope. Testing is expensive, and besides, we'd need warrants. We've got to narrow it down. The good news is, once we have a good suspect, DNA on the murder weapon will certainly do a lot to help our case."

"The handwriting guy will be here by two o'clock," Dave said, pulling on his jacket. "I'm off to Durham."

My shower would have to wait. By the time I got all the way out to my house, showered and changed and drove back again, I'd miss my appointment with the handwriting analyst entirely. Nancy called in just as I was deciding whether or not to go over to The Slab and drown my sorrows in a cup of coffee.

"Any news from the hospital?" she asked. "Did Kenny make it?"

"I called over to the Emergency Room, but they didn't know anything. There wasn't any answer at the main desk. Figures. I'll call after a while."

"I'm at the farm now. He might have been shot out here. There's some blood on the ground by where his truck was parked," said Nancy. "I went out behind the barn and followed a path into the trees. Kenny cleared a half-acre field right in the middle of the woods. I'd never have found it, if I wasn't snooping around."

"Any of his crop left?"

"Nope. The feds have been up here with bulldozers. They dug everything up, including most of Kenny's winter wheat. I guess they thought he'd hide some of the plants in with the wheat."

"That's stupid," I said. "You can't hide a marijuana plant in winter wheat."

"Well, they didn't much care I suppose. Government regulations and all that."

"What about the blood?" I asked.

"I'm still looking around. I don't see a blood trail or anything, but I'll look in the house and the barns and let you know."

"Okay," I said. "Be careful."

I still had about an hour before the handwriting analyst showed up and that was *if* he was on time. I headed over to The Slab.

"I just heard," said Pete when I came in the door. I waved a vague hand toward Collette and an idle coffee pot.

"Yeah," I said, with a shake of my head. "Bad business."

Pete nodded sadly. "Did you bring me any?"

"Any what?" I asked.

"Any pie. Noylene makes the best pie in three states. I heard she was out."

"Out of pie?"

"Yeah. I didn't get over there in time."

I looked at him with incredulity. "You heard about Kenny, right?"

"Kenny Frazier? No. Why?"

"Here's your coffee, Hon," said Collette, picking up Noylene's mannerisms quickly, now that Noylene had tendered her resignation.

"Thanks, Collette," I said, turning back to Pete. "Kenny Frazier was shot. He was shot, ran over a parking meter, crashed into a streetlight, and staggered into Noylene's."

"Really?" asked Pete. "Is he all right?"

I shook my head. "The ambulance happened to be right outside and took him down to the hospital, but he wasn't breathing when I got to him."

Collette put her hand to her mouth and, in the same motion, dropped the almost-empty coffee pot. It shattered on the black and white tiles with a crash. "Oh my God," she said. "They've killed Kenny."

"Those bastards," muttered Pete.

The forensic handwriting analyst's name was Margaret Meyerson, a fact that I learned immediately following her entrance into the station. She thrust her hand forward, grabbed my own, and shook it vigorously.

"Chief Konig," she said. "Margaret Meyerson. I'm so glad to meet you."

"Miss Meyerson," I acknowledged, trying in vain to dislodge my hand from a grip that would put even Nancy to shame.

"Call me Margaret," she said. "I hear that you have a handwriting sample you'd like me to look at."

"I do," I said. "If you'll just let go of my hand for a second..."

"Oh, sorry," she said, relinquishing my hand with a smile. "Tell me about the sample."

"It's not that much really." I was over at Dave's desk, rooting around for the copy of the note. "Three lines. Unsigned."

"Well, I'll be happy to help if I can."

"Found it," I said. "Here you go."

Margaret took the note. "Do you have somewhere I can sit down?"

"Sure. Come on into my office." I led the way, sat down behind my desk and watched as Margaret settled into the chair across from me and, with both hands, spread the note out on the flat surface of the desk.

"This isn't the original," she said. I shook my head.

"We had to send it to the lab. It should be back on Tuesday."

"Hmm," she said, looking intently at the note. "A confession. Do you have a sample to compare it to?"

"Nope."

"Here's the thing," she said, still studying the piece of paper. "Forensic handwriting analysis is a science. That is to say that when an expert can compare two signatures or samples of handwriting, he or she can make a decision as to whether the two samples were written by the same person. This is especially valuable in forgery cases or in cases where the suspect is already known. It is evidence that can be offered in court, although some federal judges have disallowed the evidence."

"We don't have a suspect yet," I said. "We're looking for clues."

"Ah," said Margaret. "What you're looking for is a graphologist — someone who can divine personality traits from the reading of a handwriting sample."

"Yep," I said. "That's it exactly."

"Fortunately for you, I am such a person," said Margaret, looking up for the first time since I'd handed her the note, "although it's not my specialty. Let me say up front, however, that graphology enjoys about the same credibility in a court of law as palm reading."

"That's okay," I said. "We have some DNA and other evidence. We just need to know where to look."

"It would be better if I had the original sample," Margaret said, her eyes going back to the note. "There's only one well-documented case of a bad guy actually being caught by a graphology profile — George Metesky, the "Mad Bomber" of New York City in the 1950s — and he was really nabbed because he'd revealed too many clues about his past in a letter to a newspaper. Of course, things were different then. The courts accepted graphology as a legitimate forensic technique."

"We've got a few people we're looking at. We just need a little direction," I said.

"Okay." She shook her head. "It's not a lot of script. I wish the sample was larger."

"Whatever you can give us would be appreciated."

I killed the organist. I had no choice. Please forgive me.

"First of all," said Margaret, "I think the writer is left-handed. If there were maybe ten more words, I could say for sure. With this, an eighty percent chance. Also, I think it's a woman, although I could be wrong. Women tend to have more refined penmanship than men, so it's a pretty good guess. Don't hold me to that, though."

I started taking notes. "Probably left-handed, probably a woman," I said, writing quickly. "Anything else?"

"You want more? The rest is all conjecture," she warned.

"Give me all you've got," I said.

Margaret sat forward in her chair, holding the piece of paper in both hands. Then she sighed and nodded.

"See this slant? It's indicative of a lefty. But, beyond that, it tells me that the outstanding elements of this writer's personality are her extroverted drive together with inner emotional turmoil."

"Emotional turmoil?" I said.

"There are some characteristics that tell me that. Very irregular writing, variable form and variable size, irregular baseline, lack of continuity, writing stops and starts," said Margaret. "I think that the writer is always responding to outside events with the underlying motive being to win social approval."

"You can tell all that?"

"Yes, look." She pointed to the paper. "Irregularity of form and movement coupled with exaggerations of the slant. This is classic. The writer is driven to favorably impress everyone who crosses his path in order to gain their admiration of his abilities. But inwardly the writer feels inadequate."

"There are only eleven words," I said, astonishment evident in my voice.

"Yeah, it'd be better if I had more to work with. When the writer hides his feelings and intentions, she not only hides her emotions from others but suppresses them within himself. See the distorted middle zone letters?"

I nodded.

"Although outwardly she tries to play the role of the perfectionist, inwardly she is a risk taker — see the strong rightward drive, the sudden burst of writing speed on the word 'please?' She welcomes new ventures, wishing to be free from the fetters of convention."

Margaret sat back in the chair and relaxed, no longer looking at the note.

"I would say that neither inner peace nor outer predictability are within the writer's reach. In personal relationships, her reactions are probably unbalanced. All her energies are applied to defending an uncertain self-image whose defects she refuses to admit."

I had stopped writing and was now simply staring at her. She shrugged and smiled.

"Changing forms of letters and the connections between the letters themselves. A variable base line coupled with a shifting emphasis of writing pressure. It's quite simple, really."

"Quite simple," I agreed.

"I've also changed my mind. The writer is probably a man. Either that or a *very* strong-willed woman."

"That's amazing."

"And all inadmissible in court," said Margaret, with a smile. "But I hope it helps. Does this analysis fit any of your suspects?"

"To a tee. Would you mind writing all of that down? I'm afraid that I missed some of it."

"My pleasure."

Nancy called at about five o'clock. I was still hanging around the office, going over the notes that Margaret Meyerson had given me. If she was as good as she appeared to be, she'd given us a pretty good description of a couple of our suspects.

"Hi, boss," Nancy said, when I answered the phone. "I think I discovered what happened."

"Yeah?"

"I'm in Kenny's barn. Not the main one by the road. The little one about two hundred yards behind the house."

"I didn't know he had another one."

"Yeah. It's where he keeps his backhoe and some other equipment. Anyway, I followed the blood trail back here. It was sporadic but pretty easy to follow. There's a spring gun set up in the rafters and aimed at the back door of the barn. It's been fired and there's blood on the ground. Kenny must have forgotten about it or thought the feds had found it. It looks as though he set it off himself."

"Any other footprints or anything?"

"Yeah," said Nancy. "Lots. Probably from all the FBI agents. A can of bug spray, too."

"Well, bring the gun in. Maybe it was an accident. Apparently, Kenny wasn't the brightest bulb on the tree."

"Have you heard anything from the hospital?

"Yeah. He didn't make it."

Chapter 18

It was time to answer some questions. The first question on my list had to do with the murder of Memphis Belle. Who killed her and why? I had some ideas, but I might be way off base.

If there was one rule in detective work, it was to follow the money. Someone was going to a lot of trouble to work this liturgical color scam, and I needed to know the reason. Who'd be in the chips if the deal went through?

There was Raoul, of course, and the rest of the decorating boys, but they were just patsies working for Miss Bulimia Forsythe. The contract would be worth millions. None of the current colors would be allowed under canon law, and the Methodists, Lutherans and Presbyterians would fall right in line like a quaver of ecumenical baby ducks. Even the Catholics would eventually make the switch. They liked to think of themselves as "cutting edge," even though they were usually about twenty years behind.

So who wanted Memphis Belle dead? I thought it was pretty obvious, and I was going after the culprit.

"Would you like to go down to The Ginger Cat for lunch?" Meg asked. "There's no sense in writing any more today. Your muse has clearly left the building."

"It's Saturday, and I'm finished writing," I said. "It's a day for college basketball. A day for knockwurst, bratwurst, and kielbasa — all grilled and consumed with a modicum of really good beer. I'm thinking Tuppers' Hop Pocket Pils. I have some in the fridge in the basement."

"But then you wouldn't have the pleasure of my company," said Meg. "Bratwurst or me — you decide. But I must warn you: choose wisely."

"Do you think they would have some kielbasa at The Ginger Cat?" I asked, hopefully.

"No, but you could probably sneak one into the restaurant in your expando-pants," said Meg, with a giggle. "Is that your lunch, or are you just...?"

"Enough," I said. "I shall endure another sprout-ridden lunch for the sake of your company. And, by the way, I'm *not* wearing expando-pants."

"That's what *you* say."

"Hello, Cynthia," I said, as Meg and I found a table in The Ginger Cat and sat down. "You're looking particularly swarthy today." Meg kicked me under the table.

"Look at her," I whispered to Meg. "I'm not wrong, am I?"

"I went into Noylene's Dip 'n Tan," said Cynthia, bringing a couple of menus over to the table. "I don't think she has the mixture right yet. I'm a little darker than I wanted."

"It looks very nice," said Meg. "Very smooth. You look as though you just got back from vacation."

"Yeah, two years in the Ecuadorian rain forest," I added under my breath, only to be kicked again. I didn't bother looking at the menu. "I'll have a pork chop and some German potato salad." I wasn't hopeful. I was just trying to make Meg feel guilty.

"You're in luck," said Cynthia. "We have some weisswurst and kraut left. It's grilled with red peppers and onions."

"Really?"

"Really."

"I don't know," I said, scratching my chin. "Maybe I'd rather have a watercress and radicchio sandwich with a side of bok choy."

"Okay. There's not much left anyway," Cynthia said. "Do you want it, Meg?"

"Wait!" I almost shouted. "Please give me the weisswurst! Pleeease!"

"Apologize for your comments about my tan," said Cynthia.

"I do. I apologize," I said quickly. "Your tan is ravishing. Thou art dark, but comely, O daughter of Jerusalem, dark as the tents of Kedar, dark as the curtains of Solomon." I could see Cynthia blush, even under her Nubian countenance.

"Tell me, O thou whom my soul loveth, where thou feedest, where thou makes thy flock to rest at noon. If thou know not, O fairest among women, go thy way forth by the footsteps of the flock, and feed thy kids beside the shepherds' tents."

"That's just about enough of *that!*" said Meg.

"Wow!" said Cynthia. "What an apology! You sure know how to make a girl feel special."

"Well," I said, modestly. "I didn't actually write it."

"I've heard it before," said Meg. "And I'd better not hear it again."

"But Meg," I said. ""Didn't you hear her? They have weisswurst! *Weisswurst!*"

"I heard, but you didn't have to spout the Song of Solomon."

"Weisswurst!"

"Okay, okay. I knew they were serving it for lunch. I even brought you one of your beers." Meg reached into her purse, pulled out a brew from my secret stash, and placed it on the table.

I was overcome. Tuppers' Hop Pocket Pils and weisswurst. "Thy lips, O my love, are as the honeycomb. Honey and milk are under thy tongue and the smell of thy garments is like the smell of Lebanon."

"Enough already," said Meg. "Before you get to the part where you say that my belly is like a heap of wheat."

Chapter 19

"Marilyn," I called, "Call me a tow truck, will you? Some jamoke skizzed my jalopy slot."

"You know, most of the time I have no idea what you're talking about."

"Listen, Marilyn, it's no fun being a detective if my own secretary doesn't get the lingo. Now hustle your pins down to Sheila's Hard-Boiled Supply and get yourself a dictionary."

"Okay," she said. "I'll do it this afternoon." She was lying--lying like the Clinton commemorative presidential impeachment rug, but I was too tired to care.

"There's someone in your office to see you," she said. "She's got the color chart."

"Yeah?"

I went into my office, and there she was--Miss Bulimia Forsythe, looking like a six-foot tall, red-haired, watermelon tree.

"Hi, Bulimia," I said, flopping into my chair. "It's been a while. What have you got for me?"

"It's the color chart for the new liturgical calendar. Care to give it a look?"

"Yeah. Let's see it."

Bulimia spread the chart out on my desk, and I looked it over. It was worse than I thought. The color for Advent was titled "Shrimp." Lent was "Sunset Blush." Epiphany was changed to "Seafoam." The other colors on the chart included Cricket, Cranberry Spice, Cobalt, Butterscotch, Mauve and Puce.

Bulimia put a skeletal hand over mine. "There's enough money here for all of us," she said. "Just let it alone."

"Can't do it, Bulimia. Not after you killed Memphis."

"I didn't kill anyone." She seemed surprised. "And I don't know anyone named Memphis."

"What about your boys?" I asked.

She shook her head, and her teeth rattled like seeds inside a pumpkin. "Of course not. They're good boys. Graduated first in their class at the C.L.A.M. That's the Christopher Lowell Academy of Mincing. C'mon," she said, flipping me half a flirt. "Sure, I'd like the cash, but I'm not going to kill someone over a bunch of fabric swatches."

I may be a sucker for a couple of falsettos in a Lycra tube sock, but I think I almost believed her.

I woke up early on Easter morning, pulled on my bathrobe and walked into the kitchen for a cup of coffee. I opened the door to let Baxter outside and stared across the field at two feet of new snow. I was on the phone to Meg as soon as my coffee was ready.

"Good morning and Happy Easter!" I said. "Did you guys get any snow in town?" Although I was only about twenty miles from St. Germaine, the difference in precipitation was sometimes astounding.

"Happy Easter, yourself! And the answer is yes. Yes, we did," said Meg. "It looks like a couple of feet. I haven't seen this much snow since December. Are you going out jogging?"

"Not this morning. I'm going to leave here early. The roads are bound to be pretty bad. I'll stop by and pick you up."

"Okay. Drive carefully."

I drove up to Meg's door with about an hour to spare. I must admit that it didn't seem much like Easter. Easter was all about rebirth and resurrection, and here I was, on the first Sunday in April, driving through snowdrifts to get to the Easter service. It wasn't April Fool's Day, but it was close enough for me to envision St. Mednard, or whichever Catholic saint was currently in charge of weather control, chuckling over his prank. At least, I thought to myself, I didn't have to play for the sunrise service. They were on their own for that one.

Since I was early, Meg, Ruby and I decided to enjoy a leisurely cup of coffee before I drove everyone to the church. Meg only lived about a half-mile away, and normally we would have walked. Ruby, who attended the Baptist church, decided that it might be better to go with us on this particular morning. She would have had to make a five-mile commute in her old Buick, and her car lacked the four-wheel drive capability that made my old truck so serviceable. I offered to drive her, but she said that she'd just as soon go with us.

135

"They're having a performance of an Easter cantata by John W. Peterson," said Ruby. "I went to a couple of rehearsals, but I just couldn't do it. Hang on. I have a flyer here somewhere."

"Do you have any donuts?" I asked. "I'm starved."

"There's a cheese danish in the fridge," said Meg, "but it's about a week old."

"Great!"

"Here it is," said Ruby, finding the flyer and reading it out loud. *"The Glory of Easter* by John W. Peterson premiered in 1962. It will be performed by our Sunset Choir on Easter morning at the eleven o'clock service."

"The Sunset Choir?" I asked, munching happily on my danish.

"That's the old folks choir," explained Ruby.

"So I gathered," I said. "But isn't that a bit morbid? That's like calling them the 'Eternal Rest Choir' or maybe the 'One Foot Already In Heaven Choir.'"

"That's good," laughed Ruby. "I prefer to call them the 'Sit In My Seat and Die Choir.' They're very possessive."

"So, you don't want to hear *The Glory of Easter?"* I asked.

"They've sung it every other year since 1962. It never gets any better."

For a cold, wintry morning in April, it looked as though attendance at St. Barnabas would be surprisingly good. It was almost like every other Easter that I had experienced in the small Episcopal church, except fur coats, earmuffs and mittens replaced the usually festive Easter hats and spring outfits. Meg and I walked into the nave and were heading toward the choir loft when I saw Benny Dawkins.

Benny was practicing with the thurible, something he did for about fifteen minutes before the congregation arrived. He didn't have it lit, so the effect wasn't quite as dramatic as when the incense pot was sending smoke cascading through the sanctuary, but I watched in appreciation as Benny walked down the center aisle, whipping the thurible through its various orbits, before stopping it on a dime just before it crashed into the altar. It was a pleasure to watch a true professional at work.

Benny had finished his warm-ups and was walking back to the sacristy to fill the pot with incense when Russ Stafford walked into the sanctuary.

"Hey, Benny!" he called loudly, from six pews away. "I heard about your violin. What was it worth? A cool quarter million?"

Benny ignored him and continued toward the door leading into the sacristy.

"I wish that *I* would have bought it from you, but I didn't know you only wanted eight hundred bucks!" Russ laughed the raucous guffaw of the boorish real-estate salesman.

"I don't think that I would make Benny too angry," I whispered to Meg. "He's got quite a temper. Russ is on thin ice."

I met with the choir, and we went over the *Messiah* choruses, tuning up a few spots that I felt could use a little tuning up. I hadn't chosen the hymns, but Marilyn had given me a "heads up." One of the hymns, *Up From The Grave He Arose*, isn't actually found in the Episcopal hymnal, but Father George had printed the words in the bulletin, hoping, I presume, that everyone knew the tune. I was pretty sure that some people did, at least the congregants that came to the Episcopal church later in their ecumenical experience. The cradle Episcopalians, or the "frozen chosen" as they are referred to by the Episco-Come-Latelys, had probably never sung it. I had copied the hymn out of a United Methodist hymnal, knowing that I, at least, would need the music in front of me.

My prelude was by G.F. Handel, in keeping with our mostly Baroque theme — a transcription of the *Arrival of the Queen of Sheba* from *Solomon*. The choir then sang the *Hallelujah Chorus* as a choral introit from the balcony, and I launched into the processional hymn, *Jesus Christ Is Risen Today*. The choir had to scramble down the stairs to be part of the procession, then, as usual, once around the church and back up to the loft.

I could see, out of the corner of my eye, that the crucifer was in the lead, followed by a couple of acolytes, Benny Dawkins swinging the thurible and sending clouds of smoke billowing upwards, Father George and the choir.

I noticed Russ Stafford sitting toward the front of the church, right on the aisle. He was hard to miss, his Easter finery consisting mainly of a green and yellow plaid sport jacket. All of a sudden, I had a flashback.

Back, a few years ago, when Benny Dawkins was learning the *Doubly Inverted Reverse Swan,* the trick that won him third place in the International Thurifer Invitational in London a few years back, he was perfecting the maneuver at St. Barnabas when, one Sunday morning, he happened to catch poor Iona Hoskins behind the ear with the pot, knock her out cold and catch her wig on fire. Iona was sitting on the aisle, and, as I suddenly recalled, didn't care for Benny very much. In fact, she had lodged a complaint with Father Tony Brown because Benny had been sneaking into the church kitchen on his way to work and eating a bowl of cereal — cereal that Iona bought especially for her breakfast club. We all assumed that it had been a terrible accident, but now, as I watched the thurible tumble and pirouette on its chains in almost slow motion, I suddenly had another thought — a thought that was interrupted by a terrific "CLANG!"

I looked up from my music long enough to see Benny glance down at an unconscious Russ Stafford. He never broke his rhythm or his stride, executed a perfect *Skin The Cat*, and continued up to the front of the church. Father George, however, didn't know what to do. He didn't want to stop the Easter procession, but Russ was clearly knocked cold. Not only that, but Russ' hair was beginning to smolder just as Iona's had done. Father George didn't stop the procession, but he did pause long enough to pat Russ' head and put out the embers of incense that had escaped from the pot during the collision.

I could hear Russ moan during the pause between stanzas, and I figured he was all right. A couple of ushers followed the choir in, helped him out of his seat and out the front door. I looked back at Benny. He was completing his patented *Spank The Baby In The Bell Tower,* the thurible flying around the altar like a smoking Sputnik. Suddenly, as the hymn came to an end, Benny stopped the pot dead in its course. Then he gave it three short swings symbolizing the Trinity and hung it on its stand.

The choir came up the stairs to the loft. Meg walked over to me and whispered, "Did you see that?"

"Yes," I whispered back. "I told you I wouldn't want to make Benny mad."

"Is Russ okay?"

"I think so. He walked out on his own with just a little help."

"Did you ever think that maybe Agnes Day was killed with the incense pot instead of the handbell?" Meg asked.

I didn't have time to think about it. It was time to play the *Gloria*.

In the Episcopal liturgy, there's quite a lot of music that goes on at the beginning of the service. There's the prelude, the opening hymn, the *Gloria* or *Kyrie*, and the Psalm accompaniment. Then there's the gradual hymn, neatly sandwiched between the Epistle and Gospel lessons. As an organist, you have to stay on your toes. Added to all that, on this particular morning, the choir sang the *Hallelujah Chorus* as the introit. It was a full day of playing and singing even before we got to the sermon.

It was during the gradual hymn that we all received our Easter surprise. This was the hymn that Father George had printed in the bulletin. I was right. About half the congregation knew it — about half of the choir as well. The verses were slow, and the chorus was a lot more animated. At least in *my* rendition.

Low in the grave He lay, Jesus my Savior,
Waiting the coming day, Jesus my Lord!
Up from the grave He arose,
With a mighty triumph o'er His foes,

When we got to "Up from the grave He arose," who should come walking down the center aisle but Kenny Frazier. He walked up to the third pew and took the seat recently vacated by Russ Stafford.

"Hey, Kenny!" yelled Moosey McCollough, from the back of the church with a seven-year old's enthusiasm, "we thought you was dead!" Kenny just smiled and waved at him with the arm that wasn't bandaged. I could imagine Ardine clamping a hand over Moosey's mouth to keep him quiet.

He arose a Victor from the dark domain,
And He lives forever, with His saints to reign.
He arose! He arose!
Hallelujah! Christ arose!

Meg pointed at Kenny walking in. She had a huge smile on her face. I nodded and kept playing, the smile spreading across mine as well. As an Easter miracle, it wasn't bad.

"Wanna see my drawings?" said Moosey, running up to me as I came down out of the loft.

"You bet," I said. "Let me get my vestments off, and I'll give them a good look."

"Oops," he said, shoving the stack of papers in my hand. "I forgot. I've gotta go get some Easter candy in the parish hall." He was already at a dead run when he shouted back over his shoulder, "Before those other guys get it all." Moosey was out the door and gone before I could answer.

I hung my robe up in the sacristy and waited for Meg, who was schmoozing with church members that she saw only once or twice a year. The rest of the crowd, though, seemed to be concentrated around two particular members. There was one group of people surrounding Kenny Frazier, patting him on the back and asking him what on earth had happened. The other group of people was surrounding and congratulating Rhiza and Malcolm Walker. The Walkers had been in attendance on Thursday night, but since the congregation left in silence after the Nailing Service, I suspected that this was the Walker's first real public appearance since the big Powerball news.

I had put Moosey's drawings in my pocket. Now, as I waited for Meg, I pulled them out to look through them — at least enough to tell Moosey that I thought they were almost masterpieces. He had drawn them on two pages that he had torn out of the attendance pads. The first was a picture of what I thought might be the Easter Bunny, but it might just as well have been a penguin with antlers or an anteater standing on his hind legs. It was the second picture that stopped me cold.

In my hand I held a drawing of some trees, or what I thought might be trees. But, the trees were not the important part of the picture. Moosey had used the side of his pencil to shade the leaves of his drawing, and his shading had revealed an underlying text. I could make out a couple of words in the corner — *please forgive me.*

"What did you think about Benny leveling Russ with the incense pot?" Meg asked.

"He said it was an accident. I talked to him in the sacristy."

"Yeah. Right," said Meg. "I don't think so."

"Well, I tend to agree," I said. "But we have no real proof. It *could* have been an accident."

"What about Agnes Day?"

"If Benny did kill her, he didn't do it with the incense pot. She was definitely killed with the handbell. The DNA samples came back last week, and Kent Murphee says the dent in her skull matched the handbell perfectly. There were three samples on the bell. Agnes Day's, an unknown man's and an unknown woman's."

"Any idea who the unknowns might be?"

"Nope. Could be anyone."

"Well," said Meg, "back to the drawing board."

"Not quite," I said.

I called Nancy and Marilyn and told them to meet Meg, Ruby and me in the church office at one o'clock. That gave us time to brave the snowdrifts, walk over to The Slab, and get a couple of grilled cheese sandwiches and some fries. We made it back to the church office just as Nancy was coming in the door. Marilyn came in a couple of minutes later.

"Here's what I have," I said, spreading Moosey's picture out on Marilyn's desk. "Look here at this corner. It's very faint, but the shading brought up the indentation of the words written on the piece of paper that was on top of it. These are the last three words of the confession note." I turned to Nancy. "Did you bring it?"

"Here it is," said Nancy, pulling out our photocopy of the original note. I laid it next to Moosey's drawing. The words were difficult to make out, but we could all see that they were a match.

"Moosey drew his pictures on the attendance forms," I said. "The forms are in these pads, and there's one pad per pew. When Father George asks everyone to be sure to sign the attendance pad, they,

in theory, sign the form, and pass it down to the next person. After every service, Carol collects the forms so we know who's been here. I don't know what we do with the information," I said, "but in this case, it may be just what we're looking for. If the form that Moosey wrote on had this indentation, then it's reasonable to assume that whoever wrote the confession note used the attendance pad as his or her writing desk."

"I get it," said Nancy. "The original attendance form would have the same indentation."

"And would tell us who was sitting in the pew," added Meg.

"Bingo," I said. "Now, Marilyn, give us some good news. We still have the attendance forms from Thursday night, right?"

"I have them right here." Marilyn opened a drawer in her desk and pulled out a stack of papers. "Even if we do find out who wrote the note, is that a confession? Will it put the killer behind bars?"

"I doubt it seriously," I said. "There's always deniability where an anonymous note is concerned, and, even if the person admits to writing it, they can always say it was a prank. What it *will* do is point us in the right direction. Then we can look for other, more compelling, evidence."

"What's the plan?" Meg asked. "Do we have to shade all these forms? That'll take hours."

"No need," I said. "Nancy?"

"Got it right here, chief," said Nancy as she reached into her jacket and pulled out a fingerprint kit.

"We'll just put some black fingerprint powder on the brush and dust each of the forms," I said. "The indentations should pick up the powder and make the writing easy to spot."

We watched Nancy dust the notes one at a time. She'd finished about thirty or so when she said, "That's the one." The powder dropped into the indentations and we could read most of the words. There, on the note, in black fingerprint powder, we could all read *killed the...had no choice...forgive me.* I put our copy of the confession next to the words. They were a match. I blew off the excess powder and all of us squinted to read the names on the pad.

There were four people sitting in that pew — Malcolm and Rhiza Walker and Annette and Francis Passaglio.

Chapter 20

Nancy and I were in the office on Monday morning when Kenny came in. I'd found him in the parish hall after the service on Sunday. He was being mobbed by all the well-wishers that had heard the grim news of his demise, so I asked him to come on down to the office in the morning. He walked in with one arm bandaged and in a sling, but other than that, looked pretty healthy.

"Man, Kenny," said Nancy. "I thought you were dead."

"We all did," I added.

"I very nearly was," said Kenny. "It was the darndest thing. I saw this bright light, and I was just walking towards it."

"Do you remember what happened?" Nancy asked. "I mean, before the bright light."

"Sure," said Kenny, smiling at us. He smiled at us for about fifteen seconds before Nancy realized he needed more prompting.

"Do you think you might tell us?" she growled.

"Oh, yeah. Sorry. Some of this I can remember, but when I got into town, everything went black. Then I remember some more in the hospital." Kenny smiled at us again.

I didn't wait the fifteen seconds. "Okay, Kenny," I said slowly. "You need to tell us what happened."

"Pothead," muttered Nancy, under her breath. "Medical marijuana, my Aunt Millie's butt!"

"Oh yeah. Sorry," Kenny said again, still smiling. "I saw this bright light..."

"Before that," I said. "When you got shot."

"Oh yeah. Sorry. Let's see...where was I?"

Nancy was getting tired of waiting. "You went into the barn," she prompted. "You went in the back door..."

"Yeah," said Kenny. "No, wait a minute. I went in the front door and walked to the back of the barn. I was gonna clean out this hornet's nest that I saw the other day. I had some bug spray and a rake. I went into the barn and sprayed the nest. But they weren't hornets. They were bees."

"Was that a problem?" I asked.

"For me it is. I'm allergic to bee stings."

"But not hornet stings?" I asked.

143

"Nope. The weird thing is, these bees were in a hornet's nest."
Kenny shrugged. "I guess they found it and moved in."

"Yeah," I said, "sometimes they'll do that. What happened
next?"

"Hey, did I tell you guys about the bright light? It was amazing!"

"Before the light," Nancy said. "You sprayed the nest."

"Oh yeah. I sprayed the nest, but I guess I missed a couple of
those little guys. They stung me on the arm." Kenny stopped talking
and smiled again.

"And?" Nancy prompted.

"And my arm started to swell up. That's how I knew they were
bees. I usually have a shot I can give myself up at the house, but I
remembered I used the last one in the summer. I have about twenty
minutes before I pass out. So then I figured I'd better get to town as
quick as I could." Kenny stopped and smiled again. "You guys have
any donuts? I've got the munchies something fierce."

"Sorry," said Nancy.

"I thought all police stations had donuts," said an obviously
disappointed Kenny.

"Nancy'll take you down and get you one after we hear your
story," I said. Nancy glared at me. "So what happened after you got
stung."

"My arm started to swell up. That's how I knew they were bees.
You see, I have this shot that I can give myself..."

"We remember!" barked Nancy. 'The bees stung you, you
didn't have a shot, you were going to drive to town, you had twenty
minutes left to live...which is about what you have right now unless
you finish this story!"

"Here's the thing," said Kenny, with another genuine smile. "Did
you know that when you're dying, there's this really bright light?
You sort of walk toward it and..."

"Arrrgh!" said Nancy.

"Kenny," I said, calmly, "after you decided to drive to town, what
happened?"

"I went out to the truck, got in and started it up."

"You didn't get shot?"

"Umm...yeah. I'm getting to it. I started the truck up, and then
I remembered that the emergency room guys like to have one of
those bees that stung me. So they can see which kind it is, I guess. I

drove around to the back of the barn, opened the back door and —
Ka-Blam!"

"You got shot," I said.

"Finally," said Nancy.

"Sure did," said Kenny. "A shotgun. Lots of pellets. The good thing was that it went off when I was opening the door, so most of the pellets had to go through the wood to get to me. It's a pretty thick door."

"Was that your shotgun, Kenny?" I asked. "Did you set it as a trap?"

"Nope. I don't own a gun."

"You didn't set a spring gun to protect your grass?" asked Nancy.

"'Course not," said Kenny. "Why would I do that? It's perfectly legal. Anyway, I knew I wasn't hurt bad although there was a lot of blood. The doc said that the pellets in my chest only went in about a quarter inch. They just popped them out with tweezers. I did get some into my arm. That's why it's in a sling."

"So you drove into town," I said.

"Yeah. But I think I passed out when I got to the square. Lucky that ambulance was there, huh?"

"Very lucky."

"The doc said that once Joe and Mike cleaned me off, they could see it wasn't bad, and they got a tube down my throat. That's what happens with these bee stings. My throat closes up, and I can't breathe. We got to the hospital, they gave me a shot, and took these pellets out. But then, that night, I had another reaction to the bee sting, and they sent me down to Kingsport."

"Why did the hospital say you were dead?" asked Nancy.

"Don't know. Maybe they just lost the paperwork."

"Do you still have the gun?" I asked Nancy.

"It's in my car. I'll send it down to the lab."

"You can do that after you take Kenny in for some donuts," I said, with a grin. "One more question, Kenny."

"Yeah?"

"Why'd you come to St. Barnabas on Sunday? I haven't seen you in church for ten years."

"Well, it's like this. It was Easter and I just had a narrow escape from death."

"That's a good enough reason," I said, with a nod.

"That, plus I've been dating one of the singers in the choir," added Kenny.

"Really," I said. "Who is it?"

"Renee Tatton. She really likes me. She says I remind her of an actor named Tab Hunter."

"Hello, Hayden. This is Gary Thorndike. I have some news for you," said the voice on the other end of the phone. "The lab's really busy, but I moved your case to the head of the line."

"Hi, Gary," I said, recognizing the voice right away. "Thanks. I hope the news is good."

"Mixed," said Gary. "The note you sent down?"

"Yeah."

"Nothing on it we could come up with. There were a couple of partial prints but they're unreadable. If you have a handwriting sample we could compare it to, we can probably match it up."

"We don't have one. So, let me get this straight...we've got three DNA samples on the bell and nothing on the note."

"I'm afraid that you are correct. But I do have some other news that might be of use."

"Yeah?"

"I had our guys look closely at the note. You know, put it under a microscope, do an ink analysis...that sort of stuff."

"What did you find?"

"It was written by a ball point pen. Probably by a southpaw."

"Good to know," I said. I didn't tell him we already knew about the lefty.

"Here's the part you'll like," said Gary. "The inky part."

"Yeah?"

"The ink's from a certain kind of pen. Specifically a Montblanc Miesterstuck Solitare. This would be the original cartridge, not a refill. The refills have a slightly different chemical makeup. So you might be looking for one that's fairly new. Maybe a Christmas present."

"You can tell this from the note?" I was astounded.

"Sure. Ink, even black ink, is a mixture of several different

dyes. We use thin layer chromatography to break it down. It's a big business with all the medical malpractice cases going on. Lawyers have to know who checked what on which patient chart and who wrote which bad prescription. All the Montblancs are in our database. Apparently, it's a very popular pen with doctors."

"How much does one of those pens go for?" I asked.

"They're out of my league, but I'd say maybe five hundred. The ball points aren't as much as the fountain pens."

"That's still a lot of cash for a pen," I said.

"Not if you've got it," said Gary.

Chapter 21

I was missing something—that much was obvious. The clues were all there. They had to be and I oughta know. I was the one that wrote them. I lit a cigar and walked down the street, mulling over the case like it was a jug of last year's Christmas wine. Maybe I had left a clue out. It wouldn't be the first time, I thought to myself. I should have put it into Chapter 10, but if I'd forgotten, no wonder I couldn't solve this case. I turned into Buxtehooters and whistled for the waitress. I went with Scarlatti's Little Fugue in D minor. It seemed to work. I had a beer in my hand before my fundament hit the chair.

Pedro was waiting for me. "Did you remember to put the clue into Chapter 10?" he asked. "I don't think we're getting anywhere."

"I can't recall," I said. "I certainly hope so."

"Well," said Pedro, thinking hard. "I wasn't in Chapter 10, so I don't know. Who have we got?"

"We've got Miss Bulimia Forsythe, but I don't think she killed Memphis," I said. "She's in the color scam up to her lilac-colored eyeshadow, but she's not a murderer."

"How about her boys?"

"Raoul, Biff and D'Roger?"

"Yeah, them," said Pedro, gulping down a bottle of Schnitzenfahrt.

"Nah. They're harmless. They may be a danger to some bolts of velveteen, but only if they don't run with the scissors."

"We gonna quash the color scam?"

"Yep."

I looked up from my typewriter, chomped down on my cigar and surveyed my domain. Meg was sitting on the old, worn, leather couch, working on her laptop, Rachmaninov's second piano concerto was on the WAVE, a fire was blazing in the hearth, and all was right with the world.

"I can see that your writing career is blossoming," said Meg, closing up her computer. "I just read *The Alto Wore Tweed* on your

new blog page." She got up and jostled the embers with the poker. A fire in April wasn't uncommon for these parts, but this one might be our last of the season. Channel Four was calling for temperatures in the low eighties by the end of the week.

"Pretty great, huh?" I answered. "It's only a matter of time before I win it all. The big enchilada. The Bulwer-Lytton extravaganza. World-wide fame shall be mine."

"Yes, well...I hate to tell you this, but there's a counter down at the bottom of your page. I was visitor number eight. And I suspect you've already visited the page a couple of times yourself."

"Two or three," I admitted. "Traffic'll pick up. It won't be long before a major publisher will be wanting to have a look at my collected works."

"With a pub called Buxtehooters selling beer called Schnitzenfahrts, I wouldn't hold my breath."

"Speaking of Buxtehooters," I said, "I need you to go out to lunch with Annette."

"What has Annette got to do with Buxtehooters?" said Meg, accusation hanging heavily on every word.

"Nothing," I said. "It was just that 'stream of consciousness' thing you were doing. Remember?"

"Well, I don't like it."

"See?" I said. "Anyway, I need you to take Annette to lunch and find out if she's left-handed."

"Obviously, you think she's the one who wrote the note. But didn't your handwriting expert say that she thought it was a man?"

"Or a very strong-willed woman. Do you know any women that are more strong-willed than Annette?"

"No," said Meg. "I can't say that I do."

"See if you can get her to write something."

"You want me to get a handwriting sample?"

"Sure. That'd be great. But I really just want to know if she's left-handed and if she uses a Montblanc ballpoint pen."

"How will I know if it's a Montblanc?" asked Meg.

"Just ask her," I said. "Ooooo, Annette. I just *love* that pen. Wherever did you get it?"

"Harumph," said Meg.

149

I pulled up my usual chair at our usual table on a bright and breezy Tuesday morning. Business at The Slab Café was beginning to pick up. It was that time of year. The temperature had climbed back into the sixties, the snow had melted and there wasn't even any slush left behind. Just wet sidewalks, slightly wilted shrubs and trees that were still trying to decide if it was safe to send their leaves out to play. Dave and Nancy came in together. Collette had our coffee poured before we even sat down.

"How about biscuits and gravy?" asked Collette. "And some grits? I made them myself."

"Then I'll have some," said Dave, with a little too much enthusiasm for Nancy's taste.

"Yeah. Fine. Whatever," she grumbled.

"Sounds good to me, too." I said to Collette, before turning my attention to my fellow officers. "We have two very serious crimes to solve. Let's get cracking. First on the list is the murder of Agnes Day."

Nancy pulled her pad out of her breast pocket. "She was killed with a handbell on Palm Sunday shortly after the service had ended. We have three DNA samples from the bell — the victim's, an unknown male and an unknown female. We currently have a number of suspects, all who had likely reasons to want to see Agnes Day dead," Nancy said.

"Who's first?" said Dave.

"Russ Stafford," Nancy continued. "He'll be broke before the end of the year. His real estate development is going belly up. He sure could have used some of St. Barnabas' sixteen million to jump start sales over at The Clifftops. He was trying to finagle a deal for St. B.'s to buy a new rectory out there. It would have kept him floating for a while, anyway."

"It was a slim hope," I said. "Even though Agnes Day hated him, and she was Lucille Murdock's nurse, there wasn't any chance that any of that money was going to Russ. Add to that, I don't think he was even in attendance at the Maundy Thursday service. At least I didn't see him there."

Dave looked puzzled.

"You know...the Nailing Service? The confession?"

"Oh, yeah," said Dave. "Scratch him off the short list." Nancy nodded.

"Then there's Ruthie Haggarty," said Nancy. "She's going to get

off for killing Little Bubba on a domestic abuse self-defense plea. At least, I think she will. I'm sure not going to testify against her. Quite frankly, Little Bubba needed killing."

"I wouldn't go that far," I said. "But she is going to inherit Agnes Day's estate. Still, I don't see her murdering for money."

"It's a lot of money, though, isn't it?" asked Dave.

"A quarter million bucks, give or take," I said. "People have been killed for a whole lot less."

"Was she there on Maundy Thursday?" asked Dave.

"Nope," I said. "She was at St. Joseph's Catholic Church. I checked with the priest. They had a service that evening, and Ruthie was in attendance."

"I'm glad," said Nancy. "I like Ruthie."

"Scratch her off," Dave said, as our food arrived at the table. I'm sure Dave was looking forward to being served by Collette, but it was Pete who was acting as our garçon.

"Here's your grub," said Pete, setting down the food and pulling up a fourth chair. "Hope you don't mind me joining you, but these biscuits looked too good to pass up."

"Anytime, Pete," I said. "You are, after all, picking up the tab. Pull up a chair for Meg, too. She'll be along in a bit."

"Of course I am," grumbled Pete in mock irritation. "My pleasure. It's the least I can do for our city's finest." Then his voice brightened. "You guys still working on the Handbell Murder?"

"We are," I said, as we all filled our plates. That was the great thing about The Slab. They still served "family style" breakfasts, and no one ever went away hungry.

"How about Benny Dawkins?" Nancy asked. "He's in bad shape financially as well. And I heard what he did to Russ on Sunday."

"I'm not saying that Russ had it coming, but he was pretty rude to Benny right before church," I said. "Still, I know that Benny was pretty upset with the violin thing."

"What happened?" asked Pete. "I don't know anything about the violin thing."

Nancy flipped a few pages in her pad. "Benny took his great-grandfather's violin to Agnes Day to get her opinion on it. He said he needed to sell it so he could make a couple of overdue farm payments."

"Yeah?" said Pete, as he spooned some more grits onto his plate.

"She offered him eight hundred dollars for it, and he took it. She made him sign a bill of sale."

"Sounds like a good deal to me," said Pete. "Those old violins aren't usually worth very much."

"Then she sold it for two hundred fifty-five thousand," said Nancy.

"Yikes!"

"It was a Guadagnini, whatever that is."

"A very expensive fiddle," I said. "Benny, shall we say, was not amused. He went and asked for the money, and she turned him down flat."

"So, do we think he killed her?" asked Dave.

"Here's what *I* think," I said. "Killing Agnes Day wouldn't get his money back. And it's my opinion that if he wanted to get back at her, he would have done something that she'd have to live with for a while. Like maybe whack her on the head with the incense pot, or burn down her house or something. I don't see him killing her." I took a sip of coffee. "But that's just me," I added.

"Here's a wrinkle," said Nancy. "I saw Benny and Ruthie in Benny's truck about an hour ago. And she wasn't hugging the window, if you get my drift."

"Well, that *is* something," I said. "Benny might just have found a way to get his money back after all. We can't scratch him off the list just yet. I still don't think he did it, but let's leave him on. Until we come up with someone better."

"Maybe they were in it together," said Pete, happily munching on a biscuit.

"We didn't think of that," said Nancy, looking over at me.

"No we didn't," I said. "Put them both back on."

"How about Kenny Frazier?" asked Nancy.

"He didn't do it," I said, "and that brings us to our other case."

"The mysterious case of *Who Killed Kenny*?" said Nancy. "Or who tried to, anyway."

"Someone tried to kill him?" asked Pete.

"Last Friday. When he came into Noylene's all bloody, we'd assumed he'd been shot, and he had. But that wasn't why he stopped breathing. He was having an allergic reaction to a bee sting."

"So, being shot was just a coincidence?" asked Pete.

"Not entirely, but yes," I said. "He would have gotten shot eventually and maybe worse, although the gun was set up pretty badly. Someone set a spring gun in Kenny's barn, trying to make it

look as though he had forgotten about it and blundered into his own trap. Whoever set it up, though, didn't know much about spring guns. You have to keep them close to the door so they'll blow a hole right through it. This one was too far back. Most of the shot stuck in the door, and the pellets that made it through didn't go very far into Kenny. Just enough to cause a lot of blood."

"How do you know that Kenny didn't set the trap himself?" asked Dave.

"He says he doesn't own a gun, and I tend to believe him," I said.

"Plus, the feds were all over the place a couple of weeks ago," added Nancy. "They cleaned everything out. They sure wouldn't have missed a spring gun. It was in plain sight, hanging up in the rafters. And there wasn't any reason for Kenny to set it after they'd gone. He didn't have anything left to guard."

"Makes sense," said Pete. "I'm getting some more biscuits. Anyone else want any?" All our hands went up. "Be right back."

"By the way," said Nancy. "The lab pulled a print off that shotgun. Nothing to match it to, though. It's not Kenny's. You think it's all a big coincidence?"

"Nope," I said. "Not this time."

"So, whoever tried to kill Kenny is involved in Agnes Day's murder as well."

"I think so. We need to figure out what Kenny and the killer have in common. They're tied together somehow."

"How about Renee Tatton? Kenny's dating her, and she's another one of our suspects," Nancy said.

"There you go," I said.

"But why would she want to kill Kenny?" asked Dave.

"No idea," I said. "Perhaps we should ask her."

"Hi, guys," said Meg, suddenly appearing at the table. "Did you save me any breakfast?"

"Pete's on his way back," said Dave.

"With seconds?" Meg asked.

"Seconds or thirds," said Nancy. "Depends on how you count."

"Hey!" said Dave, "Maybe Kenny and Renee Tatton are in it together. You know, like Benny and Ruthie."

Nancy and I looked at each other. "Nah," we said in unison.

"These are really good biscuits," said Meg. "I can see why you're having thirds. Now, back to business. I have news."

We all turned our attention from the plate of biscuits and sawmill gravy to Meg.

"I met Annette for coffee, and guess what? She's left-handed. I didn't get a handwriting sample, but she did pull out a lovely pen to sign her credit card slip. 'Ooooo, Annette,' I said. 'I just *love* that pen. Wherever did you get it?'"

"She fell for that?" asked Nancy.

"Of course she did," I countered. "It's a brilliant ploy. What did she say?"

"Francis gave it to her for Valentine's Day. It's a Montblanc. She let me look at it. It was gold. Three rings in the middle of the barrel and the inlaid white Montblanc star on the end."

"Ball point?"

"Yes."

"Well, that's about it then," said Nancy, closing her pad. "She was sitting in the exact row where the confession was written, and we have a DNA sample on the bell. If we can match it up to Annette, it's pretty much a done deal."

"We still don't know why she would try to kill Kenny," I said. "There's no connection there at all."

"I think we've got enough for a warrant," said Nancy. "I'll go talk to Judge Adams."

"Hang on," I said. "We may not want to lay out all our cards just yet."

"You may not have to," said Meg. We all looked at her as she opened her purse and pulled out a coffee cup wrapped in a napkin.

"Here's the cup she was drinking from. It was sitting on the table when she left, so I picked it up. I didn't touch it. Can you get some DNA from that?"

"I believe we can," I said with a grin. "Thank you, Miss Farthing."

"My pleasure, Detective."

I sent Dave back to Durham with the coffee cup with instructions to personally deliver it to Gary Thorndike. I had called Gary, and he promised to let me know the results the next morning. Nancy was

sitting in my office, and we were still puzzling.

"I still can't figure out the connection between Kenny and Annette," I said.

"Well," Nancy answered, "they could be totally unrelated. Maybe Kenny has an enemy that we haven't considered. Maybe one of his distributors got mad because Kenny wasn't supplying anymore. Maybe the people he's in business with don't want him talking to the feds."

"Maybe," I agreed. "It certainly seems plausible. Kenny doesn't seem to possess much guile, and he'd probably give up everyone in his organization in two shakes of a donkey's tail. But, if I was a drug dealer and I wanted Kenny dead, I wouldn't have used a spring gun. I'd have walked in and shot him in the head. Someone wanted it to look like an accident. No," I said, "there's something about the handbell. Something I'm missing."

Chapter 22

"Marilyn," I said, dragging into the office like it was a Wednesday and I had spent Tuesday taking my mind off Monday, "I can't get a handle on this case, and it's driving me nuts."

"That reminds me of a pirate joke," said Marilyn.

"Not in the mood," I muttered. "Bring me some joe, will you?"

Marilyn skipped in carrying a steaming mug of coffee and a cinnamon bun shaped like the Virgin Mary. "I thought you could use this, boss. You look as bad as...as bad as a bad looking...um...goat. No, wait...that's not very good. Shoot. I can't think of these similes as easily as you."

"Keep trying. You'll get the hang of it quicker than a freshman jack-rabbit on a promdate," I said. "Now, got any suggestions on this color caper?"

"Did you check for clues?" Marilyn asked.

"Yeah. Can't find them," I grumbled.

"Chapter 13?" she asked.

"Nope. I was looking in Chapter 10."

"Look in 13," she said, skipping back out of the office. "That's where you put them."

I laughed like King-Kong on helium.

"Have I told you how good you're looking lately?" said Meg. "Your running program is really paying off."

"Yeah," I said. "I've dropped a few pounds."

"And rearranged a few more. I swear, I can hardly keep my hands off you."

"What's stopping you then?" I asked. "Self-control? A court order?"

"The first one," laughed Meg. "That, and I don't want you to think that I'm easy."

"Ha!" I said. "Too late for that."

"How's the Pirate Eucharist coming?"

"Pretty well, I think. I've completed my English to Pirate translator. Now I can simply plug in the collect for the second

Sunday of Easter and all the lessons. Oh yeah," I added, "also the Nicene Creed."

"The creed?"

"Allow me to demonstrate," I said, assuming what I thought was a perfectly credible pirate accent. "Arrrgh! We gives the nod to one baptism fer the fergiveness 'o sins. We look fer the return voyage from Davy Jones' Locker, and the life 'o the world t'come. So says one, so says us all. Aye, aye!"

"Oh, no!" Meg said.

"Oh, yes, me buxom beauty. Now will ye join me in a rousing sea chantey?"

"Did you write it?"

"You mean, 'Did *ye* write it?'" I corrected.

"Yes, did *ye* write it?"

"Aye."

"What's it called?" Meg asked.

"How Great Thou Arrrgh!"

"Gary Thorndike called," said Nancy, as soon as I entered the police station. "He wants you to call him back."

"I'll do it right now," I said. "Sorry I'm late. I've been working on the Pirate Eucharist. There's a rehearsal tonight."

"I remember," said Nancy. "I have a hymn for you. Dave and I have been working on it all week."

"Okay," I said. "Let's hear it."

Nancy cleared her throat and began.

Arrgh! The herald pirates sing,
Glory to the Heav'nly King!
As we sail the seven seas,
Yo, ho, ho is our reprise;
Buckles swashed and timbers shivered,
Legs all pegged and lilies livered.
With a pillage and a loot,
Pirates really give a hoot.
Arrgh! The herald pirates sing,
Glory to the Heav'nly King!

I nodded. "Other than 'Pirates really give a hoot,' that's not bad. But, I think it's a little too Christmasy."

"Yeah," said Nancy. "We were afraid of that."

"I have two hymns," I said, "and some service music. It'll be very distinctive."

"Go in and call Gary Thorndike, will you?" Nancy said, with a laugh. "We need to get these crimes solved."

"Hi, Gary. This is Hayden."

"Hey there. I think I've got some news for you."

"Great. What's the verdict?"

"Well, you know the coffee cup that Officer Vance brought up yesterday?"

"Yes?" I said. "Was it a match to the DNA on the bell?"

"Nope."

"No?"

"Not even close," said Gary.

"Well...that qualifies as news, I guess." I was disappointed.

"But the DNA on the bell finally came back with a name. Sometimes it takes a while. DNA is as easy as fingerprints to match, but the databases aren't nearly as complete yet. It takes a few days, in most cases, to match the DNA with a name."

"So which is it? The man or the woman?"

"The female. Her name is Olga Spaulding. The reason that we have her DNA in the database is that she had to give a sample when she applied for a work visa in Egypt. Apparently she was working for the State Department in 2002. At least, they're the ones that have her sample on file."

"Olga Spaulding? Never heard of her."

"Really? She's one of the people who handled the bell."

"Can we get a picture?"

"You can call the State Department in DC and see if they have a picture. They may have one on file. The passport office does, I'm sure, but I don't know if you'll be able to get a copy anytime soon. Sorry. I thought this information would help."

"Thanks, Gary," I said. "I'm sure it does. I just don't know how yet."

I gave Nancy the news and the assignment of weaseling a picture out of the State Department as quickly as possible.

"So, it's not Annette."

"It's not her DNA on the handle of the bell."

"I guess that would have been too easy."

"I guess. I'm going down to The Slab for lunch. Let me know if you hear anything from the passport office."

"Hi, Collette," I said, as I sat down at my table. "I almost didn't recognize you. You're looking particularly...umm...obsidiastic today."

"Obsidiastic?" said Collette.

"Onyxian," I said, searching for just the right inoffensive word. "Melanoid, nigrescent. Downright piceous."

"Huh?"

"Collette," I said. "You are definitely a darker shade of pale. What happened?"

"I went down to Noylene's Dip 'n Tan. She was giving me a free one."

"She still doesn't have the formula perfected?"

"Oh, yeah. She really does. My hands just slipped when she was dippin' me. I fell into the tank and couldn't get out for a couple of minutes."

"How long is that color going to last?"

"It should start to wear off in a couple of weeks. Faster, if I take more showers."

I nodded. "Cleanliness is next to godliness. What's the special today?"

"Pete got some rainbow trout," Collette said. Then she lowered her voice. "He bought them out of this guy's trunk around back."

"What did the guy look like?" I asked.

"Medium build. Sort of old. Short hair, glasses and a gray beard. The weird thing was that he was wearing a leisure suit from the '70s. One of those yellow ones with the white stitching. He even had the white belt and the white shoes."

I nodded. "That'd be Cleamon Downs. He sells fish out of his trunk. I wouldn't worry about it. His fish are usually fresh. The trout producers think he robs their farms at night, but we've never been able to prove anything."

"You want it, then?" asked Collette.

"Absolutely."

I sat by myself for ten minutes, waiting for my lunch and doodling notes on the pad I'd brought with me. I was still missing something. Collette brought me a cup of coffee I hadn't asked for and set it down in silence. I put down the pad when my lunch arrived.

I sat at the table and looked deep into the eyes of my entrée — a beautiful rainbow trout, made even more enticing by an orange teriyaki sauce. Pete came and sat down across from me.

"Collette says you're thinking really hard."

"Well, I was *trying* to."

"Yeah, yeah. How do you like the trout? Nice, eh?"

"Much better than your usual fare," I said.

"I got a couple of dozen from Cleamon. He had some nice ones. Still wriggling."

"He must have been busy last night."

"I guess. I haven't had any calls from the trout farms," said Pete. "Usually, when they're missing some stock, I get calls giving me a heads up and asking me not to buy any free range trout that might turn up."

I tasted the trout. It was delicious.

"How's the Pirate Eucharist coming along?" asked Pete.

"Good. The rehearsal's tonight. I have everything ready I think."

"Do you need a ship's bell?" asked Pete. "I have one in the back. You could use it for the Sanctus. Or even the Psalm."

I held up a finger, put down my fork and opened my cell phone.

"Hi, Nancy. Get me Fred May's number, will you? Yeah. At the bank." I waited while she looked it up, then said "Thanks," and dialed.

"Fred? This is Hayden."

"Hey there. What can I do for you?"

"You remember a couple of Sundays ago? The Palm Sunday service?"

160

"Yes. I think so. That was the Sunday Agnes Day was killed."

"Yeah. Do you remember who was in the choir? There were only about six of you, as I recall."

"I think that's right. There was Marjorie and me. Renee Tatton was there 'cause she sang a solo." He paused. "I'm pretty sure that Steve was there. Judy and Michelle. I think that was it."

"You remember singing the Psalm? You know, 'Blessed is he who comes,' 'horns up to the altar' and all that."

"Yeah. I remember."

"There was a handbell that someone used to give a pitch before every refrain."

"Yep. I remember."

"Who was ringing the handbell?"

"Why," said Fred, "I was."

"Fred's coming to the station in about a half hour," I said to Pete, as I continued attacking my lunch. "And I've alerted Nancy. If his DNA matches the male sample we found on the bell, we can exclude it from the equation. Then we just have to find the female."

"Unless, he's the one who killed her," said Pete.

"Now, Pete, why would you say that and ruin my lunch?"

"I was thinking last night how hard you'd have to hit someone with a bell to kill them. It's a heavy bell, sure, but it's not solid. There's a lot of give in the metal. I mean, it's not like hitting someone with a pipe. With a piece of pipe, you've got leverage and an unyielding material. It'd be fairly easy for anyone to exert enough force to crush somebody's skull."

"You're absolutely right," I said. "There was only one whack. It had to be a doozy."

"By someone who was pretty strong."

"A man, then."

"Or a big ol' woman," said Pete.

"Or a little woman with big ol' Popeye arms."

The door of The Slab opened, and Carol Sterling came in.

"I've been looking everywhere for you," she said, pointing in my direction. "I just heard that you aren't going to be at St. Barnabas on Sunday."

"Nope. I was just subbing for Holy Week and Easter. I have a Pirate Eucharist to play at Holy Comforter in Morganton."

"Well, that's just *great!*" she said, in disgust. "A Pirate Eucharist on the very day that my granddaughter is getting baptized. We put it off because we thought you would be there. Who have they gotten to play the organ?"

"I've no idea. If you could put it off a few more weeks, I might be able to schedule it in."

"Nope. Can't do it. The whole family's coming up. This baby's almost three months old. We've got to get her legal."

"Why don't you take him up to Morganton?" said Pete. "He could be baptized as part of the service. Show her, Hayden."

"Glad to," I said. "Arrrgh, me fine little laddie. Are ye prepared t' walk the plank in t' name o' Jesus?"

"I don't think that would go over so well," said Carol.

"You're baptizin' a baby?" said Collette, wandering up with a pitcher to refill my water glass.

"Is that you, Collette?" asked Carol, squinting hard at her. "I thought that Pete had finally caved in to the Affirmative Action Commission."

"There was a little accident at the Dip 'n Tan."

"Sorry to hear that," said Carol, doing her best to hide her grin. "And the answer is 'yes.' We're baptizing my granddaughter on Sunday morning."

"Do y'all dunk him all the way under?" asked Collette. I'd never seen her so interested in Episcopalian beliefs. Something was afoot. She had been going to a non-denominational fellowship since Pete had hired her about a year ago.

"We don't dunk infants," I said. "Usually, we pour water on their heads. But most priests don't mind dunking older folks if they want to be dunked. We just have to find another place to do it. Episcopal churches don't have a tank big enough."

Well," said Collette, with a sniff. "We have a big baptism pool. Big enough for five grown people. Pastor Kilroy says that he don't believe in infant baptism. I don't either."

"I don't mind who gets baptized," I said. "Baby or non-baby, I'm happy either way." I ate the last bite of my fish. "How about you Pete?" I asked. "Do you believe in infant baptism?"

"Believe in it?" said Pete, with a snort. "Hell! I've *seen* it!"

Nancy was just finishing with Fred as I walked into the station. She had taken two DNA swabs and was packing them into their cases in the prescribed manner.

"Hi, Fred," I said. "I'm sure Nancy told you what was going on. We just need to exclude your DNA from the samples we have."

"Okay with me. The thing is, though, somebody handed me that bell. And if my DNA is on it, I sure don't know how it got there."

"Why is that?" Nancy asked.

"I was wearing handbell gloves."

Chapter 23

I knew three things. I knew who killed Memphis. I knew who was ratting out the Bishop. And I knew that I wasn't about to wear puce on the Feast of the Transfiguration.

I walked past the Possum 'n Peasel. It didn't look like the same place. They had changed the name to TJ Frumpett's and had hung ferns in all the windows. There was a line around the block, and they now had a bouncer standing at the door behind a velvet rope. It was Pedro LaFleur.

"Pedro," I asked, "Is this your new gig?"

"Just on weekends. Any news on the murder?"

"Yeah. I found the clue. It was in Chapter 13."

"Ahhh," he said. "Well, who did it?" He lifted the rope for a 38C.

"Can't tell you yet. I'm not to the end of the story."

"Oh, yeah," he said. "Did I mention that I also checked on the Soprano Enhancement Franchise for the lower East side? Guess who's got it?"

"Who?" I asked.

"Bulimia Forsythe Enterprises, Inc. They're running infomercials selling a book called <u>What The Singing Teachers Don't Want You To Know</u>. Wanna know what's in it?"

"I'll bet it's something to do with breath support."

"You got THAT right," said Pedro, eyeballing a 36B up and down before flagging her in.

"It looks like they're doing a brisk business in falsettos," I said, looking down the line.

"They're running a special. Buy two, get one free," smirked Pedro.

"So that's the scam," I said. This case was clearing up like a sixteen-year-old's face at a Clearasil clambake.

"What?" asked Pedro, holding the rope aside for a 40 double D.

"You have bigger sopranos, you need more liturgical fabric..."

Pedro nodded, and shooed away a 32A. "And the more fabric you sell, the more money you make."

"It's simple economics."

"Did you hear the news?" asked Meg.

"I don't think so," I answered. "What news?"

"Dave Vance and Collette are engaged."

"No! Really?"

"Yep. Collette announced it at The Ginger Cat. She has a ring and everything."

"That's great. I'll bet that was why Collette was so interested in Episcopal baptism. Dave may have to get re-dunked before the big day."

"Really? They do that?"

"All the time," I said. "If you're dunked when you're a baby, it may not have taken."

"Really?"

"Really. It's in the Bible somewhere. Maybe in Second or Third Fallopians."

"Well, that explains it then. By the way, how did your Pirate thingy rehearsal go last night?"

"I think it'll be fine," I said. "The men's choir is very good, and they all have their outfits."

It was Friday when I got a call from Gary Thorndike. The verdict was in on Fred's DNA. No match.

We weren't back to square one, but we weren't much past square two. I called Nancy into my office.

"Okay," I said, with a sigh, "let's go back over what we've got."

"Suspects," said Nancy. "We've got suspects and a few clues. Whoever wrote the confession was left-handed and maybe a man."

"But maybe a strong-willed woman."

"Probably a man," said Nancy, "if we include Pete's theory that if the person who wrote the note was also the murderer, he had to be strong enough to kill the old coot with one blow to the head with a bell that, although it was heavy, still had a lot of bounce."

"Old coot?"

"Umm, sorry...Agnes Day."

"I have an idea," I said, grabbing a roll of duct tape off the shelf. "Let's go."

We walked down the sidewalk and into The Slab. I went into the kitchen and came out with a cantaloupe, a coconut and an old broomstick.

"Ah," said Nancy. "Brilliant! But we don't have the bell."

"We have the next one up the scale. It's probably only a few ounces lighter."

We walked over to St. Barnabas, Nancy carrying the cantaloupe and the coconut and me spinning the duct tape on the broomstick and whistling the *Dies Irae*. I had a key to the back kitchen door, a key that I hadn't relinquished despite my resignation before Christmas, and we went in and put our produce on the counter.

"Hang on. I'll be right back," I said. "The bells are in the choir room."

A few minutes later, I walked back into the kitchen carrying G#3, another four-pound handbell, although slightly lighter than our murder weapon.

"Let's take these outside. It's going to be pretty messy," I said. Nancy nodded in agreement and we took our experiment out into the alley behind the kitchen. I set three concrete blocks onto the steps by the kitchen door and stuck the cantaloupe on top of the old broomstick that I'd broken off to the appropriate length. The makeshift Agnes Day dropped neatly into the holes in the blocks.

"That's about where her head would be," I said. "Sneak up behind her and give her a whack."

"Me?"

"You're a woman, aren't you? And pretend you're mad. Make believe it's Collette."

"Arrr," Nancy growled. She measured the distance, took the bell in two hands and absolutely demolished the cantaloupe.

"Well," I said. "That didn't take much effort. I think you killed her."

"Yes," Nancy smirked. "Yes, I did. You know, it didn't make much sound either."

"No, it didn't," I agreed. "Okay, then. That wasn't much of a challenge, and there are those that would argue that a person's head is stronger than a cantaloupe. We're going to have to tape the coconut onto the broomstick."

166

It didn't take long, and in a couple of minutes, Nancy was measuring her next attack.

"Hang on," she said. "That's a hard shell. It's going to ding up this bell. This thing has to cost a few hundred bucks."

"You're right," I said. "On the other hand, perhaps it won't hurt it at all. People have actually dropped them on the floor before. If we ding it up, we'll pay to get it re-furbished."

"Shouldn't we ask permission?" asked Nancy.

"Absolutely. We'll absolutely ask permission. Now hit the coconut. Remember," I said, "it's still Collette."

Nancy growled again, went into a two-fisted wind-up and smacked the coconut with a swing that would make Joe DiMaggio proud. The resulting clang reverberated in the alley, and although duct tape covered the entire coconut — we had wrapped it completely — seeping out of the silver-gray tape and running down the broomstick was the unmistakable evidence of Nancy's success.

"Coconut milk. Let's take the tape off," I said, "but I'm fairly sure you killed her again."

After the tape was removed, it was pretty clear to both of us that a woman could have finished Agnes Day off with the handbell in question.

"Look at that," said Nancy, "The bell smashed the coconut and cut right through the shell. There's nothing left of this whole side."

"Not only that," I added, "but Agnes Day had a lot less damage than this. You absolutely creamed her."

"It," Nancy corrected. "I creamed *it*. Not *her*."

"Yeah. How's the bell?"

"Looks okay to me," Nancy said, looking at it carefully. "I don't see a mark on it."

"There wasn't any damage to the other bell either," I said.

"So," said Nancy, "either a man or a woman could have done this. We're back to square one."

"Square one and a half."

Back at the office, we resumed our deliberations.

"Whoever hit her," said Nancy, "didn't hit her as hard as I hit that coconut."

"Maybe, they couldn't hit her as hard," I said. "She was sitting

on the bench and someone came up behind her and hit her on the right side of the head. But if they were left-handed, they would have hit her on the left side."

"So, it was a righty?"

"Not necessarily. They couldn't have gotten to her from the left side. Too many steps down and they'd be exposed to the view of the congregation. But swinging right-handed if you were a lefty would account for the relative weakness of the swing. There's no doubt though, that you could have easily killed her with either hand."

"I agree," said Nancy. "Although I probably would have done less damage with my left. You want to go back and try it?"

"No need," I said. "You, or any other woman in reasonably good shape, could have killed her with either hand. That handbell is heavy. Back to the suspects and clues."

"Right," said Nancy, flipping open her pad. "Here's what we know. Whoever wrote the confession was left-handed. We have, or had, a bunch of suspects. First, Russ Stafford."

"Cross him off," I said.

"Second, Ruthie Haggarty."

"Nope. Cross her off."

"Next," said Nancy, "Benny Dawkins."

"Nope. Didn't do it."

"Bennie and Ruthie together in a Bonnie and Clyde scenario?"

"I don't see it," I said.

Nancy drew her pen across her pad.

"Kenny Frazier."

"Nope."

"Should we worry about who shot him?" asked Nancy.

"I think," I said, slowly, "that if we figure out who killed Agnes Day, we'll know who shot Kenny. So let's use the fact that he *was* shot to find Agnes Day's murderer, but for our purposes right now, let's not worry about who shot him. That make sense?"

"As much sense as anything else," said Nancy. "How about Renee Tatton? She's dating Kenny, she was at the Palm Sunday service, she was at the Maundy Thursday service, she's left handed..."

"She's left handed? You never told me that!"

"Oh. Sorry, boss. I guess I forgot. I checked on all our suspects. There were two that were left-handed. Renee Tatton and Annette Passaglio."

"So, Renee's a viable suspect," I said.

"How about Annette?"

"Absolutely. If we assume, and I think we must, that whoever wrote the confession note was, indeed, the murderer, then Annette is our number one suspect. She was at both services, she owns a Montblanc pen — indeed, the very one that wrote the note — she was sitting in the pew where the note was written, she hated Agnes Day..."

"But," said Nancy, "her DNA wasn't on the handbell."

"Aye, there's the rub."

"So, even if she *did* do it, we wouldn't be able to prove it."

I nodded.

"Back to Renee," I said. "She was there at both services, left handed, Agnes Day knew about her voice-lift and who knows what else." I paused. "Hey, what about this? What if she came down from the choir loft with the others when the people were going forward for the Nailing Service, stopped at the back row, picked up the pad and scribbled her confession as an afterthought. Then went up to the front and nailed it to the cross with everyone else. No one would have noticed her with everyone else milling about and standing in line."

"And the pen?" asked Nancy.

"Well," I said, "maybe she saw it lying on the pew where Annette was sitting. Or maybe it was sticking out of Annette's purse. She could have borrowed it, written her note and put it right back."

"I can see it," said Nancy, with a nod. "It could have happened like that."

"How about the DNA on the bell? Any word from the passport office?"

Nancy shook her head. "They said it'd probably be the beginning of next week."

"We still don't have a match on the male sample," I added. "And I'm anxious to see a picture of Olga Spaulding."

Chapter 24

"Arrrgh!" said Father Owen, beginning the Liturgy of the Black Spot as the Pirate Eucharist was being called. This followed my prelude — variations on the hymn tune *Melita*, better known as *Eternal Father, Strong To Save*. It was the Navy Hymn, and it was our processional.

"Arrrgh! Alleluia, Christ, he be risen!" Father Owen was dressed in a stunning black and gold coat, pirate boots, a red vest and a plumed hat worthy of Leona Helmsley. He had a couple of pistols stuck in his belt, a shiny silver hook where his right hand should have been, a sword buckled around his waist, and he was accompanied by two acolyte cabin boys hoisting a couple of old-timey lanterns on poles. I, on the other hand, had chosen to be a bit more inconspicuous, donning my black cassock — the one with the hood.

"Arrrgh! The Lord, he be risen indeed. Alleluia!" replied the congregation.

I began the introduction to the hymn. The Pirate Choir consisted of the men from the Holy Comforter choir as well as several men from the St. Barnabas choir who had insisted on singing and had even come down for the rehearsal on Wednesday evening. The congregation joined in with enthusiasm. It was a hymn they knew well.

Eternal Father, strong to save,
Whose arm hath bound the restless wave,
Who bidd'st the mighty ocean deep
Its own appointed limits keep;
Oh, hear us when we cry to Thee,
For those in peril on the sea!

"Almighty God," said Father Owen. "T' ye all hearts be open, all desires known, an' from ye nay secrets be hid: Cleanse th' thoughts o' arr hearts by th' inspiration o' yer Holy Spirit, that we may parfectly love ye, an' warthily magnify yer holy Name; through Christ arr Lord. Aye aye."

This was the cue for our "song of praise" that I had adapted from *The Pirates of Penzance.*[†] The men sang like...well, like pirates!

All glory be to God on high,
We sing from under the flag we fly,
And peace to all your people on earth,
As long as they give us ample berth.
We worship you, we give you thanks,
From cabin boy through all the ranks.
But we'll be true to the song we sing,
Indeed you are the King of Kings!
For......He is the King of Kings!
And it is, it is a glorious thing to serve the King of Kings!
He is the King of Kings!
(HE IS! Hurrah for the King of Kings!)
And it is, it is a glorious thing to serve the King of Kings!
(IT IS! Hurrah for the King of Kings!)
Hurrah for the King of Kings!

[†] Download the music to *The Pirate Eucharist* at www.sjmpbooks.com

There was applause in the church after we finished, and more than a few "Arrrghs." When the people had come into the sanctuary and picked up their bulletin, they were also given an eye-patch and a small plastic parrot to pin to their shoulders. Although some of the more staid members of the congregation had eschewed the patch and the gift of the Holy Parakeet, most of the folks were definitely getting into the spirit of the service. "Most folks" included Meg and her mother, Ruby, both of whom were wearing their parrots and eye patches and sitting behind the organ, out of sight of the congregation, but with a fine view of the festivities. The rest of the St. Barnabas choir — the ones that weren't singing — were scattered through the congregation. I had seen Michelle, Rebecca, Marjorie, Bev, Georgia, Elaine and Billy Hixon, and a few others before the service had started.

"A readin' from t' Book o' Acts," said the lay reader, a gentleman named Joshua Williams. He was clad in a yellow shirt, sporting a red bandana and a sash across his chest.

"Peter, standin' wi' th'eleven," the reader began, "raised his voice and addressed th' multitude, "Ye that be landlubbers, listen t' what I be sayin': Jesus o' Nazareth, a man attested t' ye by God wi' deeds o' power, wonders, and signs that the Admiral did through him among ye, as ye yourselves know — this man, handed o'er t' ye accordin' t' the definite plan and foreknowledge o' God, ye keelhauled and killed by the hands o' those outside th' law. But the Admiral be raisin' him up, havin' freed him from Davy Jones' Locker, because 'twas impossible fer him t' be held in its power, says I. Fer David says concarnin' him, 'I be seein' the Admiral always before me, for he be at me starboard hand so that I will not be shiverin'.'"

"Yar, it be so," said Mark Wells, who had come down from St. Barnabas to see the show. He and the rest of the choir were in pirate costumes, but Mark had brought a special guest with him — his pet, a Scarlet Macaw named Reefer.

"Yar, yar," agreed some of the other choir members. Meg started to giggle. At Holy Comforter Episcopal, the choir sat in the stalls in the front of the church and was in full view of the congregation. They had spent a great deal of time on their outfits. There were several eye patches to be sure, but also a couple hooks-for-hands, a peg leg, tri-corner hats, velvet coats, plumes, capes, and sword. They were a motley, but well-costumed crew. Reefer was the only parrot.

"He's a freeflyer," Mark had informed me, when I'd met Reefer a few months ago. "I think he's about twelve years old, but I just got him last year. Actually," he added, scratching his bearded chin and pushing his baseball cap back a few inches, "I *think* it's a 'him.' It might be a 'her.' You can't tell just by looking at 'em, and I'm not about to go rootin' under those feathers. He'll take your hand clean off, if he doesn't like what you're doing."

I believed it. Reefer was a huge Macaw and stood a good three feet long from crest to tail. He sat happily on Mark's shoulder snapping walnut shells like they were bubble wrap. He was a beautiful animal to watch, mostly scarlet-red with yellow and blue on his wings and white patches around his eyes. The rest of the Pirate Choir was quite jealous of Mark's living accoutrement.

The reader continued. "Tharfore me heart be glad, and me tongue rejoiced; more o'er me flesh be livin' in hope. For ye will not be abandonin' me soul t' Davy Jones, nar let yer Holy One be seein' corruption. Ye be makin' known t' me the ways o' life; ye be makin' me full o' gladness wi' yer presence." He paused. "This be the word o' the Lord" he concluded. "And all the people replied..."

"Arrrgh!" thundered the congregation. "Awwwwk!" screeched Reefer. This was followed by laughter and more applause. I had to agree. Joshua Williams was a *very* good pirate.

We said the Psalm, accompanied by Pete's ship's bell and a choral refrain *Yo, ho, ho, to the Father and Son.*

"Avast, me hearties!" said the congregation in unison. "I will be givin' thanks t' the LORD wi' me whole heart, in the assembly o' the upright, in the congregation."

"Yo, ho, ho, to the Father and Son," sang the choir.

"He has shown his swabbies the power o' his works in givin' them the lands o' the nations," said the congregation.

"Yo, ho, ho, to the Father and Son," sang the choir.

"Yar," said Mark, as we finished up. "This be the best Psalm I sung in many a moon."

"Yar, yar," agreed members of the choir. Reefer snapped another walnut.

Reefer, Mark had informed us at the rehearsal, was a talking parrot, or so he had been told when he bought the bird from a friend

of his in Greenville. Mark hadn't heard him speak, although he'd been trying to teach him a few phrases.

"I'm his second owner," Mark explained to the choir. "He has to really like you to start talking. I've had him for about eight months and we're just now starting to bond. I even took him freeflying a couple of weeks ago. I wouldn't have done it if I wasn't sure he'd come back."

"What phrases are you teaching him?" asked one of the Morganton Pirates, a stalwart fellow with a stick-on church nametag that proclaimed "Hi, I'm Pegleg Pete."

"When I heard we were invited to a Pirate Eucharist, I started trying to teach him to say 'the gifts of God for the people of God,'" said Mark. "I haven't gotten him to do it yet, but he'll be ready next year. You can bet your stump on it!"

The gospel lesson for the second Sunday of Easter is always the same — the story of Doubting Thomas, slightly different when translated to piratese.

"A readin' from the Gospel Accordin' to Cap'n John," said Father Owen.

"Aye, aye!" said the crowd.

"When 'twas evenin' on that day, the first day o' th' week, and the hatches o' the house where th' disciples had met were battoned fer fear o' the fleet, Jesus came and be standin' among 'em and said, 'Peace be wi' ye.' After he said this, he be showin' them his hands and his side. Then th' maties rejoiced when they saw th' Lord. Jesus said to 'em again, 'Peace be wi' ye. As the Admiral has sent me, so I send ye.' When he had said this, he breathed on them and said t' them, 'Be receivin' th' Holy Ghost. If ye forgive th' sins o' any, they be forgiven them; if ye be hoardin' th' sins o' any, they be hoarded.'"

"I'm starting to understand him," whispered Meg. "This is not a good sign."

The lay reader — Joshua Williams — stood up. He was going to be playing the part of Thomas. Father Owen continued the reading.

"But Thomas the Bos'n's mate, was not wi' them when Jesus came. So th' other disciples told him, 'We be havin' seen th' Lord.' But he said t' them..."

"Unless I see th' mark o' th' nails in his hands, me hearties," said Joshua, "and put me finger in th' mark o' th' nails and me hand in his side, I will not be believin'." Joshua had his part memorized. It was a nice touch.

Father Owen took over again. "A week later, the Lad's disciples were again in th' foc'sle, and Thomas was wi' them. Although th' hatches be battoned down, Jesus came and stood among 'em and said, 'Peace be wi' ye.' Then he said t' Thomas, 'Put yer finger here and see me hands. Reach out yer hand and put it in me side. Do not be doubtin' but believe.' Thomas answered him."

"Me Lord and me God!" bellowed Joshua.

"Jesus said t' him, 'Ha'e ye believed because ye be seein' me? Blessed be those who ha'e not seen and yet ha'e come t' believe.'" There was a pause and then Father Owen finished the reading with "This be the word o' th' Lord! And all th' people replied..."

"Aaarrrgh!" shouted the congregation.

"Arrrgh and aye, aye!" echoed the choir.

"Awwwwk!" screeched Reefer.

Father Owen's sermon was a good one, incorporating the analogy of the ship on turbulent waters as a metaphor for the church. He threw in Thomas' doubt and Peter's failure to trust Jesus during the storm for good measure.

"Now we be takin' a portion o' your ill-gotten booty," said Father Owen in one of the most succinct "offertory sentences" I'd ever heard. "Let the pillagin' commence!"

The offertory solo would be sung by Brad Jefferson, a college voice student at Mars Hill College. Brad had a lovely baritone voice, and his parents had volunteered him after hearing his Senior Recital earlier in the semester. His performance had included a song by John Ireland on a famous John Mansfield poem entitled *Sea Fever*. We had rehearsed it on Wednesday, and I was pretty sure this morning's rendition would be just as gratifying.

Brad, a blonde, strapping young man, stood on the steps of the nave, surrounded by pirates, dressed in an old fashioned navy shirt with blue and white horizontal stripes, black trousers and a red neckerchief.

"He looks just like Billy Budd," whispered Meg.

"Yes, he does," agreed Ruby. "If I were forty years younger..."

"Mother!" hissed Meg.

I must go down to the seas again,
to the lonely sea and the sky,
And all I ask is a tall ship
and a star to steer her by,
And the wheel's kick and the wind's song
and the white sail's shaking,
And a grey mist on the sea's face,
and a grey dawn breaking.

It's a nice song and Brad did a great job. The ushers, or bos'ns, as they were being called, stopped passing the plates after the first three lines, turned around and stood transfixed through the remainder of the three stanzas. This left me, at the end of the song, with some improvising to do, to get the plates passed and the booty collected, but I didn't mind.

"That was wonderful," said Meg. "How come we never do that song at St. Barnabas?"

"It's not a religious piece," I said. "But it sure was appropriate for this service."

"Yar," said Mark, from the choir loft. "That chanty be so beautiful, it brung a tear to me wooden eye."

"Yar, yar," answered the choir. "It were beauty itself."

"Awwwwk," said Reefer, snapping another walnut shell.

The *Sanctus — Holy, Holy, Holy Lord —* was sung to the tune of *What Shall We Do With A Drunken Sailor?* and was led with vigor and verve by the Pirate Choir, swinging swords, muskets and more than a few flagons. If any of the singers got lost, they simply threw in a few arrrghs and jumped back in when they could. The congregation wasn't being shy either, and the church shivered its timbers with the sound.

"On th' night he be handed o'er t' sufferin' an' Davy Jones' locker," said Father Owen, "our Lord Jesus Christ took the hardtack; an' when he had beat the weevils out, he give thanks t' ye, broke it,

gave it t' his maties, an' said, 'Take and be eatin'. This be me Body, which be gi'en fer ye. Do this fer th' remembrance o' me.'"

"Arrrgh," muttered the crowd. "Aye, he did that fer us."

"After mess he took th' cup o' grog; an' when he had given thanks, he gave it t' them, an' said, 'Be drinkin' this, all o' ye: This be me Blood o' th' new Covenant, which be shed fer ye an' fer many fer th' forgiveness o' sins. When ever ye be drinkin' do this fer th' remembrance o' me.' Tharfore, we proclaim th' mystery o' faith!"

"Christ has sank t' Davy Jones' locker!" said the crowd. "Christ be risen! Christ will come again!"

"The congregation is really into this," said Meg. "Just listen to them. This is much better than the Clown Eucharist."

"Arrrgh," I replied, with a nod. "And why not? The entire church is built like a boat. Upside down, I grant you, but look up. The word *nave* is derived from the Latin *navis*, a ship, probably an early reference to the ship of St. Peter or Noah's Ark. In Gothic, as well as Romanesque churches, the sanctuary — the place where people gathered to worship — was built to resemble the vaulted keel shape of an inverted ship."

Meg nodded, looking up at the roof.

"Alleluia! Christ our Passover be sacrificed fer us!" said Father Owen in a thunderous voice. He brought his hook down into a small, round loaf of bread with a resounding THUNK! Then he hoisted it above his head. "Tharfore let us keep the feast! And all the people replied..."

"Aaarrrgh!" cheered the congregation.

"Arrrgh and aye, aye!" answered the choir.

It was at that moment that Reefer chose to speak for the first time in eight months.

"Reefer want a cracker!" he cackled, leaping off Mark's shoulder in a flurry of feathers and stretching his wings to their full five-foot span. In two beats he had cleared the choir, soared gracefully over the communion table, snatched the loaf off a surprised Father Owen's upraised hook and headed for the open rafters.

"Yar," said Mark, shaking his head. "I been afraid this would happen."

"Did you see that?" Meg asked.

"Did I ever!" replied Ruby. "That was great! Do you think he'll bring it back?"

"I don't think so," said Meg. "He's already pulling it apart and eating it."

I looked up. Meg was right. Reefer had the loaf in one claw and was tearing pieces off with his beak. Crumbs rained down on the congregation like manna from heaven.

"Reefer want a cracker," he screeched again, pulling off another chunk and gobbling it down.

"The gifts o' God fer the people o' God," said Father Owen, picking up a second loaf and watching Reefer carefully lest he make another unadvertised swoop. "Take them in rememberin' that Christ sank t' Davy Jones' Locker fer ye, an' feed on th' Lad in yer hearts by faith, wi' thanksgivin'."

"Give us a swig!" screeched Reefer. "Make it a double." The choir, unable to keep their buckaniacal glee contained any longer, let out a roar of laughter.

"I never taught him that," said Mark Wells. "It must have been the guy before me. That guy was a bartender."

The crowd, mostly giggling and keeping a sharp eye toward the rafters in case Reefer had any more surprises in store, stood to make their way forward to take communion. I began to play a quiet meditation on *Shenandoah* at the same time Meg and Ruby got up and followed the choir up to the communion rail.

"Great knockers!" screeched Reefer.

"Can't be arguin' wi' that, me buxom beauties," muttered Mark, under his breath, as the rest of the pirates were trying desperately, yet unsuccessfully, to control their mirth.

"To whose knockers was the parrot referring?" asked Ruby, politely. "Meg's or mine?"

"Mother!" said Meg. "Obviously, mine."

"Knowin' Reefer, it'd be one of each," said Mark, looking up. "He'll be comin' down when he's finished 'is grub." Crumbs were still raining down on pew number three, but the occupants had found a safer port. "At least, he always has before."

"Damn the torpedos!" shrieked Reefer. "Blow me down a rathole! Awwwwk!" The pirate communicants were now in hysterics.

"How many phrases do you think he knows?" asked Meg.

Mark shrugged. "I have no idea. I been thinkin' he didn't know nary a one. He must like it here."

The choir finished up at the rail and headed back to the loft.

The rest of the congregation made their way forward, eye patches dutifully donned and a green plastic parakeet firmly pinned to each person's left shoulder.

"Yar," said Mark. "Look at 'em all. It do me heart good. This be the finest churchin' we seen since we had a run a t' white whale, says I. I just hope that young Reefer thar don't have no more colorful phrases that he care to be sharin'."

"Yar, yar," said the choir.

"Yar," said Meg and Ruby, both of them nodding in agreement.

"Awwwwk!" clacked Reefer, loudly, from the rafters. He dropped what was left of the bread, soared down to the choir loft, and landed heavily on Mark's outstretched arm. Then he took the proffered walnut, hopped up to his astonished owner's shoulder, cracked the walnet open and gobbled it down. "The gifts of God for the people of God," he said.

"Well, I'll be a peg-legged porcupine," said Mark. "He learned it after all."

"Great knockers!" squawked Reefer, and followed his outburst with a loud wolf-whistle.

"I think he likes me better," said Ruby.

"Mother! Really!" huffed Meg.

Chapter 25

I couldn't put Miss Bulimia Forsythe out of business. That much was clear. She hadn't really done anything illegal, but I'd make sure the Liturgical Color Bill never made it out of committee. I still had friends in high places and more than enough dirt on all of them to make the pork dinner they were all looking forward to seem like a plate of undercooked buzzard a-la-mode with turnip toppings.

Bulimia had already made millions on her book sales and another million or so on her line of custom falsettos. She'd bow out gracefully. Of course, "Naves by Raoul" would be out of business, but I didn't much care. There was plenty of interior decorating work out there for a couple of androgynous mincers with good connections. Who knows? They might even get their own TV show.

I walked down to Bishop's Towers, opened the glass doors, walked right up to the Right Reverend Sherman and slugged him in the mush.

"I'm calling the police," he mumbled through what was left of his teeth.

"Do that, Padre," I answered, "and then we'll all sit down and explain your part in Memphis Belle's murder."

He turned white. "It was a suicide."

I slugged him again just for meanness.

"You called her and buzzed me up. But she'd already been dead for a couple of hours."

"She made me do it! She said she'd kill me."

"Who?" I asked. "Memphis?"

"No," he said, shaking like a robin laying goose eggs. "That nurse."

Your second story is up on the mystery blog," said Nancy. "I saw it last night. Pretty cool. First *The Alto Wore Tweed* and now *The Baritone Wore Chiffon*."

"Thanks. *The Tenor Wore Tapshoes* should be up next week, and I've got to get this one finished to complete the quartet. Another couple of chapters should do it."

"By the way, we just got a call from the State Department.

They're faxing the picture of Olga Spaulding in a couple of minutes. Any guess as to who it is?"

"I have a pretty good idea."

"Yep," said Nancy. "Me, too. Want to put a little wager on it?"

"You seem pretty sure of yourself. Do you know anything I don't?"

"I don't think so."

"Okay, then," I said. "Dinner at the Hunter's Club. Here, write your pick on a piece of paper and put it in your pocket. I'll do the same."

We barely had time to scribble our choices when the fax machine beeped and started spitting out a piece of paper.

"Okay," said Nancy, "don't bother putting it in your pocket and don't look yet. Who have you got?"

I opened my paper and showed it to her. "Renee Tatton," I said. "How about you?"

Nancy opened her paper and tossed it on the desk. "Same person. Renee Tatton. Great minds think alike, I guess."

"Well, let's confirm our brilliant detective work and go get some breakfast." I went over to the fax machine and picked up the paper that had just come in from the State Department. Printed on the fax was a copy of the inside of a passport. The name said Olga Spaulding, but the picture was someone we knew by a different moniker.

"Should I pick up Renee after breakfast?" asked Nancy. "You know, for a little chat."

"You can, if you want," I answered, "but maybe we should talk to this person instead." I handed the fax to Nancy.

"Holy Moses!"

"Holy Moses, indeed," I said, taking the fax back from Nancy and studying it again. Looking back at me from the piece of paper was St. Germaine's head librarian, Rebecca Watts.

Nancy and I walked over to the library.

"Do we have any reason to think that Rebecca Watts would want to kill Agnes Day?" I asked.

"None that I've come up with. It seems like everyone in town had a gripe against her though."

"But not Rebecca."

"No. Not Rebecca," Nancy said.

"Then let's just ask her," I said.

"Sounds like a plan."

We entered the library and made our way up to the desk. Rebecca looked up from her work as we approached, smiled and pushed her glasses up onto the bridge of her nose with one finger.

"Hi guys. What's up? By the way, Hayden, that Pirate service was *fabulous!* When are we going to do it at St. Barnabas?"

"Oh, I don't know," I said, with a shrug. I looked around the library. It was empty. "We have a couple of questions for you, Rebecca. It's about Agnes Day's murder."

"Terrible business," Rebecca said. "How can I help?"

"Here's the thing," I said. "We got some DNA off the handbell that was used to kill Agnes Day. One of the samples came back with a positive ID."

Rebecca bit her lower lip and waited for the bad news.

"Olga Spaulding."

"Terrible name, isn't it?" said Rebecca, accompanying her answer with an embarrassed smile and a shrug of her own.

Nancy smiled. "Yeah," she agreed.

"You need an explanation, don't you?"

"It wouldn't hurt," I said.

"Okay," Rebecca said, "but I'm giving you the short version. I worked for the State Department until two years ago. Then I retired, changed my name for security reasons and moved to St. Germaine."

"Witness protection?" asked Nancy.

"Not exactly. But I did have to drop out of sight. You can check all this with the FBI if you have to, but then I'd probably have to move again."

"No need for that," I said. "It's our secret. What about the bell? Did you pick it up? Maybe on the day that Agnes Day was killed? That would have been Palm Sunday."

Rebecca thought for a moment and then nodded. "Yep. I handed the bell to Fred right before the Psalm. He was on the other side of the organ. I picked it up by the handle and gave it to him."

"Did he hand it back when he was finished?"

Rebecca thought again. "No," she said. "No, he didn't, because

I had moved. He gave it to someone else I suppose or maybe put it back himself."

"Okay, then," I said, with a smile. "We just needed to check."

"You know," said Rebecca, "I wasn't kidding. If this gets out, I'll have to relocate. And I really like it here."

"You aren't a contract killer for the AGO, are you?" asked Nancy. "You know, trained to kill bad organists in seventeen different ways?"

"AGO?"

"American Guild of Organists," I answered. "It's a terrorist group, actually.

"If I was, would I have left my DNA on the murder weapon? Nope. I was a secretary in the Egyptian consulate. But I *can* make a killer basboosa," Rebecca laughed. "That's an Egyptian cake, by the way."

"Your secret is safe with us," I said. Nancy nodded in agreement.

"What do you think?" Nancy asked, as we walked back to the office, by way of The Slab Café.

"I think...Belgian Waffles."

"Me, too," she said.

Our waffles were good, the coffee was good, the service was good, and Nancy had stopped growling at Collette.

"I'm actually glad she and Dave are getting married," Nancy said. "Maybe it will give him some ambition."

"Maybe, but I don't think so," I said, mixing maple syrup with the quickly melting butter sitting atop my scrumptious repast. "Dave's got a trust fund. I don't even think he has to work. He just does it for something to do."

"That'd be nice," said Nancy. "Seems like I'm the only one who has to actually work for a living around here."

"Yeah," I agreed. "That's tough."

"Speaking of never working again," said Nancy, just before a forkful of waffles disappeared into her mouth. She nodded toward the door. Walking into The Slab, and headed for our table, was Rhiza Walker.

"Hello, Rhiza," I said, standing up and pulling out a chair. "Join us, won't you?"

"Wow," said Nancy, swallowing. "I've seen him stand up and offer a chair to only one other person in the ten years that I've known him. And that's because he thought he was going to get lucky."

"I did get lucky," I said. "And speaking of lucky, we certainly are lucky to have this lovely multi-millionaire joining us here at the Café du Slab."

"Oh, stop it," said Rhiza, "I've been a millionaire for years. Order me some of those waffles, will you?"

I nodded to Collette who was doing her best not to hover, but she'd never been in the same room with a Powerball winner before. She scurried into the kitchen.

"I guess you'll have to move to the Riviera or somewhere to escape all the publicity," Nancy said.

"Nah," replied Rhiza. "It's not that bad. We got a bunch of calls from salesmen early on, but Malcolm knows how to handle them. Mostly, the furor has died down."

"Great," said Nancy, finishing up her plate of waffles and draining the last gulp from her coffee cup. "By the way, can I borrow six million dollars?"

"Nope," said Rhiza.

"I didn't think so," said Nancy. "Back to work then."

"We need to talk," said Rhiza, after Nancy had left.

"We're talking, aren't we?"

"Nope. We're not. But we need to. At your house."

"How about tomorrow?" I asked. "Nine o'clock?"

"I can't tomorrow. Can we do Thursday?"

"I can't Thursday. I'll be in Asheville. Friday?"

"Friday it is," Rhiza said. She stood up and walked out of The Slab just as her plate of waffles arrived.

"It'd be a shame to throw these out," said Collette, putting them down in front of me.

"A real shame," I agreed.

"Are you losing weight?" asked Marilyn. I was at St. Barnabas to have a chat with Father George. He'd asked me to come in, and I

suspected that it was concerning their recent opening in the church music department.

"Nice of you to notice," I said. "Pete Moss tried to talk me into expando-pants, but I decided to start exercising. I've been running a couple of miles every morning."

"So, what kind of pants are those?" asked Marilyn, peering closely at my waistband.

"Just never you mind," I laughed. "But they're not expando-pants. And stop ogling me. That's sexual harassment, you know."

"I know. Father George made me watch the video...again. Hey," she added, "did you hear the news? Lucille Murdock is going to make her announcement on Monday night."

"She finally decided what to do with the sixteen million?"

"Apparently. Father George and the vestry are pretty nervous. She won't tell anyone anything until Monday night."

The door to Father George's office opened, and the rector motioned me into his office.

"Come in, come in, Hayden. It's so good to see you. I hope you've been doing well."

I knew schmoozing when I heard it, and this was it in spades.

"Yeah," I said. "You, too." I looked back at Marilyn and gave her a wink.

Father George gestured to the chair across from his desk and I sat down. "I've been talking with the vestry," he said, folding his hands, then raising them to his chin and tapping it with his two index fingers. "Also with Beverly Greene, our administrator, and we've decided to offer you your job back. You did a fine job substituting during Easter, and we think you'd be an excellent addition to the staff."

"I was on the staff. You fired me."

"Well, technically, you resigned," said Father George, still tapping his teeth.

"Yeah," I said, "I guess I did."

"But circumstances have changed since then. Now we'd like for you to come back."

"No thanks," I said, standing up and walking back to the door.

"Wh...what?" sputtered Father George.

"No thanks," I repeated. I opened the door and walked out past Marilyn, giving her another wink.

I walked back to the office. The weather that, just ten days ago, had laid down a blanket of snow across the region, had now definitely turned to spring, and there was no going back. The leaves had burst forth, almost unnoticed, sometime during the last week, and the reflection of the sunlight off the new growth bathed the entire town in a sort of luminescent green.

Nancy was out on patrol, but Dave was waiting for me when I came in.

"Hi, boss," he said, handing me a message. "You need to call Gary Thorndike. That's the number."

"Yeah, I have it. Congratulations, by the way."

"Thanks," Dave said. "I think."

"Hello, Hayden," said Gary, after I'd identified myself. "Guess what?"

"What?" I said.

"We got another hit on the DNA sample."

"You mean Olga Spaulding?"

"No, the other one. You remember what I said? Sometimes these matches take a while."

"Yeah, I remember," I said. "So who is it?"

"It came back from a database in Virginia. The person's name is Renee Tatton."

"Wait a minute," I said. "There were three DNA samples — the victim's, a female that we identified as Olga Spaulding, and an unknown male."

"Right. But he's not unknown anymore. His name is Renee Tatton."

Chapter 26

I had been waiting for Nancy's reaction, and it was as good as I'd hoped.

"You mean..." she started, "that she...he...she...Renee...holy crap!"

"Well put," I said, with a grin. "We've been barking up the wrong tree. You can change your sex, but you can't change your DNA."

"So Agnes Day knew Renee's *real* secret."

"Since she was the head nurse at Dr. Camelback's office, I'd go out on a limb and say that she did."

"Now we've got a real motive."

"And a good one," I said. "Motive, opportunity, and a pretty good explanation for the confession note. She's left-handed and she left DNA on the murder weapon."

"Yeah, we're a couple of geniuses," said Nancy. "Should I pick her up?"

"By all means. The only thing I can't figure out is why she tried to kill Kenny."

"They were dating. Maybe her surgery couldn't hold up to that kind of scrutiny."

"Maybe," I said. "Before you pick her up, go ask him, will you?"

"Sure."

"But not in so many words," I said. "Just in case he doesn't know."

"Got it."

Francine was waiting for me in my office when I walked in.

"I heard you were over at Buxtehooters," she said accusingly.

"I had a few drinks," I admitted. "Pedro and I were trying it out."

"I thought we had something special."

"We do, Francine," I said, sitting down behind my desk. "Real special."

"Then why did you step out on me with that dame,

Memphis Belle? Don't try to deny it!" Francine was a woman scorned.

"I didn't mean anything by it, Francine. It was just one of those things."

Suddenly Francine had a flash of light in her hand. I recognized it right away--a hospital razor. I shivered in remembrance of the last time I saw one. If there's one thing you don't quickly forget, it's getting prepped for a hernia operation by a three-hundred pound Jamaican woman named Black Ethel.

It had been two days since we received the news about Renee Tatton. Neither Nancy nor I could find any sign of her. We had gone to Judge Adams and gotten a warrant to search her apartment, but she was gone. There were a few of her belongings in the apartment, to be sure, but most of her clothes were gone, along with her toiletries. I was afraid she'd flown the coop, but I wasn't ready to put out an All Points Bulletin just yet.

I was sitting at my kitchen table, eating my scrambled eggs and pushing a dead mouse around the table with a fork, waiting for Archimedes to show as much interest in his breakfast as I had in mine. It was a good thing that I wasn't married, I thought. If Meg had been in the kitchen with me, she would have wanted me to use a different fork. Archimedes tilted his head, but made no move toward his rodent repast.

I kept thinking about Renee Tatton. I had sure been fooled. I was pretty sure that everyone was. Nancy and I had decided that this information was not for public consumption, and so we had kept it to ourselves. I'd done some research in the meantime, doing a search of graduate degrees conferred by accredited music schools in the United States. Renee Tatton, or rather, William Renee Tatton, had received a Master's degree in voice performance at the University of Minnesota in 1972. I had gotten a copy of her graduate recital program from the music library's archives. She was, or had been, a countertenor. The first half of the program was Baroque, consisting of the Pergolesi *Stabat Mater,* sung with a soprano and accompanied by string quartet and harpsichord. The second half

included Handel, Scarlatti, some Finzi songs and a performance of Benjamin Britten's *The Journey of the Magi.* If Renee had been a talented countertenor, which she seemed to be, it would not have been that difficult to switch to the mezzo-soprano repertoire once the estrogen therapy had kicked in and the voice-lift had been performed.

I was still thinking about Renee when Baxter barked and the front door opened.

"Anyone home?" called Rhiza, walking into the den.

"In the kitchen," I said, picking up the mouse and quickly tossing him back into the coffee can. I popped on the plastic lid and stood up to put the can back into the fridge. Archimedes wasn't interested anyway. He hopped up on the windowsill and stared at Rhiza as she walked in.

"I see the gang's all here," she said with a dazzling smile as she dropped her coat off the back of her shoulders and hung it on an unused chair at the table. Baxter had followed her in, wagging his tail like he'd just discovered his dearest friend.

"All present and accounted for," I said. "Although the owl doesn't seem to be hungry this morning. Now, what can I get for you?"

"A cup of coffee and a cigar. And not one of those cheap ones either," she said.

"I believe I'll join you," I said. I got up and went into the den.

"Put some music on, will you?" Rhiza called. "Some Strauss. Richard Strauss, please. You know how I hate Johann. How about the *Romance for Cello and Orchestra?*"

"It'll take me a little while to find it," I called back.

"Take your time. I'll fix the coffee."

It didn't take me but a few minutes to find the CD, put it on the WAVE and get a couple of my best *Romeo Y Julieta*s out of my humidor.

"Here you are," I said, offering Rhiza one of the newly clipped cigars.

"What else is on the CD besides the *Romance?*"

"*Don Quixote,*" I said.

"That'll do," said Rhiza, lighting her cigar carefully. I followed suit as the strains of Strauss — Richard, not Johann — filled the room.

"Remember," began Rhiza, "when I told you that I checked on Malcolm's accounts?"

"Yeah. You found his passwords and logged in every month or so."

"Just to know where we stood," said Rhiza. "Financially speaking. Malcolm doesn't share that kind of information willingly, even with his wife."

"Force of habit, I guess."

"Maybe," said Rhiza. "I asked him right after we got married if I could have a say in our financial future. He said 'sure,' but never did anything about it. He gave me an allowance and a checking account and, if I ever wanted anything, he always gave it to me — no questions asked."

"So what did you want to see me about?"

"I checked his accounts earlier this week."

"Yeah?"

"Malcolm's broke."

This caught me completely by surprise.

"He doesn't know I know. I went in and brought up all his accounts. He's been juggling funds and pushing money back and forth for a few months now."

"And you know this...?"

"Because I have an MBA from UNC-Chapel Hill. Duh!"

"Oh, yeah," I said with a laugh. "I forgot. Did you find out what happened?"

"Oh, yes." Rhiza took a long puff on her cigar and blew a smoke ring across the table. "Malcolm invested everything he had into a casino in Gulfport, Mississippi. It should have been a slam-dunk. I checked the prospectus. Solid company, huge returns — no reason not to, really. Malcolm hadn't done well in the stock market in the past several years."

"No one did," I said. "So what happened?"

"The hurricane last September. They weren't up and running yet and the construction insurance didn't cover floods."

"It wasn't a flood," I said. "It was a hurricane."

"Technically, it was a flood," said Rhiza, "and the insurance

company won't pay off. There's a lawsuit pending, of course, but these lawsuits are filed after almost every hurricane by people who have hurricane insurance, but don't get the flood coverage. The insurance companies hardly ever have to pay."

"So how much did Malcolm lose?" I asked.

"About eight million."

"Man," I said, leaning back in my chair and puffing on the cigar. "It's a good thing you won the Powerball, isn't it?"

"Well, here's the thing about that."

"You mean you didn't win?" I asked.

"Oh no," Rhiza replied. "I won, all right. Thirty-four million, one hundred eighty thousand dollars and change."

"So what's the deal?"

"The money is mine. Malcolm has no claim on it."

"North Carolina's an equitable distribution state," I said. "What's yourn is his'n and what's his'n is yourn. At least what you've garnered since you've been married. I presume that would include lottery winnings."

"Ordinarily that would be true, but do you remember that unpleasantness with Mother Ryan a couple of years ago?"

"How could I forget?" I said. "At least she's been defrocked."

"Yes, she was, but that didn't stop her from opening a psychotherapy practice in Greensboro. And it didn't stop Malcolm from going up there for sessions once a month."

"Yeah," I said. "I remember you telling me. But I didn't know he was still seeing her."

"It's not something I wanted to talk about." Rhiza said. "How about a cup of coffee?"

I nodded and took another long puff. Rhiza got up, pulled two mugs down from the cupboard, set them on the table and poured us both a cup.

"So," continued Rhiza, sitting back down and taking a sip of her coffee, "do you also remember when I told you that Mother Ryan suggested to Malcolm that we should have a post-nuptial agreement?"

"Uh-huh. And you agreed to it. But I still don't understand why you'd agree to a post-nup."

"I don't know either. I was just sad, I guess. Besides, if we get divorced, the settlement is very generous. Half a million dollars,

whatever car I'm currently driving, one of the houses...you know, stuff like that."

"Enough to keep you comfortable."

"Sure," she said. "It never was about getting all the money. I really loved him." She took another sip of the coffee. "The post-nup states that I get to keep whatever I bring into the marriage at any time. I thought, back then, that I might like to try my hand at selling real estate. Malcolm thought it was a good idea. You know, keep the little woman busy and she won't notice the occasional infidelity. So, our agreement states that, in case of divorce, I keep one hundred percent of everything I bring in. I guess Malcolm didn't expect me to win the lottery."

"I guess not. And now, he's broke."

"Well, not exactly broke. We have the two houses. But, from what I can gather, Malcolm has liquidated his other assets. And one of the houses will have to go pretty soon, unless I agree to put the lottery money in his account so he can 'manage' it for me. Like I said before, he doesn't know that I know."

"What are you going to do?" I asked. "If you give him the money, does it become marital property?"

"My lawyer says it does. So I've been putting him off."

"But he's starting to push." I said.

"He is. He has to, I suppose. It would have been nice if he just would have confided in me. I'm just not sure if I still want to be married to him."

"Is there something else?" I asked.

Rhiza sighed. "You know that he's been cheating on me for about a year."

"Yes. You told me. There was a lot of money missing from his accounts. Before the hurricane, I'm guessing."

"Yes, before the hurricane. Anyway, I finally went into his on-line banking account and looked at the checks on the Internet. Did you know that you could do that now?"

I nodded.

"So, in the past sixteen months, there were three checks written to Dr. Camelback totaling forty-six thousand dollars."

"Man!" I said. "Any of those for you?"

"You must be joking. Just look at me!" She stood up and struck a fashion model's pose. "Do I look like I need plastic surgery?"

"Umm," I said, looking her up and down very carefully. "No."

"Well, Malcolm thinks I do. But the money wasn't spent on me. And I'm pretty sure Malcolm didn't get any calf or pec implants. I would have noticed."

"So, did you find out who it was for?"

"Nope. There wasn't even any way to ask that wouldn't give me away. I think I know who it is anyway," she said. "In addition to the checks to Dr. Camelback, there's been one check a month written to someone else. Someone in town."

"Big checks?" I asked.

"Five thousand dollars a month. This is another thing that Malcolm doesn't know that I know."

"Wow. Want to tell me who it is?"

"Yeah," Rhiza said. "You know, if I leave Malcolm, he won't have a dime. He'll have to sell the house and his car just to catch up on his debts. I'll get the other house, my car and he'll still owe me five hundred thousand bucks."

"Are you going to leave him?"

"He thinks I will if I find out about his bimbos."

"You told him that?"

"In no uncertain terms."

We had smoked our cigars down to the ends.

"So?" I asked. "Are you going to tell me who it is?"

"I guess."

I waited.

"Her name is Renee Tatton."

My cigar fell out of my open mouth and into my coffee cup.

Chapter 28

"Calm down, Francine," I said. "We can talk this over."

"I'm not going kill you," she snarled. "I'm just going to make you a little bit less attractive. Then you won't have any takers when you go out philandering."

A shot rang out and Francine dropped to her knees like a nun on a hot tin roof. Marilyn was standing behind her, a .38 in her hand.

"I never did like her," said Marilyn as Francine toppled over onto her face. "Ever since she gave me this bottle of Peptobimbo for my upset stomach."

"Peptobimbo?"

Marilyn nodded. "It didn't even work."

"Is that it?" asked Meg. "Have you finished the story?"

"Not quite. A short postlude and that should do it."

"Thank God! By the way, did Father George talk to you about coming back to St. Barnabas as the organist?"

"He did. I told him 'no, thanks.'"

"You did?"

"Yes, I did. I don't really want to be tied down. Now that I've had a taste of freedom, I kind of like it."

"Well, would you come on Sunday and play?"

"I don't know if I should. No one called me to sub."

"Umm," said Meg. "That would be my job. I just assumed that you would say yes to Father George, so I forgot to ask you."

"Who played last week?" I asked. "When we were in Morganton?"

"I have it on good authority that no one did."

"Ah, so that's the reason that Father George had such a change of heart."

"I heard that he did try to find someone, but he was unsuccessful."

"You mean that if I don't show up, there won't be any music?"

"Yes," said Meg, sorrowfully hanging her head in mock-dejection. "That's it exactly. And this time, it will be *my* fault. I am at your mercy."

"Aw," I said. "I guess I'll help you out." Meg smiled.

"Five thousand a month!" exclaimed Nancy. "You think it was blackmail?"

"I don't think so," I said. "Malcolm also paid for a lot of plastic surgery."

"So what was the money for?"

"Ever heard of a sugar daddy?"

"And you think that's why Renee moved to St. Germaine?"

"Pretty sure," I said.

"Do you think Malcolm knows about her...um...gender swap?"

"I don't think so," I said. "Did Kenny?"

"Definitely not," Nancy said, shaking her head. "And he's not that good a liar."

"So Agnes Day was the only one that knew. And she might have spilled the beans."

Nancy nodded. "So she had to go. Did you tell Rhiza about her hubby's little surprise?"

"Nope."

"Why would she be dating Kenny if she had Malcolm on the hook for five grand a month?"

"Well, just because you have a sugar daddy doesn't necessarily mean you have to be exclusive. Lord knows, Malcolm wasn't."

"Has anyone seen Renee?" Nancy asked.

"Nope."

All the members of the choir were back on Sunday morning when I showed up at ten o'clock. I figured it was all Meg's doing. She was playing on my guilt — well, what she could find of it.

"Hayden," said Elaine, "we're so glad you're back."

"I'm not back," I explained. "I'm just here because Meg forgot to find someone else."

"We practiced on Wednesday, even though you couldn't make it," said Michelle. "We went over *King Jesus Hath a Garden,* but we didn't learn a communion piece. You'll just have to play something."

"Yeah," I said. "That's great, but I'm just here for today. Then I'm finished."

"We were thinking about doing the Haydn *Little Organ Mass* next month. We all probably still remember it. We'll need a couple of violins, though," said Bev. "Do you have the names of the people who played it the last time we did it?"

"Yeah, but..."

"What service music are we doing?" asked Georgia. "It's not in the bulletin."

"All right," I said. "Sit down and be quiet. Let's get started."

We were halfway through the first hymn when Renee walked into the choir loft. She smiled, waved and glided her way down to the soprano section wearing the same gown she had worn the last time I'd seen her sing — the purple one, the one covered in sequins. She stopped and said hello to a few of the choir members as she wandered past, and when she got to her chair, she shook her dress to straighten it out before she sat down. I chuckled as I watched more than a few more sequins drop to the floor.

That gown hadn't been in her apartment when we searched it, so I figured she hadn't been home. If she had been in her apartment since we'd been there, she would have known we'd searched it, and she certainly wouldn't have come up to the choir loft. But, if Renee was singing in the choir, I could certainly keep an eye on her until the service was over.

I looked over at her, as soon as the opening hymn was finished, trying to see any vestiges of remaining masculinity. Sometimes, a prominent Adam's apple was a dead giveaway for a transsexual, but Renee's was no more noticeable than any of the other sopranos. Nope, I decided, she was definitely a very good-looking woman. Still, if she was a murderer, she was one cool customer. I scribbled a note to her, asking her to stay after the postlude and talk to me, passed it down the row and watched her read it. She gave me a big smile, nodded her head and gave me a little wave. Cool as the other side of the bed.

The anthem at the offertory went surprisingly well. The choir wasn't singing a communion anthem, and after Father George had

offered the invitation to the table, they made their way downstairs. I looked down from the choir loft toward the altar. Father George was celebrating, as usual, but Father Tony Brown, our retired priest, was assisting. Malcolm Walker was one of the Lay Eucharistic ministers, holding the cup on Father George's side. Carol Sterling was the other, helping Father Tony, directly opposite.

I had played through a couple of hymns by the time the choir came back to the loft. The choir at St. Barnabas, whether they were singing or not, always went down to communion first — before the rest of the congregation. They sat down in their seats and waited for the congregation to finish, my cue for the final hymn. I looked across the soprano section.

"Where's Renee?" I whispered to Meg.

"She was right behind me," said Meg, looking around.

I had come to a stopping point, so I cadenced and looked out over the congregation. Father George's side of the nave was backed up, congregants lined down the center aisle, all the way to the back. He had the cup in one hand and the plate of bread in the other, doing his best to juggle them as carefully as he could. Malcolm was nowhere in sight.

"Here's the MIDI disk," I whispered to Meg. "You remember how it works?" She nodded back at me, waited until I had climbed off the organ bench, then slid the disk into the slot. I smiled at the choir, gave them a few reassuring hand signals and made my way down the stairs, punching Nancy's number into the speed dial of my cell phone.

I went out the front door, stripping off my cassock as I ran around the building toward the fellowship hall. I didn't know where I was going, but I knew that Malcolm and Renee already had a head start. Who knew? I might get lucky.

I circled the building and, not seeing anyone, went down the alley behind the kitchen and opened the back door to the sacristy. I could hear *Be Thou My Vision* being played on the organ, via the MIDI disk, and the choir and congregation singing along. Malcolm's cassock was draped over the banister rail leading up to my old office. I hadn't been up to my office since I'd left the employ of St. Barnabas. It was situated in the old organ pipe chamber above the front of the nave. When the organ was moved from the front of the church to the rear loft, I commandeered the space. I walked up the

stairs and tried the door. It was locked.

The hymn was going into the last stanza. I ran back down the stairs and out the side door of the sacristy, looking up and down the street that ran beside the church as I came out of the door. I spotted Malcolm's dark green Jag at the corner and started walking toward it. At the same time, Malcolm and Renee came around the other side of the church. Malcolm had Renee's arm by the elbow, and he was hustling her along at a slightly faster pace than her high heels were allowing. They hadn't seen me and weren't expecting to. Malcolm had unlocked the car and had the passenger door open for Renee when I walked up as nonchalantly as I could, given my harried pace to get there.

"Hi, Malcolm," I said. "Hi, Renee. You guys are leaving early today. I'd hoped to talk to you after the service." I directed the last statement to Renee. She smiled thinly and nodded. Malcolm let go of her arm, and I watched a couple more sequins drop to the ground.

"We're in sort of a hurry," said Malcolm. Then he looked confused. "Aren't you playing the rest of the service?"

"I have someone covering for me."

"Well, we have to go," he said. I stepped to the car and pushed the passenger door closed.

"You can't go, Malcolm."

"Why not?"

"Because I know who killed Agnes Day." I looked at Renee Tatton.

"I didn't kill her," Renee said in alarm. "Why would I?"

"A couple of reasons," I said, "the most obvious being that she knew about your secret."

Renee went white and bit her lower lip.

"She was the surgical nurse for Dr. Camelback when you had several of your surgeries. She knew about your sex change operation."

Now it was Malcolm's turn to go white. "Your *what?!*"

"Ah. You didn't know," I said. "Renee is a transsexual."

"Malcolm," said Renee, an air of desperation in her voice, "it doesn't change anything. If two people love each other..."

"Oh my God!" said Malcolm. *"Oh my God!"*

Renee turned back to me. "You...you...I suppose you've told everyone in town!"

198

"No, I haven't," I said, "But I've known Malcolm a long time. I figured he should know."

"I didn't kill Agnes Day."

"I think I'm going to be sick," said Malcolm. I looked over at him. He was green, sure enough.

At that moment, Nancy pulled her Harley in behind Malcolm's Jag.

"I didn't kill her," said Renee, again.

"I know you didn't," I said. Malcolm was leaning against his car in shock. I reached over, took his right arm, pushed the sleeve of his sport coat up over his wrist and looked at his Rolex. Then I opened his coat and pulled a Montblanc Miesterstuck Solitaire out of his inside breast pocket.

"Check his car, Nancy," I said. "It's already open."

"Do we need a warrant?" asked Nancy.

"Nope." I said. "He's double parked and he's getting a ticket. That's reasonable cause for a search. You see, Malcolm, labs can now check the composition of ink and trace it to a particular pen. I'm betting that this is the pen that wrote the confession note. You were feeling pretty guilty, and you never thought it'd be traced back to you."

Malcolm didn't say anything, but his eyes darted from side to side. "Renee..." he started. "Renee killed the organist..."

"I don't think so," I said. "She was wearing the same outfit on Palm Sunday that she's wearing today. If she had been the one who hit Agnes Day with the bell, there would have been sequins all over the organ keys and down into the pedal board. Those things are dropping off like it was molting season at a majorette convention. We found sequins, all right, but they were all in *front* of the organ."

Nancy came walking around the front of Malcolm's car holding a .45 automatic. "This yours?" she asked Malcolm. "I found it under the front seat."

"Yes," said Malcolm. "I want my lawyer."

"You'll need one, I think," I said. "We got a fingerprint off the shotgun at Kenny's farm. I'm betting that it's yours.

"Are you left-handed?" asked Nancy. Malcolm didn't answer.

"I'm pretty sure he is, but we can ask Rhiza," I said. "His watch is on his right arm. That's a pretty good indicator."

"Why'd he have the .45?" Nancy asked me.

"He had to get rid of Renee," I said, watching Renee's eyes go wide.

"You were going to kill me?" Renee asked Malcolm. Malcolm didn't reply, or even look at her. "But why?"

"He had no money," I said. "He thought that if Rhiza found out about you, he'd be out thirty-four million dollars. Also, he couldn't take the chance that you might have told Kenny about your affair. He's broke."

"Broke?"

"Broke. No more plastic surgery for you, I'm afraid."

"Broke?" asked Renee, again, looking at Malcolm as if she'd never seen him before. "And you were going to kill me?" The service had finished and people were starting to come out of the church. She turned to me. "I'd like to get out of here. Am I under arrest?" she asked.

"Nope," I said. "But don't leave town. One more thing, though. Why was Malcolm paying for all that extra surgery? I mean, you were already a woman, right?"

"Sure. Malcolm just liked bigger, better and younger. Didn't you, Hon?" She blew him a sarcastic kiss.

Nancy had the cuffs on Malcolm, and we watched Renee disappear around the corner of the church.

"I just have one question, Malcolm," said Nancy. "Could you *really* not tell that she used to be a man? I mean, once push came to shove?"

"So to speak," I added.

Malcolm ignored the question.

"Those surgeons are very good," I said. "I don't know the particulars, but from what I've read in the past couple of days, I can see how he'd be fooled."

"I guess. How come we didn't find his DNA on the handbell? And why was Renee's DNA on it?" Nancy asked me, now ignoring Malcolm as if he wasn't even there."

"Easy," I said. "Renee was the one who handed the bell to Fred right before the Psalm. And when Malcolm came upstairs, he was wearing gloves."

"Handbell gloves?"

"No, regular gloves. It was pretty cold that morning. Right Malcolm?"

Malcolm Walker didn't say anything. He just turned and walked across the street toward the police station. Nancy and I looked at each other, shrugged in unison and followed him.

Chapter 29

Monday night meetings at St. Barnabas were notoriously ill attended, but this one proved the exception to the rule. As Senior Warden, Billy Hixon was presiding, and the parish hall was as full as it was for the meeting just a few short weeks ago.

Mrs. Murdock was sitting in a chair at the front of the hall. She had both her hands in her lap, clutching her black purse that looked, in her diminutive lap, big enough to carry a good-sized badger. She peered out across the hall through thick, black-rimmed glasses. Father George was sitting next to her.

"Let's come to order," said Billy. "This won't take too long. Mrs. Murdock has an announcement to make."

"Before she does," said Jed Pierce, from the back of the room, "I'd like to make a motion. I move that if we don't agree with what Mrs. Murdock decides, we take another vote on what to do with the money."

"That's not going to happen," said Billy.

Father George stood up. "The congregation has already voted, and the vestry met last week and upheld that decision," he said. "That's it. We're just waiting for Mrs. Murdock."

"This is a parish meeting, isn't it?" hollered Jed. "We can vote on anything we want."

"Why don't you just shut up, Jed," said Bear Niederman. "You're really a jackass."

"Yeah," said Phil. "Shut up for once in your life."

With no support for his motion, Jed crossed his arms and plunked down into his chair.

Billy reached down and helped Mrs. Murdock to her feet. She handed her purse to Father George and walked up to the microphone.

"I have given this matter careful prayer and consideration," she said in a wavering voice, "and I have decided that St. Barnabas would be a better place without sixteen million dollars in the bank. Yes, it would make the life of our church much easier, but where would I be if I hadn't given to the church all these years? If St. Barnabas hadn't needed the money that I gave, I probably wouldn't have given it and just think of all the blessings that I would have missed out on."

I looked around the room. There were some nods of agreement, but most people were listening intently, not showing much emotion at all.

"I have decided that the sixteen million dollars would best be spent spreading the word of God. My two nephews came up with an idea that will put the name of Jesus in front of millions of people."

We all waited expectantly.

"I've decided that St. Barnabas is going to sponsor a NASCAR racing team."

After the meeting, Meg, Ruby, Pete, Nancy and I were sitting in The Slab eating pecan pie.

"Excellent!" I said. "A truly excellent decision!"

"NASCAR?" said Nancy.

"It's the fastest growing spectator sport in the country," Pete said. "I've been to a few races. It's a real rush."

"How long will sixteen million dollars last? That's an expensive sport," said Meg.

"Depends on if we win or not," I said. "Even if we lose, two or three years, anyway. That's my guess."

"Who's the driver?" asked Pete.

"It's my understanding that it's going to be Lucille's nephew. His name is Junior Jameson."

"I've heard of him," said Nancy. "He's won a few races."

"His team is looking for a new sponsor," I said. "Apparently their old sponsor didn't take kindly to Junior painting religious slogans on the car — especially on the back bumper. But Junior said that it unnerved the other drivers coming up behind him and gave him an edge. Imagine driving up behind someone at two hundred miles per hour, trying to pass, and seeing 'Where will you spend eternity?' jump out at you in bright yellow letters."

"Sounds like a good tactic to me," said Pete. "Who was the old sponsor?"

"Budweiser."

"Well," said Ruby with a shrug, "maybe some good will come of it."

"This is great!" said Pete, standing up to get us some more

coffee. "It just may put St. Germaine on the map. May I suggest a *Blessing of the Racecar* service before the first race next year? We'll advertise it in the paper."

"That's a great idea," I said. "With pirates."

"No pirates!" said everyone, in unison.

Postlude

Your other stories have been up on the blog for two months now," Meg said. "What about this last one? *The Soprano Wore Falsettos?*"

"I'll finish it up right now," I said, putting down my beer and walking over to the typewriter. "To tell you the truth, I got so busy, I just forgot about it. It just needs a 'postlude' to wrap it up."

"I checked *The Usual Suspects* website. You're up to two hundred forty hits."

"That's not so good," I said. "Ah, well."

"Don't get discouraged. The Bulwer-Lytton competition is coming up. Maybe you'll get an honorable mention this year."

"Maybe I'll *win*."

"Don't get your hopes up," Meg laughed. "You're not that bad yet. While you're practicing, I'll start dinner."

Pedro, Marilyn and I sat down at our usual table at Buxtehooters. I was flush and almost sober, and I didn't care who knew it. The Presiding Bishop had coughed up the cash like a kitten getting rid of a two thousand dollar hairball.

There had been a flurry of activity in St. Germaine over the past six weeks, but we were getting ready to relax into summer. The downtown area had been spruced up, as it was every year, getting ready for the influx of tourists. There were hanging baskets filled with flowers on every corner and in front of every shop. My job, or rather Nancy's job, during the summer months, was to control the parking.

Dave and Collette had set a date for their upcoming nuptials. They would be married in October, the height of the leaf season, at New Hope Fellowship Church. Dave would have to be baptized again, but he said that he didn't mind.

"If the old one *doesn't* count, then it'll be a good thing when I

do it again," said Dave. "If the old one *does* count, then it'll be just another Sunday morning bath. I just want to cover all my bases."

Malcolm Walker had a good attorney, but he had to sell his house to be able to afford him. Rhiza filed for divorce the day after he was arrested. Malcolm's lawyer pointed out to the district attorney that, although we proved the confession note was written by Malcolm's pen and although his handwriting was a match as well, writing a confession note wasn't evidence of the crime. Malcolm was just kidding around, he said, and thought it would be funny if someone found the note nailed to the cross.

I was for sending the matter to a jury, but the case was weak at best, and since there was no direct evidence linking Malcolm to Agnes Day's murder, the D.A. made a deal regarding the attempted murder charge. We did, after all, have a fingerprint on the shotgun. We weren't complete klutzes. Malcolm would do seven to ten in a minimum security facility. Rhiza had been seen around town occasionally, but she told me that she'd be in Europe for most of the summer.

I hadn't been back to St. Barnabas to play since the day we arrested Malcolm. Meg had given up asking me, and Father George had found a substitute — not a good one, by Meg's reckoning. She had only one leg, and although she walked well enough with her prosthetic, it made her pedal work a little heavy on the treble end. I had heard that she was a retired dental assistant. St. Barnabas had extended my "leave" indefinitely, hoping, I think, that I'd decide to come back. I still hadn't made up my mind.

Benny Dawkins and Ruthie Haggarty got married a month after she was found innocent of killing Little Bubba, claiming "battered spouse" syndrome. The prosecutor was just going through the motions, and, with the quarter million dollars she inherited from her late aunt, Agnes Day, hiring a good feminist lawyer was no problem. The jury was out less than fifteen minutes.

Once we told Renee Tatton she could leave town, she did. We hadn't seen hide nor hair of her in six weeks. The word was, she moved back to Virginia.

Annette Passaglio won her civil suit against Todd Whitlock, Watauga County's foremost wedding videographer. Judge Adams had ruled that since Annette had paid for the video in advance, it was, indeed, her property. It was a good thing, too, because Misty's

About the Author

Mark Schweizer lives and works in Hopkinsville, Kentucky, where he pretends to be a composer and a writer. If anyone finds out what he's up to, he'll have to go back to work at Mr. Steak.

The Liturgical Mysteries

The Alto Wore Tweed
Independent Mystery Booksellers Association "Killer Books" selection, 2004

The Baritone Wore Chiffon

The Tenor Wore Tapshoes
IMBA 2006 Dilys Award nominee

The Soprano Wore Falsettos
Southern Independent Booksellers Alliance 2007 Book Award Nominee

The Bass Wore Scales

Just A Note

If you've enjoyed this book—or any of the other mysteries in this series—please drop me a line. My e-mail address is mark@sjmp.com. Also, don't forget to visit the website (www.sjmpbooks.com) for lots of great stuff! You'll find recordings and "downloadable" music for many of the great works mentioned in the Liturgical Mysteries including *The Pirate Eucharist, The Weasel Cantata, The Mouldy Cheese Madrigal* and a lot more.

Cheers,
Mark

wedding video won the hundred thousand dollar first prize for the funniest home video of the year. Misty and Annette split the cash fifty-fifty.

Noylene's Beautifery and Dip 'n Tan had created quite a following for itself, not only in St. Germaine, but also in the surrounding townships. Noylene expected to have a great summer, what with all the tourists coming in. She hired a couple more beauticians and even bought enough tanning fluid so that the customers didn't have to squat.

Russ Stafford couldn't make The Clifftops pay off. He declared bankruptcy at the end of May and took a job selling used cars in Asheville. He didn't have to invest in a new wardrobe.

Kenny Frazier sold his farm and moved to Santa Fe where he heard that medical marijuana, if not legal, was still readily available.

Pete Moss bought stock in the Phlabco Corporation, maker of expando-pants, so deeply did he believe in their product. The stock was holding firm at twenty-three dollars per share, but Pete figured that with the ever-increasing girth of America's baby boomers, he was bound to make a killing eventually.

Rebecca Watts continued to live in bookish anonymity. She liked it that way.

"Drinks for the house," I said to Helga over the strains of a Froberger Partita. "And bring us a round of Schwabblings."

"Ja, ja," said Helga with a wink, her T-shirt valiantly engaging in the titanic struggle between the tensile strength of cotton and Newton's third law of motion.

"Not bad," said Pedro admiringly. "I see that Miss Bulimia Forsythe is still doing a brisk business."

"Men..." said Marilyn, shaking her head in disgust.

"There's always a market for self-improvement," I said, "and I know a good soprano when I see one."

Other Liturgical Mysteries
by Mark Schweizer

Why do people keep dying in the little town of St. Germaine, North Carolina? It's hard to say. Maybe there's something in the water. Whatever the reason, it certainly has *nothing* to do with St. Barnabas Episcopal Church!

Murder in the choirloft. A choir-director detective.
It's not what you expect...it's even funnier!

The Alto Wore Tweed
The Baritone Wore Chiffon
The Tenor Wore Tapshoes
The Bass Wore Scales

**ALL FOUR now available at
your favorite mystery bookseller or sjmpbooks.com.
$12.95 each**

"It's like Mitford meets Jurassic Park, only without the wisteria and the dinosaurs..."

The Soprano Wore Falsettos

A Liturgical Mystery

by Mark Schweizer